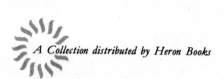
A Collection distributed by Heron Books

THE
GREATEST MASTERPIECES
OF
RUSSIAN LITERATURE

ALEXANDER KUPRIN

TALES

Translated from the Russian by
Douglas Ashby
with an Introduction by A.B. McMillin

Original Frontispiece by Jean-Pierre Meuer
Original Illustrations by Patrick Rixson

Distributed by
HERON BOOKS

This translation published
by arrangement with
Mezhdunarodnaja Kniga, Moscow

INTRODUCTION

By the end of the nineteenth century Russian literature had come to the end of an era and split into two widely different and largely hostile trends. On the one hand the Symbolists, led by Blok and Bely, rejected the tradition of psychological and social realism that had flourished in the work of the great novelists, turning instead to the mystic philosophies of Vladimir Solovyov and back to the poets Tyutchev and Fet whose work had been either unknown or rejected during the age of the novel. Their work, mostly verse, is often esoteric and obscure in meaning but always visually and musically subtle, and thus helped to restore some feeling for the harmony of the language at a time when it was in danger of becoming a purely utilitarian tool. On the other hand, opposed to these ' decadents ', were those writers who chose to continue and develop even further the well-established techniques of prose realism. It is notable that the three writers to whom Alexander Kuprin is closest are all major figures in the realistic tradition: Tolstoy, whose novels form its high water mark, was an admirer of Kuprin and influenced the younger writer in his ideas on the simple life; Gorky, bridging the gap between the classical novel and socialist realism, met Kuprin in 1900 and recognised in him ' a fine comrade and an important, sensitive writer ', and until his enforced departure abroad in 1905 encouraged and helped him, publishing his works in the journal Knowledge *of which he was the founder: later his physical absence weakened the ties between them. During the same period Chekhov, whom he regarded as his master, was also close. In his laconic, undemonstrative style, relying on effective use of detail, in his ironic but sympathetic approach to people, and above all in his apolitical, pragmatic, but generally optimistic attitude to human affairs one can perceive the inheritance of Chekhov's moral outlook. But despite these close ties with his contemporaries, Kruprin is an original, versatile and highly readable writer, whose stories, having won immediate recognition both at home and abroad, remain among the most popular of all classical works with Russian readers today.*

Alexander Ivanovich Kuprin was born on 26th August, 1870 in the small town of Narovchat near Penza in central Russia. The town was remarkable only for being mentioned in a popular jingle comparing it to a pile of logs, and, as Kuprin put it, for ' burning to the ground every two years without fail '. His parents were from the nobility, but impoverished, and before Alexander was two his father, a minor clerk, died of cholera, leaving Lyubov, his wife, to bring up Alexander and his two sisters on whatever money could be begged from more affluent friends and benefactors. This servile life of constant favour seeking and of ' having plump hands shoved into one's mouth for kisses ' was a misery for the energetic, strong-willed Alexander who, however, soon found a form of release by entering the Razumovsky Military Preparatory School (which shared with the church schools the positive attraction of providing education free of charge) ; from here he passed on to the 2nd Moscow Military Academy, which was not long after transformed into a Cadet Corps. The period following the assassination of tsar Nicholas I in 1881 was outstanding, even by Russian standards, for the black reaction prevailing in all walks of life ; the atmosphere in the educational institutions in particular was one of iron discipline and repression, and is described by Kuprin in various of his stories, particularly The Cadets, *a work which rivals Pomyalovsky's notorious* Seminary Sketches *of the 1860s in the grim and sordid existence which it depicts.*

On passing out Kuprin entered the 46th Dnepr Infantry Regiment and served in a small provincial town hardly less depressing than his native Narovchat, spoiling his chances of promotion whilst in St Petersburg for competitive examinations in 1893 by becoming involved in a characteristically scandalous prank with an obstreperous policeman. Apparently glad of the excuse, he retired from active service with the rank of lieutenant in the following year and, freed from the trammels of army discipline, began to give free rein to a multitude of powerful urges and whims. Having embarked on his literary career in 1889 whilst still at the Military Academy he continued to write whilst engaging in a range of employments comparable in number and variety only to those of his contemporary Maxim Gorky. From journalism in Kiev he moved on to a whole series of different jobs including amongst others those of loader, bailiff, labourer, dentist, chorister, surveyor, carpenter, actor and fisherman; there appeared to be no end to the activities into which Kuprin would throw himself with breathless excitement and enthusiasm, for his curiosity and energy were unbounded, a fact that finds clear and full expression in the stories, of which the great majority are set against backgrounds taken from his own first-hand experience, whilst in some cases, like for example How I Became an Actor, *they are purely autobiographical.*

In 1909, already quite well established as a writer, Kuprin came to St Petersburg and entered the literary circles of the capital for the first time. Chekhov and Gorky were particularly helpful in their criticisms and advice, whilst Tolstoy, an unconventional but often discerning critic of his contemporaries' work, numbered some of Kuprin's stories, especially the 'delicate' and 'charming' Allez! *amongst his favourite pieces, choosing them to read at literary soirées. This period was one of the most productive of Kuprin's life, with the majority of his abundant energies being turned to positive, creative activity. After the supression of the 1905 revolution, however, a certain confusion, political disorientation and general disillusionment began to express itself in meaningless pranks and elaborate practical jokes, with a perceptible decline in the general standard of his already uneven work. Occasional first class stories were still produced, but in general the promise recognised by Tolstoy and Chekhov was not completely fulfilled. A combination of personal weakness and historical circumstances decreed that Kuprin's talent as a writer never really reached the full fruition enjoyed by his great contemporaries. For this, as for everything else, Tolstoy blamed bourgeois society, observing: 'What* a fine writer he would have been if only he had not lived in an age of universal frivolousness '.

There ensued no consequent decline in his popularity as a personality or as a writer, however: his extravagant and spectacular way of life, following the powerful but erratic impulses of ' free will ', seemingly so important at that time, endeared him to the irresponsible newspaper reporters of the yellow press who seized on and exaggerated escapades, such as the time when he enticed a well-known government informer into his hotel room and dyed the wretch's hair a bright emerald hue ; as a focal point for apocryphal stories he can perhaps only be compared to his contemporary, George Bernard Shaw. The vigorous craving for knowledge and experience that took him on descents to the sea's bottom and on balloon and aeroplane flights also threw him into close contact with the lowest and most depraved elements in society; his novel The Pit about life in a brothel (which, incidentally, brought the author accusations of pornography) was preceded by a long period spent living in the prostitutes' quarter, in the course of which the fumes of the underworld gradually began to take hold and to overpower him, despite an immensely healthy physical constitution; the simple hearted admirer of Jack London and Kipling fell into bad company and soon transformed himself from a vigorous man of adventure into one of the most pathetic sights of Moscow café life, a physical and mental wreck hunched behind a row of empty bottles.

Perhaps if Gorky, for whom he felt a deep admiration, had been able to remain in Russia after the 1905 revolution he might have exercised a stabilizing influence on his impetuous compatriot, but as it was Kuprin lost his sense of direction and purpose in life. In 1919 he emigrated to France, but, pathetically homesick, returned to Moscow shortly before his death in 1938.

An uneven writer, not entirely free from lapses into banality and melodrama, Kuprin makes up in zest and enthusiasm for what he lacks in taste and literary judgement. His best stories are informed with a genuine awareness of the poetry of life whilst the truly infectious vitality and love of humanity emanating from his work ensure his continuing popularity with modern readers. Notably free from the morbid introspection of Dostoevsky and

Andreyev, the moralising of Tolstoy and Gorky and Chekhov's almost excessive abhorrence of excitement and sensationalism, Kuprin, in his best work is able to strike some new and stimulating notes. The stories in this collection, taken from the most productive decade of his life, 1897-1907, reflect many of his best and most typical qualities, and in their variety afford us considerable insight into a most interesting man and the depressing but nonetheless fascinating period in which he lived.

Allez!, *one of the first of Kuprin's works to attract widespread attention, was first published in an Ukrainian newspaper in 1897. Its theme of unrequited love, together with love in the face of social inequality, is one that recurs often with this writer, notably in* The Army Ensign, *published in the same year. Tolstoy praised* Allez! *for its formal balance and sense of restraint, but mainly ' for the way he has exposed the artificial gilt of civilisation and of false christianity', and here we feel the author of* Resurrection *reading his own convictions into the younger writer's work. The* Army Ensign *is one of Kuprin's best stories, with a difficult form sustained, and the reader's interest and conviction maintained to the end; it compares favourably with the much better known* The Garnet Bracelet *of 1906, where elements of melodrama and a generally sentimental atmosphere banish much of the poetry. With a small number of carefully chosen strokes and a laconic manner worthy of Chekhov himself, Kuprin conveys with truly masterly skill the atmosphere of army life as seen through the haze of the young officer's social and romantic day-dreams. From a series entitled* From Women's Letters, Autumn Flowers *and* A Sentimental Romance, *both published in 1901, also deal with the theme of love—as, indeed, do the majority of Kuprin's stories. Although skilfully written they belong to the world of women's magazines rather than great literature, for only an artist of Chekhov's stature could treat these stories without sentimentality; nonetheless we are forced to admire the writer's skill as a robust young man entering the mind and feelings of an emotional, tear-laden ' hospital flower'. The discrepancy between author and subject in these stories is emphasised by* Black Fog, *published in January 1905, in which Kuprin's love of the open-air, natural life is embodied in the Ukrainian Boris at the centre of the story; the purely physical significance of the sunny, healthy Ukraine is contrasted with the murk, both physical and spiritual, of the north, and the hatefulness of artificiality is brought well home in this simple, parable-like ' Petersburg happening' .*

The Jewess, *1906, is remarkable both for the very clear scene that is evoked by apparently haphazard, Chekhovian means and also for its subject matter : it was, and to a large extent still is highly untypical for a gentile living in the south of Russia to feel anything but scorn and hate for the Jews. Kiev, where Kuprin worked, was a hot-bed of the anti-semitic tradition glorified by Gogol in his historical epic* Taras Bulba *and brilliantly described in Bernard Malamud's novel* The Fixer. *The type of fanatical nationalist flourishing and, indeed, officially encouraged at this unappetizing period of Russian history is most convincingly, albeit satirically portrayed in* Measles, 1904. *A typical member of the ' Black Hundreds ' anti-semitic organisation is revealed in all his bourgeois vulgarity when confronted by the idealistic student Voskresensky, whilst Kuprin avoids mere parody or proselytising by making all the characters into rounded, human beings, with physical passions as well as abstract ideas. Once again the exact smell and flavour of the scene are excellently caught. In* The Murderer, *1906, Kuprin presents the phenomenon of man's lust to kill by the characteristic device of a story within a story; but although this grisly anecdote seems purely concerned with an abstract idea, its real significance lies in the background of political terror and reprisals following the suppression of the 1905 uprising. Set, appropriately, in the claustrophobic atmosphere of a shadowy room, the story stands in strong contrast to the feeling of lightness and spaciousness in most of Kuprin's work.*

How I Became an Actor, *first published in the journal* Theatre and Art, *1906, is purely autobiographical. In the Cadet Corps Kuprin had already shown ability as a mimic, and between spring and summer 1898 he joined a theatrical company performing in Sumy in the north east Ukraine. Chekhov thought highly of Kuprin's dramatic talent and even tried to persuade him to join the troupe of the newly formed Moscow Art Theatre, but no regular form of existence, even in the freest of all professions, could have satisfied Kuprin's restless and enquiring nature, and so the suggestion was not taken up. It is interesting to note that the picture Kuprin gives of his fellow actors reinforces Chekhov's remarks about the ' appalling ignorance ' prevalent in the profession.*

Gambrinous, *1907, is also based on fact, for it was recently discovered that there really did exist a Sasha the Musician—one Aaron Goldstein who died in Odessa in 1921 after a lifetime of experiences similar to those undergone by Kuprin's hero. The story reflects the tumultuous period between 1904 and 1906 in which the disastrous Russo-Japanese war was followed by the 1905 revolution and an ensuing series of progroms instituted by the secret police chief Plehve in the hope of ' drowning the revolution in Jewish blood '. As in Pushkin's* The Captain's Daughter *and Tolstoy's* War and Peace, *the great historical events are reflected in the lives of the ordinary people they affect, but the purpose of the story is not so much to portray the trends and movements of history as to show the strength and variety of the human spirit. Compared with the subtlety and quiet restraint of Chekhov's best stories the language here seems bright and sometimes over-saturated, but this, like the frequent enumerations and strong, direct epithets and images, is in keeping with the setting and characters in the tale, for in this story as clearly as in any other we see Kuprin's love of robust, red-blooded men, the open air and broad, heroic natures. The assertion at the end that ' you may maim a man, but art will endure all and conquer all ' is not made with a moralist's fervour but with the firm conviction of a stout-hearted optimist.*

It is clearly not enough, however, to regard Kuprin simply as a boy scout manqué, or as a pale reflection of Jack London. The positive elements in his writing have no doubt helped to secure his popularity in Russia, but his range is a genuinely wide one, as is shown by the variety of styles and themes and by the breadth of outlook in even a small collection such as the present one. Chronologically the last story is Emerald, *written and published in 1907. Based on a true happening, it is closely linked with Tolstoy's story* Yardstick *by its epigraph and the common theme*

XV

of how human society distorts and destroys all that is fine and beautiful, and reflects the writer's deep interest in and love for animals; other stories of a similar kind include The White Poodle, An Elephant's Stroll *and* The Bears. *In one story Kuprin declared: ' I would like to spend a few days as a horse, a plant or a fish '; the craving for new experiences is there, but also a belief in the value of Tolstoy's ' simple life ' taken to an extreme point in the life of animals. The ' back to nature ' idea became particularly strong in his writing after the suppression of the 1905 revolution and the break with the radical activists. In his story* The Spirit of the Times *Kuprin wrote, ' All men's sufferings arise from the fact that they are becoming ever more remote from animals. We have lost their natural beauty, their grace, their strength and agility, their staunchness in the battle with nature, their vitality. Worst of all is that consciousness has killed man's instincts '. One can point to examples of the humanising of animals in Jack London and Chekhov as well as Tolstoy, but basically* Emerald *is a hymn to natural beauty; the beauty referred to by Kuprin in* Our Justification *written on Tolstoy's death in 1910: ' He showed us, blind and dull as we are, the beauty of earth, sky, men and beasts. He taught us, disbelieving and mean creatures, how man can be good, compassionate, interesting and beautiful '.*

Kuprin won a reputation with English readers long before the Dostoevsky cult had given an automatic entrée to everything Russian in this country. A keen admirer of Jack London for his heroic adventures and of Kipling for his manliness and broad knowledge of natural phenomena, Kuprin gave expression to his idealised concept of the English in his description of the sailors in Gambrinous. *He himself prized knowledge highly and was an expert on, amongst other things, dogs, fish, trees, birds, bees and precious and semi-precious stones; his infectious longing to ' see, know and understand everything ' is reflected in the stories and enables him to attract and to hold the reader's attention immediately. Our debt to Kuprin was summed up by the distinguished Soviet writer Konstantin Paustovsky when he wrote: ' We should be grateful to Kuprin for everything—for his great humanity, for*

INTRODUCTION

his refined talent, for his love of Russia, for his unshakeable faith in the happiness of his people, and, finally, for his undying ability to take fire from the most insignificant contact with poetry, and to communicate the experience freely and simply '.

London, October 1968.   ARNOLD B. McMILLIN

CONTENTS

GAMBRINOUS

I

GAMBRINOUS' is the name of a popular beer-shop in a vast port of South Russia. Although rather well situated in one of the most crowded streets, it was hard to find, owing to the fact that it was underground. Often old customers who knew it well would miss this remarkable establishment and would retrace their steps after passing two or three neighbouring shops.

There was no sign-board of any kind. One entered a narrow door, always open, straight from the pavement. Then came a narrow staircase with twenty stone steps that were bent and crooked from the tramp of millions of heavy boots. At the end of the staircase, on a partition, there was displayed, in alto-relief, the painted figure, double life-size, of the grandiose beer patron, King Gambrinous himself. This attempt in sculpture was probably the first work of an amateur and seemed to be clumsily hacked out of an enormous petrified sponge. But the red jacket, the ermine mantle, the gold crown, and the mug, raised on high with its trickling white froth, left no doubt in the visitor's mind that he stood in the very presence of the great Beer King.

The place consisted of two long, but extremely low, vaulted rooms, from whose stone walls damp streams were always pouring, lit up by gas jets that burned day and night, for the beershop was not provided with a single window. On the vaults, however, traces of amusing

1

paintings were still more or less distinguishable. In one of these, a band of German lads in green hunting jackets, with woodcock feathers in their hats and rifles on their shoulders, were feasting. One and all, as they faced the beer hall, greeted the customers with outstretched mugs, while two of them continued to embrace the waists of a pair of plump girls, servants of the village inn, or perhaps daughters of some worthy farmer. On the other wall was displayed a fashionable picnic, early eighteenth century, with countesses and viscounts frolicking in powdered wigs on a green lawn with lambs. Next to this was a picture of drooping willows, a pond with swans, which ladies and gentlemen, reclining on a kind of gilt shell, were gracefully feeding. Then came a picture of the interior of a Ukrainian hut with a family of happy Ukrainians dancing the gopak with large bottles in their hands. Still further down the room a large barrel sported itself upon which two grotesquely fat cupids, wreathed with hop-leaves and grapes, with red faces, fat lips, and shamelessly oily eyes, clicked glasses. In the second hall, separated from the other by a small archway, were illustrations from frog life : frogs were drinking beer in a green marsh, hunting grasshoppers among the thick reeds, playing upon stringed instruments, fighting with swords, and so on. Apparently the walls had been painted by some foreign master.

Instead of tables, heavy oak barrels were arranged on the sawdust-strewn floor and small barrels took the place of chairs. To the right of the entrance was a small platform, with a piano on it. Here, night after night, through a long stretch of years, Sasha—a Jew, a gentle, merry fellow, drunk and bald, who had the appearance of a peeled monkey, and who might be any age—used to play the violin for the pleasure and distraction of the guests. As the years passed, the waiters, with their leather-topped sleeves, changed, the bar-tenders also changed, even the proprietors of the beershop changed, but Sasha invariably, every night at six o'clock, sat on his platform with his fiddle in his hands and a little white dog on his knee. And by one o'clock in the morning, always with the same little dog, Bielotchka, he would leave Gambrinous', scarcely able to stand after his beer.

There was, too, at Gambrinous', another unchanging face—that of the presider at the buffet, a fat, bloodless old woman, who, from being always in that damp beer basement, resembled one of those pale, lazy fish which swarm in the depths of sea caverns. Like the captain of a ship from his bridge, she, from the height of her bar, would give curt orders to the waiters, smoking all the time and holding her cigarette in the right corner of her mouth, while her right eye constantly blinked from the smoke. Her voice was rarely audible and she responded to the bows of her guests always with the same colourless smile.

II

The enormous port, one of the largest commercial ports in the world, was always crowded with ships. In it appeared the dark, rusty, gigantic armour-clad vessels. In it were loaded, on their way to the Far East, the yellow, thick-funnelled steamers of the Volunteer fleet that absorbed every day long trains of goods or thousands of prisoners. In spring and autumn, hundreds of flags from all points of the globe waved, and from morning until night orders and insults, in every conceivable language, rang out lustily. From the ships to the docks and warehouses and back along the quivering gangways the loaders ran to and fro, Russian tramps in rags, almost naked, with drunken, swollen faces, swarthy Turks, in dirty turbans, with large trousers, loose to the knees but tightened from there to the ankles, squat, muscular Persians, their hair and nails painted a red-carrot colour with quinquina.

Often graceful Italian schooners, with two or three

masts, their regular layers of sail clean, white and elastic as young women's breasts, would put in to this port at respectful distances from each other. Just showing over the lighthouse, these stately ships seemed—particularly on a clear spring morning—like wonderful white phantoms, swimming not on the water, but on the air above the horizon. Here, too, for months in the dirty green port water, among the rubbish of egg-shells and water-melon peels, among the flight of white sea-gulls, the high boats from Anatolia, the felligi from Trebizond, with their strange painted carvings and fantastic ornaments, swayed at anchor. Here extraordinary narrow ships, with black tarred sails, with a dirty rag in place of a flag, swam in from time to time. Doubling the mole, almost rattling against it with its side, one of these ships, lying close to the water, and without moderating its speed, would dash into any harbour, and there, amid the international insults, curses and threats, would put in at the first dock to hand, where its sailors—quite naked, bronzed little people, with guttural gurgling voices—would furl the torn sails with amazing rapidity and the dirty mysterious ship would immediately become lifeless. And just as enigmatically some dark night, without lighting its fires, it would soundlessly disappear from the port. At night, indeed, the whole bay swarmed with light little smuggling craft. The fishermen from the outskirts, and from further off, used to cart their fish into town, in the spring small *kamsas* filling their long boats by the million; in the summer the monstrous dab; in the autumn mackerel, fat *kefals* and oysters; in the winter white sturgeon from ten to twenty poods in weight, often caught at considerable risk, miles out to sea.

All these people—sailors of varied nationalities, fishermen, stokers, merry cabin-boys, port thieves, mechanics, workmen, boatmen, loaders, divers, smugglers—all young, healthy, and impregnated with the strong smell of the sea and fish, knew well what it was to endure, enjoyed

4

the delight and the terror of everyday danger, valued, above anything else, courage, daring, the ring of strong slashing words, and, when on shore, would give themselves up with savage delight to debauchery, drunkenness, and fighting. At night, the lights of the large town, towering above the port, lured them like magical shining eyes that always promised something fresh, glad, and not yet experienced, but always with the same deceit.

The town was linked to the port by steep, narrow, crooked streets, which decent folk avoided at night. At every step one encountered night shelters with dirty windows, protected by railings and lit up by the gloomy light of the solitary lamp inside. Still oftener one passed little shops in which one could sell anything one happened to have, from the sailor's kit down to his net, and rig oneself out again in whatever sailor's kit one chose. Here, too, were many beershops, taverns, eating-houses and inns, with flamboyant sign-boards in every known language, and not a few disorderly houses, at once obvious and secret, from the steps of which hideously painted women would call to the sailors in hoarse voices. There were Greek coffee-shops, where one used to play dominoes and cards ; and Turkish coffee-shops, where one could smoke narghiles and get a night's shelter for five kopeks. There were small Oriental inns in which they sold snails, *petalidis*, shrimps, mussels, large inky scuttle-fishes, and all sorts of sea monstrosities. Somewhere in the attics and basements, behind heavy shutters, were hidden gambling dens, where faro and baccarat often ended in one's stomach being slit or one's skull broken. And right at the next corner, sometimes in the next house, there was sure to be someone with whom one could dispose of anything stolen, from a diamond bracelet to a silver cross, and from a bale of Lyons velvet to a sailor's Government greatcoat.

These steep narrow streets, blackened with coal dust, towards night became greasy and reeked as though they were sweating in a nightmare. They resembled drains or dirty pipes, through which the cosmopolitan town vomited into the sea all its rubbish, all its rottenness, all its abomination and its vice, infecting with these things the strong muscular bodies and simple souls of the men of the sea.

The rowdy inhabitants of these streets rarely visited the dressed-up, always holiday-like, town, with its plate-glass windows, its imposing monuments, its gleam of electric light, its asphalt pavements, its avenues of white acacias, its imposing policemen and all its surface of cleanliness and order. But every one of them, before he had flung to the winds those torn, greasy, swollen paper roubles of his toil, would invariably visit Gambrinous'. This was sanctified by ancient tradition, even if it were necessary to steal under cover of darkness into the very centre of the town.

Many of them, truly enough, did not know the complicated name of the famous Beer King. Someone would simply say : " Let's go to Sasha's." And the others would answer : " Right-o. That's agreed." And they would shout in a chorus together : " Hurrah ! "

It is not in the least surprising that among the dock and sea folk Sasha enjoyed more respect and popularity than, for example, the local archbishop or governor, and, without doubt, if it were not his name then it was his vivid monkey face and his fiddle that were remembered in Sydney or Plymouth, as well as in New York, Vladivostok, Constantinople, and Ceylon, to say nothing of the gulfs and bays of the Black Sea, where there were many admirers of his talent among the daring fishermen.

Sasha would usually arrive at Gambrinous' at a time when there was nobody there except perhaps a chance visitor or two. At this time, a thick, sour smell of yesterday's beer hung over the rooms and it was rather dark, as they were economical in those days with gas. In hot July days, when the stone town languished from the heat and was deafened by the crackling din of the streets, one found the quiet and coolness of the place quite agreeable.

Sasha would approach the buffet, greet Madame Ivanova, and drink his first mug of beer. Sometimes she would say : " Won't you play something, Sasha ? "

" What do you want me to play, Madame Ivanova ? " Sasha, who was on the most polite terms with her, used to ask amiably.

" Something of your own."

Then he would sit down in his usual place to the left of the piano and play long, strange, melancholy pieces. Somehow it became sleepy and quiet in the basement, with only a hint of the muffled roar of the town. From time to time the waiters would jingle carefully the crockery on the other side of the kitchen wall. Then from the chords of Sasha's fiddle came, interwoven and blended with the sad flowers of national melodies, Jewish sorrow as ancient as the earth. Sasha's face, his chin strained, his forehead bent low, his eyes looking gravely up from under the heavy brows, had no resemblance, in this twilight hour, to the grinning, twinkling, dancing face of Sasha that was so familiar to all Gambrinous' guests. The little dog, Bielotchka, was sitting on his knees. She had been taught long ago not to howl to the music, but the passionately sad, sobbing and cursing sounds got on her nerves in spite of herself, and in convulsive little yawns she opened her mouth, curling up her fine pink tongue, and, with all her fragile body and pretty small muzzle, vibrated to her master's music. But little by little the public began to appear, and with it the accompanist, who had left his daily occupation at some tailor's or watchmaker's shop. On the buffet there were sausages in hot water and cheese sandwiches, and at last the other gas-jets were lit up. Sasha drank his second mug of beer, gave his order to his accompanist : " ' The May Parade,' eins, zwei, drei," and a stormy march began. From this moment he had scarcely time to exchange greetings with the newcomers, each of whom considered himself Sasha's particularly intimate friend and looked round proudly at the other guests after receiving his bow. Winking first with one eye and then with the other, gathering all his wrinkles into his bald receding skull, Sasha moved his lips grotesquely and smiled in all directions.

At about ten or eleven, Gambrinous', which could accommodate two hundred or more people, was absolutely choked. Many, almost half, came in accompanied by women with fichus on their heads. No one took offence at the lack of room, at a trampled toe, a crumpled hat, or someone else's beer being poured over one's trousers ; and if they did take offence it was merely a case of a drunken row.

The dampness of the dimly lit cellar showed itself on the walls, smeared with oil paint, and, from the ceiling the vapour from the crowd steamed like a warm heavy rain. At Gambrinous' they drank seriously. It was considered the right thing in this establishment to sit together in groups of two or three, covering so much of the improvised table with empty bottles that one saw one's vis-à-vis as through a glass-green forest.

In the turmoil of the evening the guests became hoarse and over-heated. Your eyes smarted from tobacco smoke. You had to shout and lean over the table in order to hear and be heard in the general din. And only the indefatigable fiddle of Sasha, sitting on his platform, triumphed over the stuffiness, the heat and the reek of tobacco, the gas jets, the beer, and the shouting of the unceremonious public.

But the guests rapidly became drunk from beer, the proximity of women, and the stifling air. Everyone wanted his own favourite songs. Close to Sasha, two or three people, with dull eyes and uncertain movements, were constantly bobbing up to him to pull him by the sleeve and interfere with his playing.

" Sash . . . the sad one . . . do pl . . . " the speaker stammered on, " do, please."

8

" At once, at once," Sasha would repeat with a quick nod as, with the adroitness of a doctor, he slipped the piece of silver noiselessly into his pocket. " At once, at once."

" Sasha, that's a swindle ! I've given the money and this is the twentieth time that I'm asking for : ' I was swimming down the sea to Odessa.' "

" At once, at once."

" Sasha, ' The Nightingale.' "

" Sasha, ' Marussia.' "

" ' Zetz,' ' Zetz,' Sasha, Sasha, ' Zetz,' ' Zetz.' "

" At once . . . at once."

" ' The Tchaban,' " howled from the other end of the room a scarcely human, but rather a kind of colt's voice.

And Sasha, to the general amusement, shouted back to him like a cock :

" At once."

And then without stopping, he would play all the songs they had called for.

Apparently he knew every single one of them by heart. Silver coins fell into his pockets from all sides and mugs of beer came to him from every table. When he descended from his platform to get to the bar he would be nearly pulled in pieces :

" Sashenka, one little mug, like a good chap."

" Here's to your health, Sasha ! you devil, come along when you're asked."

" Sasha come and d-r-i-i-i-nk some beer," bellowed the colt's voice.

The women, inclined, like all women, to admire professionals, would begin to coquet, make themselves conspicuous, and show off their adoration, calling to him in cooing voices and capricious, playful little laughs :

" Sashetchka, you simply must have a drink with me. No, no, no, I'm asking you. And then play the ' Cake Walk.' "

Sasha smiled, grimaced, bowed right and left, pressed

9

his hand to his heart, blew airy kisses, drank beer at all the tables and, on returning to the piano, where a fresh mug was waiting for him, would begin something like " Separation."

Sometimes, to amuse his audience, he would make his fiddle whine like a puppy, grunt like a pig, or rattle in heart-rending bass sounds, all in perfect time. The audience greeted these antics with benevolent approval : " Ho, ho-ho-ho-o-o."

It was becoming still hotter. Heat steamed from the ceiling. Some of the guests were already in tears, beating their breasts, others, with bloodshot eyes, were quarrelling over women and were clambering towards each other to pay off old scores, only to be held back by their more sober neighbours, generally parasites. The waiters miraculously found room for their legs and bodies to slide between the barrels, large and small, their hands strung with beer mugs raised high above the heads of the carousers. Madame Ivanova, more bloodless, imperturbable, and silent than ever, directed from her counter the performances of the waiters, like a ship captain in a storm.

Everyone was overpowered by the desire to sing. Softened by beer, by his own kindness, and even by the coarse delight that his music was giving to others, Sasha was ready to play anything. And at the sounds of his fiddle, hoarse people, with awkward, wooden voices, all bawled out the same tune, looking into one another's eyes with a senseless seriousness :

> " Why should we separate ?
> Why should we live in separation ?
> Isn't it better to marry
> And cherish love ? "

Then another gang, apparently hostile, tried to howl down its rival by starting another tune.

Gambrinous' was often visited by Greeks from Asia Minor, " Dongolaki " who put into the Russian ports with fish. They, too, gave orders to Sasha for their Oriental songs, consisting of dismal, monotonous howling on two or three notes, and they were ready to sing them for hours with gloomy faces and burning eyes. Sasha also played popular Italian couplets, Ukrainian popular songs, Jewish wedding-marches, and many others. Once a little party of negro sailors found their way into Gambinous', and they also, in imitation of the others, wanted very much to sing a bit. Sasha quickly picked up a galloping negro melody, chose the accompaniment on the piano, and, then and there, to the great delight and amusement of the habitués, the beershop rang with the strange, capricious, guttural sounds of an African song.

An acquaintance of Sasha's, a reporter on a local paper, once persuaded a professor of the musical school to pay a visit to Gambrinous' and listen to the famous violinist, but Sasha got wind of it and purposely made his fiddle mew, bleat, and bellow more than usual that evening. The guests of Gambrinous' were simply splitting their sides and the professor observed with profound contempt : " Clownery."

And out he went without even finishing his mug of beer.

III

Every now and then the exquisite marquises, the festive German sportsmen, the plump cupids, and the frogs looked down from their walls on the kind of debauch that one could seldom see anywhere, except at Gambrinous'.

For example, a gang of thieves on a spree after a good haul would come in, each with his sweetheart, each with his cap on one side and a defiant, insolent expression, displaying his patent leather boots negligently with all the distinction of the cabaret at its best. To them Sasha would play special thieves' songs, such as " I'm done for, poor little boy," " Don't cry, Marussia," " The spring has passed," and others.

It was beneath their dignity to dance, but their sweethearts, for the most part not bad-looking and usually young, some almost little girls, would dance the " Tchaban," squealing and clicking their heels. Both men and women drank heavily ; one thing only was wrong with them, they always finished their sprees with old disputes about money, and went off, when they could, without paying.

Fishermen, after a good catch, would come in a large party of about thirty. Late in the autumn there were such lucky weeks that each net would bring in every day up to forty thousand mackerel or *kefal*. At a time like this the smallest shareholder would make over two hundred roubles. But what was still better for the fishermen was a lucky haul of sturgeon in the winter ; this was a matter of great difficulty.

One had to work hard some thirty versts from shore, in the still of the night, sometimes in stormy weather. When the boats leaked, the water froze on one's clothes and on the oars. The weather would keep like this for two or three days if the wind did not throw you two hundred versts away at Anap or Trebizond. Every winter a dozen or so of skiffs would simply disappear, and only in the summer did the waves bring back to this or that point of the coast the corpse of the gallant fishermen.

But when they came back from the sea safe, after a good catch, they came on shore with a frenzied thirst for life. Thousands of roubles went in two or three days in the coarsest, most deafening, drunken orgies. The fishermen used to get into some cabaret or other, throw all the other guests out, lock the doors, close the shutters, and for days at a stretch, without stopping, would devote themselves to women and drink, howl songs, smash the glasses and the crockery, beat the women and frequently

12

one another, until sleep came over them anywhere—on the tables, on the floor, across the beds, among spittoons, cigar ends, broken glasses, the splash of wine and even the splash of blood. That is how the fishermen went on the spree for several consecutive days, sometimes changing the place, sometimes remaining in the same den. Having gone through everything to the last farthing, they would return to the docks, their heads bursting, their faces marked by brawls, their limbs shaking from drink, and, silent, cowed, and repentant, would enter the boats to resume that hard and captivating trade which they loved and cursed in the same breath.

Never did they forget to visit Gambrinous'. In they would throng with their hoarse voices and their faces burnt by the ferocious north-west winter, with their waterproof jackets, their leather trousers, and their top-boots up to the thighs, those selfsame boots in which their comrades, in the middle of some stormy night, had gone to the bottom like stones.

Out of respect for Sasha, they did not kick strangers out, though they felt themselves masters of the beershop, and would break the heavy mugs on the floor. Sasha played for them their own fishermen's songs, drawling, simple, and terrible, as the beat of the sea, and they sang altogether, straining to the uttermost their powerful chests and hardened throats. Sasha acted upon them like Orpheus on the waves and sometimes an old hetman of a boat, forty years old, bearded, weather-beaten, an enormous wild-animal-like fellow, would melt into tears as he gave out in a small voice the sorrowful words of :

> " Ah, poor me, little lad
> That I was born a fisherman . . . . "

And sometimes they danced, trampling always on the same spot, with set stone-like faces, rattling with their heavy boots, and impregnating the whole cabaret with the sharp salt smell of the fish, with which their clothes

13

and bodies had been soaked through and through. To Sasha they were very generous and never left him long away from their tables. He knew well the outline of their desperate, reckless lives, and often, when playing for them, he felt in his soul a kind of respectful grief.

But he was particularly fond of playing for the English sailors from the merchant ships. They would come in a herd, hand in hand, looking like picked men, big-chested, large-shouldered, with white teeth, healthy colours, and merry bold blue eyes. Their strong muscles stood out under their jackets and from their deep-cut collars rose, straight and strong, their stately necks. Some of them knew Sasha from former visits to this port. They recognised him, grinning with their white teeth, and greeted him in Russian.

" Zdraist, Zdraist."

Sasha of his own accord, without invitation, used to play for them " Rule, Britannia." Probably the consciousness that they were now in a country bowed down by centuries of slavery gave a certain proud solemnity to this hymn of English liberty. And when they sang, standing with uncovered heads, the last magnificent words : " Britons never, never, never shall be slaves," then, involuntarily, the most boisterous visitor to Gambrinous' took off his hat.

The square-built boatswain, with one earring and a beard that fringed his neck, came up to Sasha with two mugs of beer and a broad smile, clapped him on the back in a friendly way, and asked him to play a jig. At the very first sound of this bold and daring dance of the sea, the English jumped up and cleared out the place, pushing the little barrels to the walls. The stranger's permission was asked, by gestures, with merry smiles, but if someone was in no hurry, there was no ceremony with him, and his seat was simply knocked from under him with a good kick. This was seldom necessary, however, because at Gambrinous' everybody appreciated dances and was

14

particularly fond of the English jig. Even Sasha himself, playing all the time, would mount on a chair so as to see better.

The sailors formed a circle, clapping their hands in time with the quick dance music, and then two of them came out into the middle. The dance figured the life of a sailor on sea. The ship is ready to start, the weather is superb, everything is in order. The dancers have their hands crossed on their chests, their heads thrown back, their bodies quiet, though the feet mark a frenzied beat. Then a slight wind arises and with it a faint rocking. For a sailor, that is only pleasant, but the steps of the dance become more and more complicated and varied. A fresh wind starts—it is already not so easy to walk on deck—and the dancers are slightly rocked from side to side. At last there comes a real storm and the sailor is hurled from taffrail to taffrail; the business is getting serious. " All hands on deck ! Reef the sails ! " By the dancers' movements one detects with amusement how they scramble up the shrouds with hands and feet, haul the sails and strengthen the topsail while the storm tosses the ship more and more fiercely. " Man overboard, stop." A boat is lowered. The dancers, bending their heads low and straining their powerful naked throats, row with quick strokes as they bend and straighten their backs. But the storm passes, the rocking settles down, and the ship runs lightly with a following wind, while the dancers become motionless again with crossed hands as they beat with their feet a swift merry jig.

Sometimes Sasha had to play a Lezguinka for the Georgians, who were employed at wine-making in the neighbourhood. No dance was ever unknown to him. When a dancer, in a fur cap and atcherkessba, fluttered airily between the barrels, throwing first one hand and then the other behind his head, while his friends clapped in time and shrieked, Sasha, too, could not refrain and shouted joyously in time with them : " Hass, hass,

hass." Sometimes, too, he would play Moldavian dances and the Italian Tarantella and waltzes for German sailors.

Occasionally they fought, and sometimes rather brutally, at Gambrinous'. Old visitors liked to yarn about the legendary slaughter between Russian sailors on active service, discharged from some cruiser to the reserve, and a party of English sailors. They fought with fists, casse-têtes, beer-mugs, and even hurled at each other the little barrels that were used for seats. It must be admitted, and not to the honour of the Russian warriors, that it was they who first started the row, and first took to the knife, and though they were three to one in numbers, they only squeezed the English out of the beershop after a fight of half an hour.

Quite often Sasha's interference stopped a quarrel that was within a hair's breadth of bloodshed. He would come up to the disputants, joke, smile, grimace, and at once from all sides mugs would be stretched out to him. " Sasha, a little mug ; Sasha have one with me. . . ."

Perhaps the kind and comic goodness, merrily beaming from those eyes that were almost hidden under the sloping skull, acted like a charm on these simple savages. Perhaps it was an innate respect for talent, something almost like gratitude. Perhaps it was due to the fact that most of the habitués of Gambrinous' were never out of Sasha's debt. In the tedious interludes of " dekocht," which, in sea-port jargon, means " stony broke," one could approach Sasha for small sums and for small credit at the buffet without fear of refusal.

Of course the debts were never repaid—not from evil intention, but merely from forgetfulness. All the same, these debtors, during their orgies, returned tenfold their debts in their " tips " to Sasha for his songs. The woman at the buffet sometimes reproached him. " I am surprised, Sasha, that you're not more careful with your money."

He would answer with conviction : " But, Madame Ivanova, I can't take it with me in my grave. There'll

16

be enough for us both, that is for me and Bielotchka. Come here, Bielotchka, good doggie."

V

The songs of the day could also be heard at Gambrinous'.

At the time of the Boer War, the "Boer March" was a great favourite. (It seems that the famous fight between the Russian and English sailors took place at this very time.) Twenty times an evening at least they forced Sasha to play this heroic march, and invariably waved their caps and shouted "Hurrah!" They would look askance, too, at indifferent onlookers, which was not always a good omen at Gambrinous'.

Then came the Franco-Russian celebrations. The mayor gave a grudged permission for the "Marseillaise" to be played. It was called for every day, but not so often as the "Boer March," and they shouted "Hurrah" in a smaller chorus, and did not wave their caps at all. This state of things arose from the fact that no deep sentiment underlay their call for the "Marseillaise." Again, the audience at Gambrinous' did not grasp sufficiently the political importance of the alliance; finally, one noticed that it was always the same people every evening who asked for the "Marseillaise" and shouted "Hurrah."

For a short time the "Cake Walk" was popular, and once an excited little merchant danced it, in and out between the barrels, without removing his raccoon coat, his high goloshes, and his fox fur hat. However, the negro dance was soon forgotten.

Then came the great Japanese War. The visitors to Gambrinous' began to live at high pressure. Newspapers appeared on the barrels; war was discussed every evening. The most peaceful, simple people were transformed into politicians and strategists. But at the bottom of his heart, each one of them was anxious if not for himself, then for a brother or, still more often, for a close comrade. In those days the conspicuously strong tie which welds together those who have shared long toil, danger, and the near presence of death, showed itself clearly.

At the beginning no one doubted our victory. Sasha had procured from somewhere the " Kuropatkine March," and for about twenty-nine evenings, one after the other, he played it with a certain success. But, somehow or other, one evening the " Kuropatkine March " was squeezed out for good by a song brought by the Balaklava fishermen, the salt Greeks, or the Pindoss, as they were called.

> " And why were we turned into soldiers,
> And sent to the Far East ?
> Are we really at fault because
> Our height is an extra inch ? "

From that moment they would listen to no other song at Gambrinous'. For whole evenings one could hear nothing but people clamouring :

" Sasha, the sorrowful one, the Balaklava one."

They sang, cried, and drank twice as much as before, but, so far as drinking went, all Russia was doing much the same. Every evening someone would come to say good-bye, would brag for a bit, puff himself out like a cock, throw his hat on the floor, threaten to smash all the little Japs by himself, and end up with the sorrowful song and tears.

Once Sasha came earlier than usual to the beershop. Tho woman at the buffet said from habit, as she poured out his first mug : " Sasha, play something of your own." All of a sudden his lips became contorted and his mug shook in his hand.

" Do you know, Madame Ivanova," he said in a bewildered way, " they're taking me as a soldier, to the war ! "

Madame Ivanova threw her hands up in astonishment. " But it's impossible, Sasha, you're joking."

18

Sasha shook his head dejectedly and submissively. " I'm not joking."

" But you're over age, Sasha ; how old are you ? "

No one had ever been interested in that question. Everyone considered Sasha as old as the walls of the beershop, the marquises, the Ukrainians, the frogs, and even the painted king who guarded the entrance, Gambrinous himself.

" Forty-six." Sasha thought for a second or two. " Perhaps forty-nine. I'm an orphan," he added sadly.

" But you must go and explain to the authorities ! "

" I've been to them already, Madame Ivanova. I have explained."

" Well ? "

" Well, they answered : ' Scabby Jew, sheeny snout ! Just you say a little more and you'll be jugged, there ! ' And then they struck me."

Everyone heard the news that evening at Gambrinous', and they got Sasha dead drunk with their sympathy. He tried to play the buffoon, grimaced, winked, but from his kind funny eyes there peeped out grief and awe. A strongish workman, a tinker by trade, suddenly offered to go to the war in Sasha's place. The stupidity of the suggestion was quite clear to all, but Sasha was touched, shed a few tears, embraced the tinker, and then and there gave him his fiddle. He left Bielotchka with the woman at the buffet.

" Madame Ivanova, take care of the little dog ! Perhaps I won't come back, so you will have a souvenir of Sasha. Bielinka, good doggie ! Look, it's licking itself. Ah you, my poor little one. And I want to ask you something else, Madame Ivanova ; the boss owes me some money, so please get it and send it on. I'll write the addresses. In Gomel I have a first cousin who has a family and in Jmerinka there's my nephew's widow. I send it them every month. Well, we Jews are people like that, we are fond of our relations, and I'm an orphan. I'm alone. Good-bye, then, Madame Ivanova."

" Good-bye, Sasha, we must at least have a good-bye kiss. It's been so many years . . . and, don't be angry, I'm going to cross you for the journey."

Sasha's eyes were profoundly sad, but he couldn't help clowning to the end.

" But, Madame Ivanova, what if I die from the Russian cross ? "

V

Gambrinous' became empty as though orphaned without Sasha and his fiddle. The manager invited as a substitute a quartette of strolling mandolinists, one of whom, dressed like a comic-opera Englishman, with red whiskers and a false nose, check trousers, and a stiff collar higher than his ears, sang comic couplets and danced shamelessly on the platform. But the quartette was an utter failure ; it was hissed and pelted with bits of sausage, and the leading comic was once beaten by the Tendrove fishermen for a disrespectful allusion to Sasha.

All the same, Gambrinous', from old memory, was visited by the lads of sea and port, whom the war had not drawn to death and suffering. Every evening the first subject of conversation would be Sasha.

" Eh, it would be fine to have Sasha back now. One's soul feels heavy without him."

" Ye-e-es, where are you hovering, Sashenka, dear, kind friend ? "

" In the fields of Manchuria far away . . . " someone would pipe up in the words of the latest song. Then he would break off in confusion, and another would put in unexpectedly : " Wounds may be split open and hacked. And there are also torn ones."

> " I congratulate you on victory,
> You with the torn-out arm."

" Stop, don't whine. Madame Ivanova, isn't there any news of Sasha ? A letter or a little postcard ? "

Madame Ivanova used to read the paper now the whole evening, holding it at arm's length, her head thrown back, her lips constantly moving. Bielotchka lay on her knees, giving from time to time little peaceful snores. The presider at the buffet was already far from being like a vigilant capatin on his bridge and her crew wandered about the shop half asleep.

At questions about Sasha's fate she would shake her head slowly. " I know nothing. There are no letters, and one gets nothing from the newspapers."

Then she would take off her spectacles slowly, place them, with the newspaper, close to the warm body of Bielotchka, and turn round to have a quiet cry to herself.

Sometimes she would bend over the dog and ask in a plaintive, touching little voice : " Bielinka, doggie, where is our Sasha, eh ? Where is our master ? "

Bielotchka raised her delicate little muzzle, blinked with her moist black eyes, and, in the tone of the buffet woman, began quietly to whine out : " Ah, ou-ou-ou. Aou—A-ou-ou-ou."

But time smooths and washes up everything. The mandolinists were replaced by balalaika players, and they, in their turn, by a choir of Ukrainians with girls. Then the well-known Leshka, the harmonicist, a professional thief who had decided, in view of his marriage, to seek regular employment, established himself at Gambrinous' more solidly than the others. He was a familiar figure in different cabarets, which explains why he was tolerated here, or, rather, had to be tolerated, for things were going badly at the beershop.

Months passed, a year passed ; no one remembered anything more about Sasha, except Madame Ivanova, who no longer cried when she mentioned his name. Another year went by. Probably even the little white dog had forgotten Sasha.

21

But in spite of Sasha's misgivings, he had not died from the Russian cross ; he had not even been once wounded, though he had taken part in three great battles, and, on one occasion, went to the attack in front of his battalion as a member of the band, in which he played the fife. At Vafangoa he was taken prisoner, and at the end of the war he was brought back on board a German ship to the very port where his friends continued to work and create uproars.

The news of his arrival ran like an electric current round the bays, moles, wharves, and workshops. In the evening there was scarcely standing-room at Gambrinous'. Mugs of beer were passed from hand to hand over people's heads, and although many escaped without paying on that day, Gambrinous' never did such business before. The tinker brought Sasha's fiddle, carefully wrapped up in his wife's fichu, which he then and there sold for drink. Sasha's old accompanist was fished out from somewhere or other. Leshka, the harmonicist, a jealous, conceited fellow, tried to compete with Sasha, repeating obstinately : " I am paid by the day and I have a contract." But he was merely thrown out and would certainly have been thrashed but for Sasha's intercession.

Probably not one of the hero-patriots of the Japanese War had ever seen such a hearty and stormy welcome as was given to Sasha. Strong rough hands seized him, lifted him into the air, and threw him with such force that he was almost broken to bits against the ceiling. And they shouted so deafeningly that the gas-jets went out and several times a policeman came down into the beershop, imploring : " A little lower, it really sounds very loud in the street."

That evening Sasha played all the favourite songs and dances of the place. He also played some little Japanese songs that he had learned as a prisoner, but his audience did not take to them. Madame Ivanova, like one revived, was once more courageously on her bridge while Bielinka,

22

sitting on Sasha's knees, yelped with joy. When he stopped playing, simple-minded fishermen, realising for the first time the miracle of Sasha's return, would suddenly exclaim in naïve and delighted stupefaction :

" Brothers, but this is Sasha ! "

The rooms of Gambrinous' then resounded once more with joyous bad words, and Sasha would be again seized and thrown up to the ceiling while they shouted, drank healths, and spilt beer over one another.

Sasha, it seemed, had scarcely altered and had not grown older during his absence. His sufferings had produced no more external change on him than on the modelled Gambrinous, the guardian and protector of the beershop. Only Madame Ivanova, with the sensitiveness of a kind-hearted woman, noticed that the expression of awe and distress, which she had seen in Sasha's eyes when he said good-bye, had not disappeared, but had become yet deeper and more significant. As in old days, he played the buffoon, winked, and puckered up his forehead, but Madame Ivanova felt that he was pretending all the time.

VI

Everything was as usual, just as if there had been no war at all and Sasha had never been imprisoned in Nagasaki. Just as usual the fishermen, with their giant boots, were celebrating a lucky catch of sturgeon, while bands of thieves danced in the old way, Sasha playing, just as he used to do, sailor songs brought to him from every inlet of the globe.

But already dangerous, stormy times were at hand. One evening the whole town became stirred and agitated, as though roused by a tocsin, and, at an unusual hour, the streets grew black with people. Small white sheets were going from hand to hand, bearing the miraculous word " Liberty," which the whole immeasurable confident country repeated to itself that evening.

There followed clear, holiday-like, exulting days, and their radiance lit up even the vaults of Gambrinous'. Students and workmen came in and beautiful young girls came too. People with blazing eyes mounted on those barrels, which had seen so much in their time, and spoke. Everything was not comprehensible in the words they uttered, but the hearts of all throbbed and expanded to meet the flaming hope and the great love that vibrated through them.

"Sasha, the 'Marseillaise'! Go ahead with the 'Marseillaise'!"

No, this was not at all like that other "Marseillaise" that the mayor had grudgingly allowed to be played during the week of the Franco-Russian celebrations. Endless processions, with songs and red flags, were going along the streets. The women wore red ribbons and red flowers. People who were utter strangers met and shook hands with each other with happy smiles. But suddenly all this jubilation disappeared, as if washed out like children's footsteps on the sands. The sub-inspector of police, fat, small, choking, with bloodshot protruding eyes, his face red as an over-ripe tomato, stormed into Gambrinous'.

"What? Who's the proprietor of this place?" he rattled out. "Bring him to me." Suddenly his eyes fell on Sasha, who was standing, fiddle in hand.

"So you're the proprietor, are you! Shut up! What, playing anthems? No anthems permitted."

"There will be no more anthems at all, your Highness," Sasha replied calmly.

The police dog turned purple, brought his raised index finger to Sasha's very nose, and shook it menacingly from left to right.

"None—what—ever."

"I understand, your Highness—none whatever."

"I'll teach you revolutions! I'll teach you!"

The sub-inspector bounded out of the beershop like a bomb, and with his departure everyone became flattened

24

and dejected. And gloom descended on the whole town. For dark, anxious, repugnant rumours were floating about. One talked cautiously. People feared to betray themselves by a glance, were afraid of their own shadows, afraid of their own thoughts. The town thought for the first time with dread of the sewer that was rumbling under its feet, down there by the sea into which it had been throwing out, for so many years, its poisoned refuse. The town shielded the plate-glass windows of its magnificent shops, protected with patrols its proud monuments, and posted artillery in the yards of its fine houses in case of emergency. But in the outskirts, in the fetid dens, in the rotting garrets, throbbed, prayed, and cried with awe the people chosen by God, abandoned long ago by the wrathful Bible God, but still believing that the measure of its heavy trials was not yet spent.

Down there by the sea, in those streets that resembled black, sticky drain-pipes, a mysterious work was progressing. The doors of the cabarets, tea-shops, and night-shelters were open all night.

In the morning the pogrom began. These people who, so recently uplifted by the pure, general joy, so recently softened by the light of the coming brotherhood of man, who had gone through the streets singing beneath the symbols of liberty they had won—these very people were now going to kill, not because they had been ordered to kill, not because they had any hatred against the Jews, with whom they had often close friendships, not even for the sake of loot, which was doubtful, but because the sly dirty devil that lives deep down in each human being was whispering in their ears : " Go. Nothing will be punished : the forbidden curiosity of the murderer, the sensuality of rape, the power over other people's lives."

In these days of the pogroms, Sasha, with his funny, monkey-like, purely Jewish physiognomy, went freely about the town. They did not touch him. There was about him that immovable courage of the soul, that absence

even of *fear of fear* which guards the weakest better than
any revolver. But on one occasion, when, jammed against
the wall, he was trying to avoid the crowd that flowed like
a hurricane down the full width of the street, a mason in
a red shirt and a white apron, threatened him with his
pointed crowbar and grunted out, " Sheeny ! Smash the
sheeny ! Smash him to the gutter."

Someone seized his hands from behind.

" Stop, devil ! It's Sasha, you lout ! "

The mason stopped. In this drunken, delirious, insane
moment he was ready to kill anyone—his father, his sister,
the priest, the Orthodox God himself—but he was also
ready, as an infant, to obey the orders of any strong will.
He grinned like an idiot, spat, and wiped his nose with
his hand. Suddenly his eyes fell on the white, nervous
little dog, which was trembling all over as it rubbed itself
against Sasha. The man bent down quickly, caught it
by the hind legs, lifted it up, struck it against the paving-
stone, and then took to his heels. Sasha looked at him
in silence. He was running all bent forward, his hands
stretched out, without his cap, his mouth open, his eyes
white and round with madness.

On Sasha's boots were sprinkled the brains of little
Bielotchka. Sasha wiped off the stains with his handkerchief.

VII

Then began a strange period that resembled the sleep
of a man in paralysis. There was no light in a single
window throughout the whole town in the evening, but
for all that the flaming sign-boards of the cafés chantants
and the little cabarets shone brightly. The conquerors
were proving their force, not yet satiated with their im-
punity. Savage people, in Manchurian fur caps with
St. George's ribbons in their buttonholes, visited the

restaurants and insistently demanded the playing of the
national anthem, making sure that everybody rose to
his feet. They also broke into private flats, fumbled
about in the beds and chests of drawers, asking for vodka,
money, and the national anthem, their drunken breath
polluting the atmosphere.

Once, some ten of them visited Gambrinous' and occupied
two tables. They behaved with the greatest insolence,
talked dictatorially to the waiters, spat over the shoulders
of perfect strangers, put their feet on other people's seats,
and threw their beer on the floor, under the pretext that
it was flat. Everyone let them alone. Everyone knew
that they were police-agents and looked at them with
that secret awe and disgusted curiosity with which the
people regard executioners. One of them was apparently
the leader. He was a certain Motka Gundoss, a red-
haired, snuffling fellow with a broken nose, a man who
was said to be enormously strong, formerly a professional
thief, then a bully in a disorderly house, and after that
a souteneur and a police-agent. He was a converted
Jew.

Sasha was playing the " Metelitza," when all of a sudden
Gundoss came up to him and seized his right hand firmly,
shouting, as he turned to the audience, " The national
anthem—the anthem, the anthem, the national anthem,
brothers, in honour of our adored monarch ! "

" The anthem, the anthem," groaned the other scoundrels
in the fur caps.

" The anthem," shouted a solitary uncertain voice.

But Sasha freed his hand and said calmly : " No anthems
whatever."

" What ? " bellowed Gundoss, " you refuse ? Ah, you
stinking sheeny ! "

Sasha bent forward quite close to Gundoss, holding
his lowered fiddle by the finger-board, his face all wrinkled
up, as he said :

" And you ? "

" What, me ? "

" I am a stinking sheeny ; all right ; and you ? "

" I am orthodox."

" Orthodox ? And for how much ? "

The whole of Gambrinous' burst out laughing, and Gundoss turned to his comrades, white with rage.

" Brothers," he said, in a plaintive, shaking voice, and using words that were not his own but which he had learned by heart. " Brothers, how long are we to tolerate the insults of these sheenies against the throne and the Holy Church ? "

But Sasha, who had drawn himself up compelled him with a single sound to face him again, and no one at Gambrinous' would ever have believed that this funny, grimacing Sasha could talk with such weight and power.

" You ? " shouted Sasha. " You, you son of a dog. Show me your face, you murderer. Look right at me. Well ? Well—— "

It all happened in the flash of a second. Sasha's fiddle rose swiftly, swiftly flashed in the air, and crack—the big fellow in the fur cap reeled from a sound blow on the temple. The fiddle broke into fragments and in Sasha's hands remained only the finger-board, which he brandished victoriously over the heads of the crowd.

" Br-o-th-ers, help ! Save me-e," howled Gundoss.

But already it was too late to save him. A powerful wall surrounded Sasha and covered him. And this same wall swept the people in the fur caps out of the place.

An hour later, when Sasha, after finishing his night's work in the beerhouse, was coming out into the street, several people threw themselves on him. Someone struck him in the eye, whistled, and said to the policeman who ran up :

" To the police-station. Secret service. Here's my badge."

VIII

Now for the second time Sasha was considered to be definitely buried. Someone had witnessed the whole scene outside the beershop and had handed it on to the others. And at Gambrinous' there were sittings of experienced people who understood the meaning of such an establishment as the police-court, the meaning of a police-agent's vengeance.

But now they were much less anxious about Sasha's fate than they had been before ; they forgot about him much more quickly. Two months later there appeared in his place a new violinist (incidentally, one of Sasha's pupils), who had been fished up by the accompanist.

Then, one quiet spring evening, some three months later, just when the musicians were playing the waltz, " Expectation," someone's thin voice called out in fright :

" Boys, it's Sasha ! "

Everyone turned round and rose from the barrels, Yes, it was he, the twice resurrected Sasha, but now with a full-grown beard, thin, pale. They threw themselves at him, surrounded him, thronged to him, rumpled him, plied him with mugs of beer, but all at once the same thin voice exclaimed :

" Brothers, his hand—— "

Suddenly they all became silent. Sasha's left hand, hooked and all shrivelled up, was turned with the elbow towards his side. Apparently it could not bend or unbend, the fingers were permanently sticking up under the chin.

" What's the matter with you, comrade ? " the hairy boatswain from the Russian Navigation Company asked.

" Oh, it's nothing much—a kind of sinew or something of that sort," Sasha replied carelessly.

" So that's it."

They all became silent again. " That means it's the

end of the ' Tchaban ' ? " the boatswain asked compassionately.

" The ' Tchaban,' " Sasha exclaimed, with dancing eyes.
" You there," he ordered the accompanist with all his old
assurance. " The ' Tchaban '—eins, zwei, drei."

The pianist struck up the merry dance, glancing doubtfully over his shoulder.

But Sasha took out of his pocket with his healthy hand
some kind of small instrument, about the size of his palm,
elongated and black, with a stem which he put into his
mouth, and bending himself to the left, as much as his
mutilated, motionless hand allowed, he began suddenly to
whistle an uproariously merry " Tchaban."

" Ho, ho, ho ! " the audience rocked with laughter.

" The devil," exclaimed the boatswain and without
in the least intending it he made a clever step and began
to beat quick time. Fired by his enthusiasm the women
and men began to dance. Even the waiters, trying not to
lose their dignity, smilingly capered at their posts. Even
Madame Ivanova, unmindful of the duties of the captain
on his watch, shook her head in time with the flame dance
and lightly snapped her fingers to its rhythm. And perhaps even the old, spongy, time-worn Gambrinous slightly
moved his eyebrows and glanced merrily into the street.
For it seemed that from the hands of the crippled, hooked
Sasha the pitiable pipe-shell sang in a language, unfortunately not yet comprehensible to Gambrinous' friends, or to
Sasha himself.

Well, there it is ! You may maim a man, but art will
endure all and conquer all.

A SENTIMENTAL ROMANCE

MY DEAREST FRIEND,

Here I am at our sanatorium by the sea, just as I was last spring. Even my room is the same. Only, during the winter, the wallpaper has been changed and there is a slight smell of paste still in the room. I don't know how other people feel, but this smell always brings back to me that sweet, gentle melancholy which is so indissolubly linked with the memories of childhood. Perhaps it has clung to me ever since my schooldays. I remember how, in old times, they used to bring me back after the long summer holidays. As you pass through the quite familiar dormitory, the classrooms, the corridors and everywhere, you detect the smell of paste, of fresh paint, of lime and varnish. And you feel, with a sense of troubled melancholy, that you are again stepping over a new border of life and you vaguely regret the past that has been left on the other side—grey, ordinary, unpleasant, but endlessly dear, just because it is the past and will never, never repeat itself. Ah, that past! What a mysterious, untranslatable charm it retains over one's soul! Even to you, my dearest, I only dare to write because I feel, since the morning, under the spell of last year's memories.

I am sitting at this moment at the writing-table, but I have only to lift my eyes from it to see the sea, that very sea with which you and I—do you remember?—were so poetically in love. But, even without looking up, I can feel it. It seems to be rising in a level, dark blue shroud right up to the middle of my window, which is wide open. Over it is the blue sky, quite cloudless and solemnly calm. And under the window an apple tree is in bloom. One of its branches, spreading out, covered all over with delicate blossoms, transparently white in the sunlight and faintly pink in the shade, peeps in over the sill. When a faint wind stirs the sea, it rocks slightly, as though bowing to me in a friendly greeting, and, scarcely audibly, rustles against the green barred shutter. I gaze at it and can never get enough of the swan-like movements of this white branch, covered with bloom, which, so softly, with such exquisite precision, outlines itself gracefully against the deep, strong, joyful blue of the sea. And I simply want to cry, so touched am I at its unsophisticated beauty.

Our sanatorium is drowned (forgive this antiquated comparison) in the white waves of pear trees, apple trees, almond trees and apricot trees, all in bloom. They say that in the language of the old inhabitants, the Tcherkesses, this exquisite little seaside village was called " The White Fiancée." What a delightful and fitting name ! There seems to emanate from it an atmosphere of coloured language and Eastern poetry, an atmosphere as of from something taken straight out of " The Song of Songs " of King Solomon.

The garden paths are covered with light, white petals, and, when the wind blows, the trees seem to be snowing in slowly falling, heavy flakes. These light snowflakes fly into my room, cover the writing-table, fall on my dress, my hair, and I can't—besides, I have no wish to—rid myself of these memories which agitate me and make my head turn like some old aromatic wine.

It was last spring, the third or fourth day after your arrival at the sanatorium. The morning was just as quiet, cool, and gleaming. We were sitting on the south verandah, I in the rocking-chair covered with a pale blue sailcloth (do you remember that armchair ?) and you on the balustrade, leaning against the corner post and holding it with one hand. My God, even now, after writing these lines, I stopped, closed my eyes for a few seconds, with my hand over them. And again, in front of me with extraordinary vividness, came to me your face of those days—thin, pale, with fine, distinguished features, a coil of dark hair hanging carelessly over the white forehead and with those deep, sad eyes. I can visualise even that pensive and absent-minded smile which used just to touch your lips when you said, looking dreamily at the falling petals of the white flowers, " The apple trees are shedding their blossom and the spring is only at its very start. Why does this swift, expansive bloom of the southern spring always awake in me such a maladive feeling of distress and unfulfilment ? No later than yesterday, it seems, I was watching with emotion the first swelling buds, and to-day the flowers are already scattering and you know that to-morrow will come the cold autumn. Isn't it like our own lives ? In youth, you live only on hope ; you think that now, at once, something great, absorbing, will seize hold of you, and then suddenly you seem to wake up and you see that nothing is left but memories and regret for the past, and you your-self are unable to tell at what precise period your real life swept by—the full, consciously beautiful life."

You see how well I remember your words ! Every-thing associated with you is imprinted on my soul in bright relief, and I treasure it, admire and delight in it, as a miser does in his gold. I confess even that I have come here exclusively to see once more, even from the window, a morsel of our sea and our sky, to smell the fine aroma of the apple trees in flower, to hear in the evening the dry chatter of the crickets and—to live endlessly over again in imagination those naïve, pale memories at whose faintness a healthy person would laugh aloud. Ah, those healthy people—with their rough appetite for life, their depths of strong sensation, permitted them by their strong bodies and their indifferent prodigality of soul—they cannot even imagine those untranslatably delicate, inexplicably complex shades of moods through which we pass, we who are condemned almost from our birth to the monotonous vegetation of the hospital, the health resort and the sanatorium.

Here everything is as it used to be. Only you are not here, my dear friend and teacher. Of course, you can guess that through the newspapers I have heard of your recovery and that you are back again in your University chair. Our dear doctor, as fond of life as ever, has confirmed this news, his face glowing with pleasure. Doubtless he attributes your cure to his system of hot baths and his theories of diet. As you know, I don't believe in either treatment, but all the same, I was ready to kiss this kindly and naïve egoist for his news of your health.

He, on the contrary, is not at all pleased with me. I saw it in the way he shook his head, wrinkling his lips and breathing hard through his nose with that preoccupied seriousness of his, while he was listening to my chest and tapping it. Finally, he advised me to go somewhere in the real south, to Mentone or even Cairo, advised me with an awkward and jocular prudence which was a poor mask for the anxiety that kept peeping out from his eyes. Visibly, he is afraid of the bad impression that my death will create among his patients, and he wants to save them this unpleasantness. I shall be very sorry to prejudice, involuntarily, the good reputation of his establishment, but, all the same, I do consider myself entitled to the luxury of dying in this particular place, sanctified by the poignant charm of early autumn.

All the more, because this will happen much sooner than he expects ; perhaps even before the last white petals of my apple tree have fled. I will confess to you, as a secret, that already I cannot go beyond the verandah, and even that is very difficult, though I still have the courage to answer the doctor's anxious, interrogative looks with an insouciant smile. But don't think that I am complaining to you in the selfish hope of arousing compassion for myself. No, I merely want to avail myself of the right, that a dying human being has, to discuss what healthy people are silent about from conventional shyness. Besides, I want to tell you that death does not frighten me and that it is to you, my dear friend, and only to you, that I owe this philosophic quietude. I understand now perfectly your words : " Death is the simplest and most normal of all the phenomena of life. Man comes into this world and lives exclusively through chance, but he dies only through inevitable law." This beautiful aphorism has become to me now particularly clear.

Yes, you have taught me a great deal. Without you, I should never have reached those slow, delicate delights, produced by a book one has just read, a deep and beautiful thought from a creative mind, inspired music, the beauty of sunset, the aroma of a flower, and—this first of all— the soul-communion of two refined natures, in which, owing to serious illness, nervous receptivity reaches a point of exaltation and mutual understanding passes into a silent clairvoyance.

Do you remember our long, unhurried walks along the seashore, under the perpendicular rays of the sun, in those burning, lazy, mid-day hours, when everything seems to die in helpless lassitude, and the waves just rustle and whiz on to the hot, yellow sand and go back into the dazzling sea, leaving behind a moist, dented edging, which disappears just as quickly as the traces of one's breath on glass ? Do you remember how we used to hide from the doctor, who allowed no one to be out of doors after sunset, and steal out on the terrace in the warm moonlit nights ? The moonlight would cut through the espalier of the dense vineyard and lie on the floor and the white wall, like a pattern of light, fantastic lace. In the darkness, we could not see, but only guess at each other, and the timid whispers in which we had to speak gave even to the simplest words a deep, intimate, agitating significance. Do you remember how, on the rainy days, when the sea was enveloped in a fog all day long and there was in the air a smell of wet sand, of fish and refreshed leaves, we used to tip-toe into my cosy room and read Shakespeare, just a little at a time, like real gourmets, tasting the savour of every page, revelling in every spark from this great mind which, for me, became deeper and deeper, still more penetrating, under your guidance. These books, in their soft covers of tender green morocco, are still with me now. On certain pages of them, here and there, are sharp nail-marks, and when I look at these remaining symbols, which remind me so vividly of your vehement, nervous enthusiasm for the beauties and abysses of this Shakespearean genius, I am overcome by a quiet, sombre emotion.

Do you remember? Ah, how endlessly I could repeat this question, but I am beginning to be tired already, and I have still so much to say to you.

Of course, you can imagine that here in the sanatorium, I am condemned to perpetual silence. The usual stereotyped sentences which our invalids exchange when they are compelled to meet at breakfast, at dinner, at tea, drive me frantic. They always talk about the same things : to-day one of them has had a bath two degrees lower than the day before, another has eaten a pound more of grapes, a third has climbed a steep slope leading to the sea without stopping and—imagine—without even being out of breath ! They discuss their maladies at length, with egotistic enjoyment, sometimes in disgusting detail. Unfailingly, each wishes to persuade the rest that no one else can possibly have such extraordinary complications of cruel suffering. It is a tragedy when two competitors meet, even if it is only a question of a simple headache. Scornful shrugs come into play, ironical half-hidden smiles, haughty expressions and the most icy glances. " What's this you are telling me about your headache ? Ha ! ha !

This is really funny. I can imagine what you would have said if you had endured once the cruel pain that I suffer every day ! "

Here illness is a cause of pride and rivalry, a fantastic warrant for an odd self-respect, a sort of decoration in a way. However, I have noticed this sort of thing among healthy people, but here among sick people—it becomes dreadful, repulsive, incredible.

That's why I'm always pleased when I find myself at last alone, in my cosy, impregnable little corner. But no, I'm not alone : with me there are always you and my love. There, I have said the word and it didn't burn my lips at all, as it always does in novels.

But I don't even know myself if one can call this quiet, pale, half-mystical feeling " love."

I'm not going to conceal from you the fact that girls of our class have a much more definite and realistic comprehension of love than is suspected by their parents, who watch modern flirtations through their fingers. At school, one talks a great deal on this subject and curiosity gives it a kind of mysterious, exaggerated, even monstrous, significance. From novels and the stories of married friends we learn about mad kisses, burning embraces, about nights of delight, voluptuousness and goodness knows what. All this we assimilate instinctively, half consciously, and—probably according to individual temperament, depravity, perspicacity—more or less clearly.

In that sense, my love is not love, but a sentimental and amusing play of the imagination. Sickly, puny, and weak from my very childhood, I have always had a horror of everything in which, one way or another, physical force, rough health, and the joy of life displayed themselves. A horse ridden quick, the sight of a workman with an enormous weight on his back, a big crowd, a loud shriek, an excessive appetite, a strong odour—all this makes me wince or rouses in me disgusted antipathy. And these are exactly the feelings that I experience when my thoughts are confronted by the real, sensual love of healthy people, with its heavy, inept, shameless details.

But if one is to call the exclusively soul union of two people, when the feelings and thoughts of one of them, through some mysterious current, transmit themselves to the other, when words yield place to silent glances, when a scarcely perceptible shiver of the eyelids, or the pale ghost of a smile in the eyes say sometimes so much more than a long confession of love between " ordinary folk " (I'm using your actual expression), when through the mere meeting of each other's eyes at table, or in a drawing-room, at the arrival of a newcomer or at a stupidity that has just been uttered, two people, without words, know how to share an impression—in a word, if relations of this kind can be called love, then I may boldly say that not only I, but each of us, has loved the other !

And not even with that love which one calls mockingly " brother's love." I know this because I have a very clear recollection of one instance, the one instance at which I am afraid of blushing when I talk about it. It happened on the broken cliff over the sea, in the vineyard summer-house, which is still called, just as it was last year, with faded sentimentality, " the arbour of love."

It was a quiet peaceful morning and the sea seemed green with just that alternation of bright and pale green that certain species of malachite have ; sometimes over its quiet surface there would creep an uneven purple spot—the shadow of a cloud. I had not slept well the night before and I had got up feeling broken, with a headache and my nerves overstrung. At breakfast I had quarrelled with the doctor, not so much because he had forbidden me to bathe in the open sea as on account of his self-assertive and radiant health. When I complained to you about him in the arbour I burst out crying. Do you remember the incident ? You were disconcerted and you were saying disconnected but kind, caressing

38

words, cautiously stroking my head as if I were a child. This sympathy was too much for me, and I leaned my head on your shoulder and then . . . you kissed me again and again on the temple and on the cheek. And I must confess (I knew that I should blush at this part of my letter) that these kisses, not only were not repugnant, but even gave me a pleasant, purely physical pleasure, like the sensation of a light warm wave running over the whole of my body from head to foot.

But this was the only instance of that kind. You, my friend, said more than once that for people like us, exhausted consumptives, chastity was not so much a virtue as a duty.

All the same, this love, gleaming through my sad sunset, was so pure, so tender, so beautiful in its very malady ! I remember, when I was quite a little schoolgirl, lying in the infirmary, an enormous, empty, dreadfully high room, lying there for some reason or other, apart from the rest of the sick ones, and being intolerably bored. And then my attention happened to be caught by a simple, but wonderful thing. Beyond the window, in the moss-covered recess—moss grew almost all over the saliences of that old, pre-Catherine wall—a flower had sprouted. It was a real hospital flower, with a corolla like a tiny yellow star and a long, thin, pale green little stalk. I couldn't tear my eyes from it and felt for it a sort of pitiful, pensive love. My own beloved one, this weak, sick, yellow little flower—it is my love for you.

There, this is all that I wish to tell you. Good-bye. I know that my letter will slightly touch you, and the thought of this pleases me beforehand. For, with a love like this, actually like this, no one has probably ever loved you or ever will love you. . . .

It is true that I have one wish : it is to see you in that mysterious hour when the veil will begin to lift itself from my eyes, not to cling to you in senseless terror, but so that in that moment, when the will weakens, in

the moment of involuntary fear which—who knows?
—will perhaps seize me, you might press my hand tightly
and say to me with your beautiful eyes :

" Courage, my friend—a few more seconds and you
will know all."

But I shall resist this temptation. I shall seal my
letter at once, write the address, and you will receive
it a few days after I have crossed " the enigmatic border
of knowledge."

My last feeling will be one of deep gratitude to you
who have illumined my last days with love. Good-bye.
Don't be anxious about me. I feel well. There, I have
closed my eyes, and over my body there runs once more
a sweet, warm wave as then—in the vineyard arbour.
My head swims so quietly and pleasantly. Good-bye.

THE ARMY ENSIGN

PROLOGUE

L AST summer one of my nearest friends inherited from an aunt of his a small farm in the Z—— district of the Government of Podol. After looking through the things that had fallen to his lot, he found, in an attic, a huge iron-bound trunk stuffed with old-fashioned books, with the letter " T " printed like a " CH," from the yellowish leaves of which came a scent of mouldiness, of dried-up flowers, of mice, and of camphor, all blended together. The books were chiefly odd volumes of faded Russian authors of the early nineteenth century, including an epistolary manual and the Book of Solomon. Among this assortment were letters and papers, mostly of a business nature and wholly uninteresting. But one rather thick bundle wrapped up in grey packing paper and tied carefully with a piece of string, roused in my friend a certain curiosity. It proved to contain the diary of an infantry officer, named Lapshine, and several leaves of a beautiful, rough Bristol paper, decorated with irises and covered with a small feminine handwriting. At the end of these pages was the signature " Kate," but many of them bore the single letter " K." There could be no doubt that Lapshire's diary and Kate's letters were written at about the same time and concerned the same events, which took place some twenty-five years or so ago. Not knowing what to do with his find, my friend posted the package to me. In offering it now to my readers, I must confess that my own pen has dealt only very slightly with it, merely correcting the grammar here and there and obliterating numerous affectations in quotation marks and brackets.

I

September 5th.

Boredom, boredom, and again boredom ! Is my whole life going to pass in this grey, colourless, lazy, crawling way ?   In the morning, squad drill and this sort of thing :

" Efimenko, what is a sentry ? "

" A sentry is an inviolable person, your Honour."

" Why is he an   inviolable person ? "

" Because no one dares to touch him, your Honour."

" Sit down.   Tkatchouk, what is a sentry ? "

" A sentry is an inviolable person, your Honour."

And so on endlessly.

Then dinner at the mess, Vodka, stale stories, dull conversations about the difficulty nowadays of passing from the rank of captain to that of colonel, long discussions about examinations, and more vodka.   Someone finds a marrowbone in his soup and this is called an event to be celebrated by extra drinks.   Then two hours of leaden sleep, and in the evening, once more, the same inviolable person and the same endless " fi-i-r-ing in file."

How often have I begun this very diary ! It always seemed to me, I don't know why, that destiny must at last throw into my everyday life some big, unusual event which will leave indelible traces on my soul for the rest of my life. Perhaps it will be love ?   I often dream of some beautiful, unknown, mysterious woman, whom I shall meet some day—a woman who is weary and distressed as I am now.

Haven't I a right to my own bit of happiness ?   I

am not stupid ; I can hold my own in society. I am
even rather witty, if I am not feeling shy and happen
to have no rival close at hand. As to my appearance,
naturally it is difficult for me to judge it, but I think I
am not too bad, though on rainy autumn mornings I
confess that my own face in the looking-glass strikes me
as loathsome. The ladies of our regiment find something of Lermontov's Petchorin about me. However,
this merely proves, in the first place, the poorness of the
regimental libraries and, secondly, the immortality of
the Petchorin type in infantry regiments.

With a dim presentiment of this strip of life in front
of me, I've begun my diary several times, intending to
note down every small detail so as to live it over again
afterwards, if only in memory, as fully and clearly as
possible. But day after day passed with the old monotonous sameness. The extraordinary made no start,
and, losing all taste for the dry routine of regimental
annals, I would throw my diary aside on a shelf for long·
intervals and then burn it with other rubbish when changing
my quarters.

September 7th.

A whole week has gone by already since I got back
from manœuvres. The season for open-air work has
begun and squad after squad is told off to dig beetroots
on the estates of the neighbouring landowners. Only
our squad and the eleventh are left. The town is more
dead-and-alive than ever. This dusty, stuffy heat, this
day-time silence of a provincial town, broken only by
the frantic bawling of cocks, gets on my nerves and depresses
me.

Really, I am beginning to miss the nomad life of manœuvres which struck me as so unendurable at the time.
How vividly the not very complicated pictures of Army
movements come back to my memory, and what a softening
charm memory gives to them !   I can see it all clearly now :

Early morning . . . the sun not yet risen. A cold sky looks down at the rough, old bell tent, full of holes ; the morning stars scarcely twinkle with their silvery gleam . . . the bivouac has livened up and is bustling with life. One hears the sounds of running about, the undertone of, angry voices, the crack of rifles, the neighing of waggon horses. You make a desperate effort and crawl out from under the hairy blanket which has become white from the night dew. You crawl straight out into the open air because you cannot stand in the low tent, but only lie or sit down. The orderly, who has just been beating a devil's tattoo with his boot on the samovar (which of course is strictly forbidden), hurries off to get water, bringing it straight from the stream in a little brass camp kettle. Stripped to the waist, you wash in the open air, and a slight, fine, rosy steam curls up from your hands, face, and body. Here and there, between the tents, officers have improvised fires from the very straw on which they have spent the night, and are now sitting round them, shrivelled up from cold and gulping down hot tea. A few minutes later, the tents are struck, and there, where just now " the white linen town " had sported itself, are merely untidy heaps of straw and scraps of paper. The din of the roused bivouac deepens. The whole field is swarming with soldiers' figures in white Russian blouses, their grey overcoats rolled over their shoulders. At first glance there seems absolutely no order in this grey, ant-like agitation, but the trained eye will note how gradually thick heaps are formed out of it and how gradually each of these heaps extends into a long regular line. The last of the late comers rush up to their squads, munching a piece of bread on the way or fastening the strap of a cartridge case. In another minute the squads, their rifles clinking against each other, form into a regular enormous square in the middle of the field.

And then the tiring march of from thirty to forty versts. The sun rises higher and higher. About eight o'clock the heat makes itself felt ; the soldiers begin to be bored, their marching becomes slack, and they sing listlessly the regular marching songs. Every minute the dust gets thicker, enfolding in a long yellow cloud the whole column which extends for a full verst along the road. The dust falls in brown layers on the soldiers' shirts and faces and, through this background, their teeth and the whites of their eyes flash as if they were negroes. In the thick dusty column it is difficult to distinguish a private from an officer. Also, for the time being, the difference of rank is modified, and one cannot help getting acquainted with the Russian soldier, with his shrewd outlook on all sorts of things—even on complicated things like manœuvres —-with his practical good sense and his adaptability under all sorts of conditions, with his biting word-pictures and expressions seasoned, as they are, with a rough spiciness to which one turns a deaf ear. What do we meet on the road ? A Ukrainian in large white trousers is walking lazily beside a pair of grey shorthorns and, on the roadside, a pedlar, a velvety field, ploughed for the winter crop. Everything invites investigating questions and remarks, impregnated either with a deep, almost philosophical, understanding of simple everyday life, or with pointed sarcasm, or with an irrepressible stream of gaiety.

It is getting dark when the regiment nears the place for its night camp. One sees the cooks already round the large smoky squad cauldrons placed in a field aside from the road. " Halt ! Pile arms ! " In a twinkling the field is covered with stately files of little wigwams. And then, an hour or two later, you are once more lying under the canvas, full of holes, through which you see the twinkling stars and the dark sky, while your ears note the gradual quieting down of the sleeping camp. But still, for a long time, you catch from the distance separate sounds, softened by the sad quietude of evening : at times the monotonous scraping of a harmonica reaches your ear, sometimes an angry voice, undoubtedly the

sergeant-major's, sometimes the sudden neigh of a colt . . .
and the hay, under one's head, blends its delicate aroma
with the almost bitter smell of the dewy grass.

September 8th.

To-day, my squad's commandant, Vassili Akinfievitch,
asked me whether I should like to go with him to the
autumn work. He has arranged for the squad very advantageous terms with Mr. Obolianinov's manager—almost
two and a half kopecks a pood. The work will consist
of digging the beetroot for the local sugar factory. This
does not tire the soldiers, who do it very willingly. All
these circumstances had probably put the captain in such
a rainbow mood, that he not only invited me to go with
him to the work, but even, in the event of my accepting,
offered me a rouble and a half a day out of the money
payable to himself. No other squad commandant had
ever shown such generosity towards his subalterns.

I have rather curious, I should say rather mixed, feelings
towards Vassili Akinfievitch. In the service I find him
insupportable. There he parades all his angry rudeness
almost conscientiously. At squad drill he thinks nothing
of shouting out before the men at a young officer :

" Lieutenant, please take hold of your men. You walk
like a deacon in a procession."

Even if it's funny, that sort of thing is cruel and tactless.

To the men, Vassili Akinfievitch metes out justice with
his own fists, a measure which not one of the platoon com-
manders would ever dare to do. The men like him, and,
what is more important than anything else, believe his
word. They all know very well that he will not draw a
kopeck out of the ration money, but will be more likely
to add something like twenty-five roubles a month out of
his own pocket, and that he will permit no one under him
to be wronged, but on the contrary will take up the cudgels
for him even with the colonel. The men know all this
and I am sure that in the event of war they would all follow

to the last Vassili Akinfievitch, without hesitation, even to obvious death.

I dislike particularly his exaggerated horror of everything " noble." In his mind the word " nobility " suggests the impression of stupid dandyism, unnaturalness, utter incapacity in the service, cowardice, dances and the guards. He can't even pronounce the word " nobility " without a shade of the most bitter sarcasm, drawling it out to its last letter. However, one must add that Vassili Akinfievitch has been toiling up from the ranks step by step. And at the period when he received his commission, the unfortunate rankers had a rough time of it with the little aristocrats of the mess.

He finds it hard to make friends, as every inveterate bachelor does, but when he takes a fancy to someone he opens, with his purse, his naïve, kindly, and clean soul. But even when opening his soul, Vassili Akinfievitch puts no check on his language—this is one of his worst traits.

I think he rather likes me, in his way. As a matter of fact, I am not such a bad officer of the line. When I am hard up, I borrow from him freely and he never duns me. When we are off duty he calls me " Army Ensign." This odd rank died out of the service long ago, but old officers like to use it playfully in memory of their youth.

Sometimes I feel sorry for him, sorry for a good man whose life has been absorbed in the study of a thin Army Regulation book and in a minute attention to regimental routine. I am sorry for the poorness of his mental outlook, which allows him no interest in anything beyond his narrow horizon. In a word, I feel the same sort of sorrowful pity for him that comes to one involuntarily when one looks long and attentively into the eyes of a very intelligent dog.

Here I pull myself up ! Am I aiming at anything myself ? Does my captive thought really struggle so impatiently ? At any rate, Vassili Akinfievitch has done something in his life ; he has two St. George's on his breast and the scar of a Circassian sabre on his forehead. As for the men under him, they have such fat merry mugs that it makes one cheerful to look at them. Can I say as much for myself ?

I said that I would go to the digging with pleasure. Perhaps it will be a distraction ? The manager has a wife and two daughters, two or three landowners live near. Who knows ? there may be a little romance !

To-morrow we start.

September 11th.

We arrived this morning at the railway station of Konski Brod. The manager of the estate, advised of our coming by telegram, had sent a carriage to meet Vassili Akinfievitch and myself. My word ! I never drove in anything so smart in my life before. It was a four-in-hand coach, magnificent horses, cushiony tyres, studded harness, driven by a healthy-looking lad, who wore an oil-cloth cap and a scarf round his waist. It is about eight versts to Olkhovatka. The road is perfect and smooth, level, straight as an arrow, lined on both sides with thick pyramid-like poplars. On the way, we constantly met long files of carts loaded, to the very top, with cloth bags full of sugar. Apropos of this, Vassili Akinfievitch tells me that the output of the Olkhovatka factory is about 100,000 poods of sugar every year. That is a respectable figure, particularly in view of the fact that Obolianinov is the sole proprietor of the business.

The manager met us at the farm buildings. He has a German surname, Berger, but there's nothing German about his appearance or his accent. In my opinion, he's more like Falstaff, whom I saw somewhere at an exhibition. I think it was at Petersburg, when I went there to pass my unlucky examination at the Academy of the General Staff. He is extraordinarily fat, the fat almost transparent ; it shines on his flabby cheeks, which are covered with a network of small red veins. His hair is short, straight, and grizzly ; his moustache sticks out on each

48

side in warrior-like brushes ; he wears a short imperial under his lower lip. Beneath the thick, dishevelled eyebrows his quick, sly eyes are oddly narrowed by the tautness of the cheeks and cheek-bones. The lips, particularly the smile, reveal a merry, sensual, jolly, very observant man. I think he is deaf, because he has a habit of shouting when he talks to one.

Berger seems pleased at our arrival. To people like him a listener and a boon companion are more necessary than air. He kept running up to one or the other of us, and seizing us round the waist, would repeat : " Welcome, gentlemen, you are welcome."

To my amazement, Vassili Akinfievitch liked him. I did, too.

Berger showed us into a pavilion where four rooms had been prepared for us, provided with everything necessary and unnecessary on such a large scale that we might have been coming to spend three years there instead of a month. The captain was apparently pleased with these attentions from the owner of the place. But once, when Berger opened a drawer of his writing-table and showed a whole box of long, excellent cigars, placed there for us, Vassili Akinfievitch grumbled in an undertone :

" This is a bit too much . . . This is ' nobility ' and all that sort of thing."

Incidentally, I have forgotten to mention his habit of adding " and all that sort of thing " to almost every word he says. And, taking him all round, he is not exactly an eloquent captain.

While placing us, so to speak, in possession, Berger was very fussy and shouted a great deal. We did our best to thank him. Finally, he seemed to get tired, and, wiping his face with an enormous red handkerchief, he asked us if there was anything else we wanted. We, of course, hastened to assure him that we had more than enough. On leaving us, Berger said :

" I'll put a boy at your disposal at once. You will be

kind enough to order for yourself breakfast, lunch, dinner, and supper according to your wishes. The butler will come to you every evening for this purpose. Our wine-cellar, too, is at your disposal."

We spent the whole day in installing the soldiers, with their rifles and ammunition, in empty sheds. In the evening the groom brought us cold veal, a brace of roast snipe, a sort of tart with pistachio nuts, and several bottles of red wine. We had scarcely seated ourselves at the table when Berger appeared.

" You're at dinner. That's first rate," he said. " I've brought you a little bottle of old Hungarian. My dead father had it in his cellar for twenty years . . . We had our own estate near Gaissina . . . Make no mistake about us, we Bergers are the lineal descendants of the Teutonic Knights. As a matter of fact, I have the right to the title of Baron, but what good would it be to me ? The arms of the nobility require gilt, and that has vanished long ago from ours. You're welcome here, defenders of the throne and the Fatherland."

However, judging by the measures of precaution with which he extracted the musty bottle from a side pocket of his nankin jacket, I am inclined to think that the old Hungarian was preserved in the master's cellar and not at all " on our own estate near Gaissina." The wine was really magnificent. It is true that it completely paralyses one's feet, deprives one's gestures of their ordinary ex-pressiveness, and makes the tongue sticky, but one's head remains clear all the time and one's spirits gay.

Berger tells stories funnily and with animation. He chattered the whole evening about the landlord's income, the luxury of his life in Petersburg, his orangery, his stables, the salaries he paid to his employees. At first Berger represented himself as the head manager of the business. But half an hour later he let the cat out of the bag. It seems that among the managers of the estate and the employees at the factory, Falstaff occupies one of the humblest positions. He is merely the overseer of the farm of Olkhovatka, just an accountant with a salary of nine hundred roubles a year and everything found except his clothes.

" Why should one man have such a lot ? " the captain asked naïvely, apparently struck by the colossal figures of income and expenditure that Falstaff was pouring out so generously.

Falstaff made a cunning face.

" Everything will go to the only daughter. Well, there you are, young man "—he gave me a playful dig in the ribs with his thumb. " Make up your mind to marry, and then don't forget the old man."

I asked with the careless air of one who has seen too much :

" And is she pretty ? "

Falstaff grew purple with laughter.

" Ha, ha ! He's biting. Excellent, my warrior. Excellent. Prepare to rush—rush ! Tra-ta-ta-ta. I like the military way." Then suddenly, as if a spring had been pressed, he stopped laughing. " How can I answer you ? It depends on one's taste. She is . . . too subtle . . . too thinnish . . . "

" Nobility," put in the captain with a grimace.

" As much as you like of that. And she's proud. She doesn't want to know any of the neighbours. Oh, and she's unmanageable. The servants dread her more than fire. Not that she's one to shout at you or rebuke you. There's none of that about her. With her it's just : ' Bring me this . . . Do this . . . Go ! ' and all so coldly, without moving her lips."

" Nobility," said the captain, putting his nose in the air spitefully.

We sat like this till eleven o'clock.

Towards the end, Falstaff was quite knocked out and went to sleep on his chair, snoring lightly and with a·peaceful smile round his eyes. We woke him up with difficulty and he went home, respectfully supported under the elbow by our boy. I have forgotten to mention that he is a bachelor, a fact which, to tell the truth, upsets my own plans.

It's an odd fact how terribly a day at a new place drags and, at the same time, how few impressions remain from it. Here I am writing these lines and I seem to have been living in Olkhovatka for a long, long time, two months at least, and my tired memory cannot recall any definite event.

September 12*th.*

To-day I have been looking over the whole place. The owner's house, or, as the peasants about here call it, the Palace, is a long stone building of one storey, with plate-glass windows, balconies, and two lions at the entrance. Yesterday it did not strike me as so big as it did to-day. Flower-beds lie in front of the house ; the paths separating them are spread with reddish sand. In the middle there is a fountain with shiny globes on pedestals, and a light prickly hedge runs round the front. Behind the house are the pavilion, the offices, the cattle and fowl-yards, the stud boxes, the barns, the orangery, and, last of all, a thick shady garden of some eleven acres, with streams, grottos, pretty little hanging bridges, and a lake with swans.

It is the first time in my life that I have lived side by side with people who spend on themselves tens, perhaps even hundreds, of thousands, people who scarcely know the meaning of " not able to do something."

Wandering aimlessly through the garden, I could not take my thoughts off this, to me, incomprehensible, strange, and at the same time attractive existence. Do they think and feel just as we do ? Are they conscious of the superiority of their position ? Do the trifles which burden our lives ever come into their heads ? Do they know what we go through when we come in contact with their higher sphere ?

I am inclined to think that all that means nothing to them, that they ask themselves no inquisitive questions, that the grey monotony of our lives seems just as uninteresting to them, just as natural and ordinary for us, as for example the sight of my orderly, Parkhomenko, is to me. All this, of course, is in the nature of things, but for some reason or other it hurts my pride. I am revolted by the consciousness that in the society of these people, polished up and well-glossed by a hundred years of luxurious habits and refined etiquette, *I*, yes *I*, no one else, will appear funny, odd, unpleasant even by my way of eating, and making gestures, by my expressions and appearance, perhaps even by my tastes and acquaintances—in a word, in me rings the protest of a human being who, created in the image and resemblance of God, has either lost one or the other in the Flight of Time, or has been robbed of them by someone.

I can imagine how Vassili Akinfievitch would snort if I read these reflections to him.

September 13*th*.

Although to-day is the fatal number—the devil's dozen —it has turned out very interesting.

I have been wandering about the garden again. I don't remember where I read a comparison of Nature in autumn with the astonishing, unexpected charm which sometimes permeates the faces of young women who are condemned to a swift and certain death from consumption. To-day I cannot get this strange comparison out of my head.

There is in the air a strong and delicate aroma of fading maple trees, which is like the bouquet of good wine. One's feet bruise the dead yellow leaves which lie in thick layers over the path. The trees have a bright and fantastic covering as though decked out for a banquet of death. Green branches, surviving here and there, are curiously blended with autumn tints of lemon, or straw, or orange, or pink and blood-crimson, sometimes passing into mauve and purple. The sky is dense and cold, but its cloudless blue caresses the eye. And in all this bright death-feast one catches an indefinable, languid sadness which contracts one's heart in a pain that is lingering and sweet.

I was walking along a pathway beneath acacias, interlaced so as to form a thick, almost dark arch. Suddenly my ear caught a woman's voice saying something with great animation and laughter. On a seat, just where the thick wall of acacias curved into something like an alcove, sat two young girls (I took them for girls at once and later on I found that I was right.) I could not see their faces very well, but I noticed that the eldest, a brune, had the provoking, luxuriant appearance of a Ukrainian, and that the younger, who looked like a " flapper," was wearing a white silk handkerchief negligently thrown on her head with one corner pulled down on her forehead, thus concealing the upper part of the face. All the same, I succeeded in catching a glimpse of laughing pink lips and the gay shining of her white teeth as, without noticing my presence, she went on telling something, probably very amusing, in English to her companion.

For some time I hesitated. Shall I go on, or shall I go back ? If I go on, shall I salute them or not ? Once more I was overwhelmed by yesterday's doubts of my plebeian soul. On the one hand I was thinking, if they are not the hosts of this place, these girls are probably guests, and in a way, I, too, am a guest, and therefore on an equal footing. But on the other hand, does Hermann 'Hoppe permit bowing to unknown ladies in his rules of etiquette ? Won't my bowing seem odd to these girls, or, what will be still worse, won't they regard it as the respectfulness of an employee, of " a hired man." Each point of view seemed to me equally dreadful.

However, after thinking it over like this, I walked on. The dark one was the first to catch the rustle of leaves under my feet, and she quickly whispered something to the girl in the silk dress, indicating me with her eyes. As I came up to them, I raised my hand to the peak of my cap without looking at them. I felt, rather than saw, that they both slowly and almost imperceptibly bent their heads. They watched me as I moved away. I knew this by the sense of awkwardness and discomfort which attentive eyes fixed on my back always give me. At the very end of the alley I turned round. At the same second, as it often happens, the girl with the white handkerchief glanced in my direction. I heard some kind of exclamation in English and then a burst of sonorous laughter. I blushed. Both the exclamation and the laughter were certainly intended for me.

In the evening Falstaff came to us again, this time with some wonderful cognac, and once more he told us something incredible about his ancestors who had taken part in the Crusades. I asked him quite carelessly :

" Do you know who those two young girls are, whom I met in the garden to-day ? One is a fresh-looking brune, and the other is almost a little girl in a light grey dress."

He gave a broad grin, wrinkling up the whole of his face and causing his eyes to completely disappear. Then he shook his finger at me slyly :

" Ah, my son of Mars, so you're on the fish-hook ! Well, well, well ! . . . Don't get angry. I'll stop, I will really. But all the same, it's interesting . . . Well, I suppose I must satisfy your curiosity. The younger one is our young lady, Katerina Andreevna, the one I told you about, the heiress. You can't call her a little girl. It's only to look at she's so thin, but she's a good twenty years old."

" Really ? "

" Yes, if not more. Oh, she's such an imp. But the little brunette, that's the one to my taste, all eggs and cream and butter." Falstaff smacked his lips carnivorously. " That's the kind of little pie I love. Her name is Lydia Ivanovna—such a kind, simple girl, and dying to get married. She's a distant relation of the Obolianinovs, but she's poor, so she's just staying here as a friend . . . Oh, well, damn them all ! " he wound up suddenly, waving his hand, " let's get on with the cognac."

Inwardly I had to agree with this last opinion. What do I care about those girls, whom I saw to-day, when to-morrow we may be off in different directions and may never hear of each other again ?

Late in the night, after Falstaff had left us (the boy again balancing him respectfully, this time by the waist), when I was already in bed, Vassili Akinfievitch came to me, half undressed, with slippers on his bare feet and a candle in his hand.

" Well, young man," he said, yawning and rubbing his hairy chest, " will you explain one thing to me ? Here we are, fed on all sorts of *delicatessen* and given their best old wine to drink and a boy at our disposal, and cigars and all that sort of thing, but they won't invite us to their own table, will they ? Now why is this ? Kindly solve that problem."

Without waiting for my answer, he went on in a sarcastic tone :

" Because, my dear old chap, all these ' Nobility ' people and all that sort of thing are most refined diplomats. Ye-e-es. What is their way of doing it ? I make a good study of their sort on different voluntary work. I know the type. He will be amiable to you and will serve you up dinners " (justice compels me to add that the captain mispronounced the word " serve ") " and cigars, and all that sort of thing, but all the same you feel that he looks on you as a low worm ; and notice, Lieutenant, it's only the real great ' alistocrats ' " (here, as if out of irony, he purposely mutilated the word) " who have this attitude towards our fellow men. The simpler sort, the more doubtful ones, swagger and put on more airs. Immediately that type will sport an eye-glass, round his lips, and imagine that he's a bird. But as for the real sort, the first thing with them is simplicity—because there's no reason for them to put on airs when right in their own blood they feel scorn for our fellow men . . . and it all comes out very naturally and charmingly, and all that sort of thing."

Having finished this accusing speech, Vassili Akinfievitch turned round and went off to his room.

Well, perhaps he's right in his own way, but all the same it seems to me rather bad taste to laugh at strangers behind their backs.

September 14th.

To-day I met them both again in the garden. They walked with their arms round each other's waists. The little one, her head on her companion's shoulder, was humming something with half-closed eyes. Seeing them it suddenly occurred to me that these chance rambles of mine might be misinterpreted. I turned quickly into a side-path. I don't know that they saw me, but apparently I must choose another time for my walks or risk seeming an army intruder.

September 15th.

Lydia Ivanovna started this evening for the station. She will probably not return to Olkhovatka. First of all, because she has been followed by a respectable quantity of luggage, secondly, because she and the daughter of the house said good-bye to each other rather long and affectionately. Apropos of this, I saw for the first time from my window André Alexandrovitch himself with his wife. He's quite a fine-looking type, stately, broad-shouldered, with the cut of an old Hussar ; his grey hair is worn *à la russe*, his chin is clean-shaven, his moustache long, downy and silvery, and his eyes are like a hawk's, only blue, but just the same as the hawk's—round, sunken, motionless and cold. His wife gives one the impression of a frightened and modest person. She holds her head a little on one side, and a smile, half guilty and half pitiful, is always on

57

her lips. The face is yellow but kind. In her youth she was probably very beautiful, but now she looks much older than her age. There was also a bent old woman on the balcony. She wore a black head-dress and greenish curls, and she came out leaning on a stick, and hardly able to drag her feet after her. She wanted, I think, to say something, but she began coughing, shook her stick in a despairing sort of way and disappeared.

September 16*th*.

Vassili Akinfievitch has asked me to look after the work until he can get rid of his fit of Balkan rheumatism.

" Pay particular attention," he said, " to the delivery of the beetroot ; the soldiers are already complaining because the foreman here gives them overweight. To tell the truth, I am rather afraid that in the end there'll be trouble over this."

The soldiers have been working in threes. They have already practically finished their contract. One digs out the beetroot from the ground with a shovel, while two cut it with knives and clean it. These sets of three are usually formed from soldiers of the same strength and skill. There's no point in choosing a bad one, as he would only be in the way of the others.

I've read somewhere or other, I think in the " Indicator," the reflections of a leisurely thinker, who says that there is no advantage at all in this sort of work : that clothes get torn, and soldiers undisciplined. This is absolutely false. Never is there such a confident, almost relation-like feeling between officers and privates as at this sort of free work. And if one admits that the soldier needs holidays during his hard military training, there is no better rest for him than the toil in the fields which he loves. But all the money earned in this way must go to the soldiers without any middleman . . . each knows where the shoe pinches.

And our people are admirable workers ; hired peasants wouldn't do half the work. There's only one exception, Zamochnikov, who, as usual, does nothing. Zamochnikov is the spoilt favourite of the whole squad, from the captain down to the last private, Nikifor Spassob (this same Spassob, with his lame leg and the white spot on his right eye, has been for the last four years a walking and a crying reproach to the military service). It is true that during his whole period of service Zamochnikov has been unable to master the vowels in the alphabet and has shown a really exceptional stupidity in regard to book-learning, but you could not find in the whole regiment such a spirited singing-leader, such a good teller of stories, such a jack-of-all-trades and a Merry Andrew to boot. He apparently knows what his rôle is very well and looks upon it in the light of a military duty. On march he sings almost without stopping, and his lashing, spirited talk often wrings a laugh of appreciation from the tired soldiers and gives them a moral shake-up. Vassili Akinfievitch, though he keeps Zamochnikov under arms more often than the rest, for which Zamochnikov bears him no grudge, confessed to me once that a stirrer-up like him is a perfect treasure in war-time and difficult circumstances.

Zamochnikov, however, is no mere clown and sham, and for this I like him particularly. Life in him simply boils up unrestrainedly and never allows him to sit quiet for a minute.

Here he was to-day, passing from work-party to work-party and finally arriving at a women's department. He started a long dialogue with the Ukrainians, which made the soldiers near him leave their work and roll on the ground with laughter. I can hear from a distance his imitations of the brisk, shrill quarrels of women, and then again the lazy talk of an old Ukrainian. On catching sight of me, he puts on a pre-occupied look and fumbles on the ground. " Well, my fellow-country-women," he asks, " which of you has sent my shovel to perdition ? " I shout at him and endeavour to make my face severe. He stands to attention, carrying himself, as he always does before an officer, with a graceful vigour, but in his kind blue eyes there still trembles the little fire of his interrupted merriment.

September 17*th.*

Our acquaintance has taken place, but under exceptionally comic conditions. Why should I hide it from myself ? I secretly longed for this acquaintance, but if I could have foreseen that it would happen as it happened to-day, I should have refused it.

The stage was again the garden. I have already written that there is a lake ; it has a little round island in the middle, overgrown with thick bushes. On the shore, facing the house, is a rather small wharf and near it a flat-bottomed boat is moored.

In this boat Katerina Andreevna was sitting as I passed. Holding the sides of the boat with both hands and bending forward first on one side and then on the other, she was trying to balance and shove off the heavy boat which had stuck fast on the slimy bottom of the lake. She wore a sailor costume, open at the throat, allowing one to see her thin white neck and even her thin little collar-bones, which stood out under the muscular tension. A small gold chain hid itself in her dress. But I gave her only a passing glance, and, having once more given her a half-salute, I turned away with my usual modest dignity. At that moment a girl's voice, fresh and merry, called out suddenly :

" Will you please be so kind—— "

At first I thought this exclamation was meant for some-one else who was walking behind me, and involuntarily I glanced back. She was looking at me, smiling and nodding emphatically.

" Yes, yes, yes—you. Will you be so kind as to help me to shove off this wretched boat ? I'm not strong enough by myself."

I made her a most gallant bow, bending my body forward and lifting my left leg back, after which I ran eagerly down to the water and made another bow just as ceremonious as the first. I must have looked fine, I imagine. The lady was now standing up in the boat, still laughing and saying :

" Push it away just a little . . . then I'll manage it myself."

I seize the bow of the boat with both hands, with my legs spread wide apart so as to preserve my balance, then I warn her with refined politeness :

" Will you be kind enough to sit down, Mademoiselle . . . the push may be a very vigorous one."

She sits down, stares at me with laughing eyes, and says :

" Really, I'm ashamed to trespass like this on your kindness."

" Oh, it's nothing, Mademoiselle."

The fact that she is watching me gives my movements a certain gracefulness. I'm a good gymnast, and nature has given me a fair amount of physical strength. But, in spite of my efforts, the boat does not stir.

" Please don't take so much trouble," I hear a tender little voice saying. " It's probably too heavy and it may hurt you. Really, I——."

The sentence hangs unfinished in the air. Her doubt of my strength gives it a tenfold force. A mighty effort, a push, a crash, the boat flies off like an arrow, while I, in accordance with all the laws of equilibrium, splash full length into the mud.

When I get up I find my face and hands and my snow-white tunic, worn for the first time that morning, everything covered in one long layer of brown, sticky, reeking mud. At the same time I see that the boat is gliding swiftly to the very middle of the lake and that the girl, who had fallen backwards when I shoved off, is getting up. The first object that jumps to her eye is myself. A frantic laugh rings through the whole garden and echoes through the trees. I get out my handkerchief and pass it, confusedly, first over my tunic and then over my face. But in time I realise that this only smudges the mud into me worse than before and gives me a still more pitiable appearance. Then I make an heroic attempt to burst out laughing myself over the comedy of my miseries, and produce some sort of idiotic neighing. Katerina Andreevna rocks with laughter more than ever, and is hardly able to pronounce her words :

" Go . . . go . . . quickly. . . . You . . . will catch cold. . . ."

I run off at full speed from this accursed place, run the whole way back to the house, while in my ears there still rings that merciless, ceaseless laugh.

The captain, as he caught sight of me, merely threw his arms out in astonishment.

" Ni-ce ! Well, you are a pretty sight ! How the deuce did you manage it ? "

I made no answer, banged the door of my room and furiously turned the lock twice. Alas ! now everything is all over for ever.

P.S.—Is she pretty or is she not ? I was so absorbed in my gallantry (condemn yourself to death, wretched man !) that I hadn't even time to get a good look at her. . . . Ah, but what does it matter ?

To-morrow, whatever happens, I am going back to the regiment, even if I have to sham being ill. Here I should not be able to live down my disgrace.

Kate to Lydia.

OLKHOVATKA,
September 18th.

MY DEAREST LYDIA,

Congratulate me quickly. The ice is broken. The mysterious stranger, it seems, is the most amiable in the world, a *chevalier sans peur et sans reproche*. The honour of this discovery belongs to me, since you, you

little villain, deserted me. There is no one now to keep
me out of mischief, which I have had time to get into
over and over again.

To begin with, I must confess that yesterday I arranged
the capture of my mysterious stranger. I waited in the
boat, and, when he passed by, I asked him to shove it
off from the shore. Oh, I know perfectly well that you
would have stopped short of a trick like that. You ought
to have seen the eagerness with which the mysterious
stranger rushed up to fulfil my request. But the poor
man didn't measure his strength, fell into the water and
was covered with filthy mud. He presented the most
pitiful and at the same time the most amusing appearance
you could imagine. His cap had fallen on the ground,
his hair had slipped down over his forehead, and the
mud was pouring from him in streams, while his hands,
with the fingers parted, seemed to be petrified. I thought
at once : I must not laugh ; he will be offended.

It would have been much better not to think at all.
I began to laugh, laugh, laugh. . . . I laughed myself
into hysterics. In vain I bit my lips until they bled,
and pinched my hand until it hurt. Nothing was of
any use. The confused officer took to flight. This wasn't
very wise on his part, for I had left the oars behind. I
had to float over the roughish water until the wind brought
my fragile bark into the reeds. There, by grabbing
one after the other with both hands, I succeeded somehow or other in pulling the boat in. But in jumping
out I managed to wet my feet and skirt almost up to the
knees.

Do you know, I like him very much. A strange presentiment told me that an interesting flirtation would
start between us, " l'amour inachevé," as Prévost puts
it. There is something about him manly, strong, and
at the same time tender. It's nice to have power over
a man like that. Apart from this, he's probably very
reserved—I mean to say, not gossipy ; I don't think

63

he's stupid, but chiefly one divines in his figure and movements robust health and great physical strength. While
I was muddling about in the boat, I was seized by a weird,
but very attractive thought : I wanted him terribly
to take me up in his arms and carry me swiftly, swiftly
over the gardens. It would have been no great effort
for him, would it, my little Lida ?

What a difference there is between him and the people
one meets in Petersburg, those dancers and sportsmen
in whom one always detects something worn and jaded
and disagreeably shameless. My officer is fresh, like a
healthy apple, built like a gladiator, at the same time
bashful, and, I think, passionate.

To-morrow, or the day after, I will make advances
to him (that's the way, I think, to express it in Russian ?)
Lidotchka, you must correct all my gallicisms without
mercy, as you promised ! Really I am ashamed of making
mistakes in my own language. That he tumbled so
magnificently into the lake doesn't matter a bit. I alone
was a witness of the tragedy. It would have been quite
another matter if he had been so clumsy in public. Oh,
then I should certainly be ashamed of him. This must
be our special women's psychology.

Good-bye, my dear little Lida. I kiss you.

Your KATE.

September 19*th*.

Everything passes in this world—pain, sorrow, love,
shame, and in fact it is an extremely wise law. The
other day I was sure that if, before my departure, I should
happen to meet Katerina Andreevna by any chance I
should almost die from shame. But not only have I
not left Olkhovatka, but I have even found time to seal
a friendship with this bewitching creature. Yes, yes,
friendship is exactly the word. To-day, at the end of our
long, earnest conversation, she herself said this, word
for word : " So M. Lapshine, let us be friends, and neither

of us will remember this unlucky little story." Of course " this unlucky little story " meant my adventure with the boat.

Now I know her appearance down to the most delicate details, but I cannot describe her. As a matter of fact I believe this to be generally impossible. Often one reads in novels a description of the heroine : " She had a beautifully regular, classical face, eyes full of fire, a straight, charming little nose and exquisite red lips, behind which gleamed two rows of magnificent pearly teeth." This is crude to a degree ! Does this insipid description give even the slightest hint of that untranslatable combination and reciprocal harmony of features which differentiates one face from all the millions of others ?

Here I can see her face in front of me in actual, minute, extraordinarily vivid detail : a full oval of an olive pallor, eyebrows almost straight, very dark and thick, meeting over the ridge of the nose in a sort of dark down, so that it gives them a certain expression of severity ; the eyes are large, green, with enormous short-sighted pupils ; the mouth is small, slightly irregular, sensual, mocking and proud, with full, sharply chiselled, lips ; the dull hair is gathered up at the back of the head in a heavy negligent knot.

I could not go away yesterday. The captain is seriously ill and rubs himself from morning till night with formic acid and drinks a concoction made out of some sort of herbs. It would not be sportsmanlike to desert him while in this state. All the more because the captain's concoction is nothing but a masked drinking bout.

Last night I went into the garden, without even daring to confess to myself that I secretly hoped to find Katerina Andreevna there. I don't know whether she saw me pass the gate, or if everything can be put down to chance, but we met face to face on the main path, just as I had emerged on to it from the alley.

The sun was setting, half the sky was reddening, pro-

mising a windy morning. Katerina Andreevna wore a
white dress, relieved at the waist by a green velvet belt.
Against the fiery background of the sunset her fine hair
flamed round her head.

She smiled when she saw me, not angrily, rather kindly,
and stretched out her hand to me.

" I am partly to blame for what happened yesterday.
Tell me, you didn't catch cold, did you ? "

The tone of her question is sincere and sympathetic.
All my fears vanish. I find myself even daring to risk
a joke at my own expense :

" Rubbish, a little mud bath ! On the contrary it's
very healthy. You're too kind, Mademoiselle."

And we both start laughing in the most simple, sincere
way. Honestly, what was there so terrible and shameful
in my involuntary fall ? Decidedly I don't understand
it. . . .

" No, we can't leave it like this," she says still laughing.
" You must have your revenge. Can you row ? "

" I can, Mademoiselle."

" Well, come along. Don't keep calling me ' mademoiselle.' But you don't know my name ? "

" I know it—Katerina Andreevna."

" Ah, that's too fearfully long : ' Ka-te-ri-na—and on
the top of it Andreevna. At home, everyone calls me
' Kate.' Call me simply ' Kate.' ' "

I click my heels together in silent assent.

I pull the boat to the shore. Kate, leaning heavily
on my outstretched arm, moves easily over the little
seats to the stern. We glide slowly over the lake. The
surface is so polished and motionless that it has the appearance of density. Stirred by the faint motion of the boat,
little wrinkles behind the stern swim lazily away to left
and right, pink under the last rays of the sun ; the shore
is reflected in the water upside down, but it looks prettier
than in reality, with its shaggy white willows, the green
of which has not yet been touched by autumn. At a

little distance behind us swim a couple of swans, light as fluffs of snow, their whiteness intensified by the dark water.

" You always spend the summer in the country, Mademoiselle Kate ? " I ask.

" No, last year we went to Nice, and before that to Baden-Baden. I don't like Nice ; it's the town of the dying, a sort of cemetery. But I gambled at Monte Carlo, gambled like anything. And you ? Have you been abroad ? "

" Rather ! I have even had adventures."

" Really ? That must be very interesting. Please tell me about them."

" It was about two years ago in the spring. Our battalion was quartered at a tiny frontier place—Goussiatine. It is generally called the Russian Goussiatine, because at the other side of a narrow little river, not more than fifty yards in breadth, there is an Austrian Goussiatine, and when I'm talking, by no means without pride, about my trip abroad, it is this very Austrian Goussiatine that I mean.

" Once, having secured the favour of the Inspector of rural police, we made up a rather large party to go over there, a party exclusively composed of officers and regimental ladies. Our guide was a local civilian doctor and he acted as our interpreter. Scarcely had we entered —to express myself in the grand style—alien territory, than we were surrounded by a crowd of Ruthenian ragamuffins. A propos of this, it was a chance of testing the deep sympathy which our brother Slavs are supposed to feel for us Russians. The urchins followed us to the very doors of the restaurant without ceasing for a second to spatter us with the most choice Russian insults. Austrian Jews were standing in the street in little groups with tasselled fur caps, curls falling over their shoulders, and gaberdines beneath which one could see white stockings and slippers. As soon as we approached them they began to point at us, and in their quick guttural language, with a typical snarl at the end of each sentence, there was something menacing..

" However, we reach the restaurant at last and ordered guliash and massliash ; the first is some national meat dish deluged with red pepper and the second a luscious Hungarian wine. While we were eating, a dense crowd of the inhabitants of Goussiatine trooped into the small room and stared, with genuine curiosity, at the foreign visitors. Then three people emerged from the crowd and greeted the doctor, who immediately introduced them to our ladies. After these, four more came and then about six others. Who these citizens were I have never found out but they probably occupied administrative posts. Among them there was a certain Pan Komissarj and Pan Sub-Komissarj and other Pans as well. They were all good enough to eat guliash and drink massliash with us, and they kept repeating to the ladies : ' At your service, Pane,' and ' We fall at the Pane's feet.'

" At the end Pan Komissarj invited us to stay until the evening, as a subscription ball was to take place that day. We accepted the invitation.

" All went swimmingly, and our ladies were enthusiastically whirling in waltzes with their new acquaintances. It is true we were a little surprised at foreign usage : each dancer called a dance for himself and paid the musicians twenty kopecks. We got used to this custom, but we were soon bewildered by a quite unexpected incident.

" One of our party wanted some beer and he mentioned this to one of our new acquaintances—a portly gentleman with a black moustache and magnificent manners ; our ladies had decided about him that he *must* be one of the local magnates. The magnate happened to be an extremely affable man. He shouted : ' At once, gentlemen,' disappeared for a minute, and returned with two bottles of beer, a corkscrew, and a serviette under his arm. The two bottles were opened with such extraordinary skill that our colonel's wife expressed her admiration. To her compliment the magnate replied with modest dignity : ' Oh, that's nothing for me, Madame . . . I have a post as waiter at this establishment.' Naturally, after this unexpected confession, our party left the Austrian ball hurriedly, a little informally even."

While I am telling this anecdote Kate laughs sonorously. Our boat doubles round the little island and comes out into a narrow canal over which trees, bending low on each side, form a cool, shadowy arch. Here one catches the sharp smell of marsh ; the water looks black as ink and seems to boil under the oars.

" Oh, how nice ! " Kate exclaims with a little shiver.

As our conversation is threatening to dry up, I enquire :

" You find it rather dull in the country, don't you ? "

" Very dull," Kate answers, and after a short silence, she adds negligently, with a quick, coquettish glance : " Up to now, at all events. In the summer my friend was staying here—I think you saw her, didn't you ? —and then there was someone to chatter with. . . ."

" Have you no acquaintance among the landowners about here ? "

" No. Papa won't call on anyone. It's fearfully dull. In the morning I have to read the *Moscow News* aloud to my grandmother. You can't imagine what a bore it is. It's so nice in the garden and I have to read there about conflicts between civilised Powers and about the agricultural crisis . . . and sometimes, in despair, I decide to skip some twenty or thirty lines, so that there is no sense at all left. Grandmother, however, never suspects anything and often expresses surprise : ' Do you notice, Kate, that they write quite incomprehensibly nowadays ? '

" Of course I agree : ' Indeed they do, Grandmother, utterly incomprehensibly.' But when the reading is over I feel like a schoolgirl let out for the holidays."

Talking like this we roll along over the lake until it begins to get dark. As we say good-bye, Kate, in a little parenthesis, gives me to understand that she is accustomed to stroll about the garden every morning and every evening.

All this happened yesterday, but I have had no time to write anything in my diary, because I spent the rest of the evening up to midnight in lying on my bed, staring at the ceiling, and giving myself up to unrealisable, impossible reveries which, in spite of their innocence, I am ashamed to put down on paper.

We met again to-day, already without the least embarrassment, just like old acquaintances. Kate is extraordinarily good and kind. When, in the course of conversation, I expressed, among other things, my regret that the unlucky incident of the boat made me seem comic in her eyes, she stretched out her hand to me with a sincere gesture and pronounced these unforgettable words :

" Let us be friends, M. Lapshine, and let us forget that story."

And I know the kind tone of those words will never be effaced from my memory by words of any other sort for all eternity.

September 20th.

Oh, I was not mistaken ! Kate indeed hinted yesterday that we can meet in the garden every morning and every evening. It is a pity though that she was not in a good humour to-day ; the reason was a bad headache.

She looked very tired and she had black marks under her eyes and her cheeks were paler than usual.

" Don't take any notice of my health," she said in reply to my expressions of sympathy. " This will pass. I have got into the bad habit of reading in bed. One gets entranced, without noticing it, and then there comes insomnia.

P. Rixson.

You can't hypnotise, can you ? " she added half jokingly.

I answered that I had never tried, but that I probably could.

" Take my hand," Kate said, " and look intently into my eyes."

Gazing into Kate's large black pupils, I endeavoured to concentrate and gather all my force of will, but my eyes fell confusedly from her eyes to her lips. There was one moment when my fingers involuntarily trembled and gave a faint pressure to Kate's hand. As if in answer to my unconscious movement, I also felt a faint pressure in return. But naturally this was only by chance, because she immediately withdrew her hand.

" No, you can't help me. You're thinking of something quite different."

" On the contrary, I was thinking of you, Mademoiselle Kate," I retorted.

" Quite possibly. But doctors never look at one with eyes like that. You are a bad one."

" I a bad one ! God is my witness that no evil thought, even the shadow of an evil thought, has ever come into my head. But possibly my unlucky face has expressed something utterly different from what I feel."

The strange part of it is that Kate's observation suddenly made me *feel* the woman in her for the first time, and I felt awkward.

So my experiment in hypnotism was a failure. Kate's migraine not only did not vanish but grew worse every minute. When she went away she was probably sorry for the disappointment in my face. She allowed me to hold her hand for a second longer than was necessary.

" I'm not coming in the evening," she said. " Wait until to-morrow."

But how well was this said ! What an abyss of meaning a woman can sometimes put into the most ordinary, the most commonplace, sentence ! This " wait " I translated like this : " I know that it is a great pleasure for you to see me ; it is not unpleasant to me either, but then we can meet each other every day, and there is ever so much time ahead of us—isn't there ? " Kate gives me the right to wait for her. At the very thought of it my head swims in transport.

What if mere curiosity, an acquaintance made out of boredom, chance meetings—what if all this were to pass into something deeper and more tender ? As I wandered along the garden paths, after Kate's departur , I began to dream about it involuntarily. Anyone may dream about anything, may he not ? And I was imagining the springing up between us of a love, at once passionate, timid, and confident, her first love, and though not my first, still my strongest and my last. I was picturing a stolen meeting at night, a bench bathed in the gentle moonlight, a head confidently leaning upon my shoulder, the sweet, scarcely audible, " I love you," pronounced timidly in answer to my passionate confession. " Yes, I love you, Kate," I say with a suppressed sigh, " but we must part. You are rich ; I am just a poor officer who has nothing except an immeasurable love for you. An unequal marriage will bring you only unhappiness. Afterwards you would reproach me." " I love you and cannot live without you," she answers ; " I will go with you to the ends of the earth." " No, my dear one, we must part. Another life is waiting for you. Remember one thing only, that I will never, never in my life stop loving you."

The night, the bench, the moon, the drooping trees, the sweet love words, how exalted, old-fashioned, and silly it all sounds ! And here, while I am in the act of writing these words, the captain, who has just finished his stirrup-cup, bawls out to me from his bed : " What is it that you are scribbling by the hour, Lieutenant—verses, perhaps ? You might honour us with such nobility ! "

The captain, I think, hates verses and Nature more than anything in the world. Twisting his mouth sideways,

he says sometimes : " Little verses ? What earthly use
are they ? " And he declaims sarcastically :

> " In front of me there is a portrait,
> Inanimate but in a frame,
> In front of it a candle burns . . . "

" Rubbish, fiddlesticks, and all that sort of thing."

All the same, he is not quite a stranger to art and poetry.
After an extra drink or two, he sometimes plays the guitar
and sings curious old love songs that one has not heard
for the last thirty years.

I shall go to bed at once, though I know I shall have
difficulty in getting to sleep. But are not reveries, even
the most unrealisable ones, the undeniable and consoling
privilege of every mortal ?

September 21*st.*

If anyone had told me that the captain and I would
dine with André Alexandrovitch himself, I should have
laughed in his face. But, incidentally, I have just come
back from the Palace and even now I have between my
teeth the same cigar that I started smoking in that magnificent study. The captain is in his room, rubbing
himself with the formic acid and grumbling something
or other about " nobility and all that sort of thing."
However, he is quite bewildered and apparently admits
himself a comic figure in the laurels of a toreador and
fearless rescuer of one of the fair sex. Probably fate
itself has chosen to present us in this place in comic rôles :
me in my adventure on the lake shore, him in to-day's
exploit.

But I must tell about everything in order. It was
about eleven in the morning. I was sitting at the writing-
table, busy with a letter to my people, while waiting
for the captain, who was to be in for lunch. He came
all right, but in a most unexpected state : covered with
dust, red, overwhelmed with confusion, and furious.

I looked at him questioningly. He began to pull off his tunic, railing all the time. " This is . . . this kind of . . . of stupid thing, and . . . all that sort of thing ! Imagine, I was coming from the digging. Passing through the yard, I see that old woman—well, the mother or grandmother, whoever she is—crawling out from the hedge in front of the Palace. Yes, crawling. She toddles along, quite quietly, when—goodness knows where it came from—a little calf jumps out, an ordinary little calf, not a year old . . . gallops, you know the way they do, tail up and all that sort of thing . . . simply a calf's ecstasy ! Yes, that's what had got hold of him. He sees the old woman and starts for her. She begins shouting and shakes her stick at him, which makes him still worse. There he was, dancing round her, just thinking that she was playing with him. My poor old woman rolls on the ground, half dead with fright and unable even to shriek any longer. I see that one must help, and rush up to her at top speed, chase away the stupid calf and find the old woman lying on the ground, almost breathless and voiceless. I thought that she had perhaps caved in from sheer funk. Well, somehow or other, I lifted her up, shook the dust from her and asked her if she were hurt. All she did was to roll her eyes and groan. Finally she gasped out : ' Take me home.' I put an arm round her and managed to drag her up on to the verandah, where we found the chatelaine herself, the wife of our host. She was terrified and burst out : ' What is the matter with you, Maman ? What in the world has happened ? ' Between us we got the old woman into an armchair and rubbed her over with some sort of scent. She was right enough and gradually found her breath. Then she started embroidering. I simply didn't know where to turn. ' I was going,' she says, ' along the yard, when suddenly a bull flies straight out at me—an enormous mad bull with bloodshot eyes, his mouth all foaming. He came right at me, banged me in the chest with his

horns and dashed me on the ground. . . . Beyond that
I remember nothing.'

"Well then, it appeared that I had performed a sort
of miracle, that I had sprung at this would-be bull and,
on my honour, had practically tossed him over my shoulder.
I listened and listened and at last I said : ' You are mistaken, Madame, it wasn't a bull, it was just a little calf.'
But I might have talked till I was hoarse. She wouldn't
even listen. ' It's all his modesty,' she said, and that
very moment in came their young lady, and she, too, was
in a great state. The old woman started telling her
the whole comedy over again. The deuce knows what
an idiotic business it is. They called me a hero and a
saviour, pressed my hands, and all that sort of thing.
I listened to them, feeling amused and ashamed, really.
Well, I think to myself, I am in for a pretty story and
there is nothing to say ! I had all the difficulty in the
world to get rid of them. What an idiotic affair ! I
don't believe one could invent anything sillier."

We sat down to lunch and, after a few glasses of his
mixture, the captain grew calmer. He was just starting
for the digging when, suddenly, our boy rushed headlong
into the room, his face distorted with awe, his eyes almost
jumping out of their sockets.

"The master . . . the master himself is coming
here."

We too, God knows why, got flurried, rushed about,
and began hurriedly to put on the tunics that we had
just taken off. And then, at that very moment, Obolianinov showed himself at the door and stopped with a slight
half-bow.

"Gentlemen, I'm afraid that my visit is inconveniencing
you," he said with the most natural and, at the same time,
cold amiability. "Please remain just as you were, at
home."

He was wearing loose, light trousers which suited
astonishingly well his great height and his curiously

75

youthful appearance. His face is that of a real aristocrat. I have never seen such a regular profile, such a fine eagle nose, such a determined chin and such arrogant lips.

He turned to the captain.

" Will you kindly allow me to express to you my deep gratitude ? If it had not been for your daring—— "

" Please, no ! What do you mean ? " the captain answered, quite confused, and waving his hands in incoherent gestures. " I've done nothing particular ; why thank me ? A mere calf. To tell the truth, it was simply awkward and all that sort of thing."

Obolianinov repeated his ironical, or polite, bow.

" Your modesty does honour to your manliness, Captain. In any case, I consider it my duty to express my gratitude on behalf of my mother and myself."

At this the captain grew thoroughly ashamed ; his face reddened and then seemed to become brown, and he waved his hands more incoherently than ever.

" For goodness' sake. . . . There is nothing particular in it. Simply a calf. But I—don't worry about it— I see a calf running—well, then, I at once. . . . Please don't."

I saw that the captain had become utterly mixed, and hastened to the rescue.

" Kindly take a seat," I said, offering our visitor a chair.

He gave me a fugitive, indifferent glance and a negligent " *Merci*," but did not sit down and merely placed his hands on the back of the chair.

" I'm very sorry, gentlemen, that we did not meet before," he said as he held out his hand to the captain. " In any case, it's better late than never, isn't it ? "

The captain, quite disconcerted, found no reply and merely bowed extremely low as he pressed the white, well-kept hand.

As far as I was concerned, I introduced myself rather

curtly: "Lieutenant Lapshine." And then I added, though rather indistinctly: "Delighted . . . I'm sure. Such an honour."

Finally, I'm not certain which of us came off the better, the captain or I.

"I hope, gentlemen, that you won't refuse to dine with me," said Obolianinov, picking up his hat from the chair. "We dine at seven punctually."

We bowed again and our boss retired with the same magnificent ease of manner with which he had entered.

At seven o'clock we presented ourselves at the Palace. All the way, the captain was grumbling about " nobility " and constantly arranging the order which, for some reason or other, he was wearing on his chest. To all appearances, he was in a most depressed frame of mind. However, I must admit that I was not feeling very easy myself.

As soon as we reached the house, we were shown into the dining-room, a large, rather dark room, with massive carved oak panels. The master of the house was not there, but only his wife and the old woman, the mother who had been saved from death by the captain. A slight embarrassment arose, naturally chiefly on our side. We had to introduce ourselves. We were asked to sit down. Inevitably, the conversation fastened upon the event of the morning, but, having lasted for about five minutes, it dried up of its own accord, without any hope of revival, and all four of us sat silent, looking at each other, oppressed by our silence.

Luckily Kate, accompanied by her father, came into the room. On seeing me she bit her lip with an expression of surprise and raised her eyebrows. We were introduced. I understood from Kate's glance that no one was to know about our chance meeting in the garden. Dear girl! Of course I will fulfil your silent order.

After dinner, during which Obolianinov had tried in vain to make the captain talk—for some reason or other he paid little attention to me—the old lady expressed a wish to play whist. As the captain never touched cards, I had to make the fourth, and for two hours I had to endure the most dreary boredom. During the first two rubbers, the old lady played more or less correctly. But afterwards her attention wandered. She began to play out of turn and to pick up other people's tricks. When spades were called, she played diamonds.

" But, Maman, you still have a spade," our host would observe with ironical deference.

" Well, are you going to teach me now ? " the old lady would answer in an offended tone. " I am too old to be taught, my dear. If I don't play a spade, it means that I haven't got one."

All the same, a minute later, she would herself lead spades.

" You see, Maman, you have found a spade," her son would remark with the same shade of benevolent sarcasm, while she was unaffectedly bewildered.

" I can't make out, my dear, where it came from. I simply can't make out . . . "

But I myself played absent-mindedly. All the time I was listening for the light footsteps of Kate behind my chair. She, poor girl, struggled for about half an hour in the hope of entertaining the captain, but all her attempts were broken by his stony silence. He only blushed, wiped his perspiring forehead with a check hand-kerchief, and answered to each question : " Yes, Madame. No, Madame." At last Kate brought him a whole heap of albums, and pictures in which he became entirely absorbed.

Several times Kate came purposely near the card-table.

Our eyes met each time, and each time I caught in hers a sly and tender little glint. Our acquaintance, suspected by no one, made of us a pair of conspirators, initiated in a common mystery which bound us one to the other with deep, strong ties.

It was already dark when, after finishing the whist

and having a smoke in the study, we were on our way home. The captain was walking ahead of me. Then on the balcony I suddenly felt, yes, exactly felt, the presence of someone. I pulled hard at my cigar and, in the reddish light that rose and lowered, I detected a frock and a dear smiling face.

" What a wise, good little boy ! How well he behaved himself ! " I heard in a low murmur.

In the darkness my hand seized hers. The darkness gave me suddenly an extraordinary courage. Pressing those cold, dainty little fingers, I raised them to my lips and began to kiss them quickly and avidly. At the same moment, I kept repeating in a happy whisper :

" Kate, my darling . . . Kate."

She did not get angry. She only began to pull her hand feebly away and said with feigned impatience :

" You mustn't. You mustn't. Go away. . . . Oh, how disobedient you are ! Go, I tell you."

But when, afraid of making her really angry, I loosened my fingers, she suddenly clung to them and asked :

" What is your name ? You haven't told me yet."

" Alexei ; " I answered.

" Alexei ; how nice . . . Alexei . . . Alexei . . . Alesha. . . ."

Overwhelmed by this unexpected caress, I stretched out my hands impulsively, only to meet emptiness. Kate had already disappeared from the balcony.

Oh, how passionately I love her !

Kate to Lydia.

September 21st.

You will remember, of course, my dear Lidotchka, how Papa was always against " rankers " and how he used to call them sarcastically " army folk." So you will be doubtless astonished when I tell you that they dined with us to-day. Papa himself went to the pavilion and invited them. The reason for this sudden change is that the elder of the officers saved the life of my *grand'mère* this morning. From what Grandmother tells us, there was something extraordinary about it. She was passing through the yard, when a mad bull suddenly flew in, the gallant officer dashed between her and the bull—in a word, a regular story in the manner of Spielhagen.

Honestly, I will confess to you that I don't particularly like Papa's having invited them. In the first place, they both get utterly lost in society, so that it is a martyrdom to look at them, particularly the elder. He ate his fish with his knife, was dreadfully confused at the time, and presented the oddest appearance. Secondly, I am sorry that our meetings in the garden have lost almost all their charm and originality. Before, when no one even suspected our chance acquaintance, there was in these rendezvous something forbidden, out of the common. Now, already, alas ! it will strike no one as even surprising to have seen us together.

That Lapshine is head over ears in love with me, I have now not the slightest doubt—he has verv, almost too eloquent eyes. But he is so modest, so undecided, that, whether I like it or not, I have to meet him half way. Yesterday, when he was leaving us, I purposely waited for him on the balcony. It was dark and he began kissing my hands. Ah, dear Lidotshka, in those kisses there was something enchanting. I felt them not only on my hands, but all over my body, along which each kiss ran in a sweet, nervous shiver. At that moment I was very sorry not to be married. I wanted so much to prolong and intensify these new and, to me, unknown sensations.

You, of course, will preach me a sermon for flirting with Lapshine. But this does not tie me to anything and, doubtless, it gives pleasure to him. Besides, in a week at the latest, we are leaving here. For him and for me there will be left memories—and nothing else.

Good-bye, dear Lidotchka, it's a pity that you won't

be in Petersburg this season. Give a kiss from me to
your little mite of a sister.

Yours ever,

KATE.

September 22nd.

> " Is it happiness or only the phantom of happiness ? . . .
> What matters it ? . . . "

I don't know which of the poets wrote that, but to-day
I can't get it out of my head.

And it's true ; what does it matter ? If I have been
happy, even for an hour, even for one brief moment, why
should I poison it with doubts, distrust, the eternal questions
of suspicious self-esteem ?

Just before the evening, Kate came out into the garden.
I was waiting for her and we went along the thick alley,
that very same alley where I saw for the first time my
incomparable Kate, the queen of my heart. She was
moody and answered my questions often at random. I
asked them indeed without much meaning, but only
to avoid burdening both of us with silent pauses. But
her eyes did not avoid mine ; they looked at me with
such tenderness.

When we had reached *the* bench, I said : " How dear
and unforgettable this place is to me, Melle Kate."

" Why ? " she asked.

" It was here that I met you for the first time. You
remember ? You were sitting here with your friend
and you even burst out laughing when I passed by."

" Oh, yes, naturally I remember," Kate exclaimed,
and her face lit up with a smile. " It was stupid of us
to laugh aloud like that. Perhaps you thought that it
was meant for you ? "

" To tell the truth, I did."

" You see how suspicious you are ! That's not nice

81

of you. It happened simply like this : when you passed
I whispered something to Lydia. It really was about
you, but I don't want to repeat it, as an extra compliment
might make you unbearable. Lydia stopped me for fear
of your catching the words. She is very *prude* and always
stops my little outbursts. Then, to tease her, I imitated
the voice of my former governess—a very old, stuck-up
Miss—' for shame, *shocking*, for shame.' There, that's
all, and this little bit of buffoonery made us laugh out
loud. Well, are you pleased now ? "

" Perfectly. But what did you say about me ? "

Kate shook her head with an air of sly reproach.

" You are much too curious and I won't tell you anything. As it is, I am much too good to you. Don't
forget, please, that you must be punished for your behaviour
yesterday."

I understood that she had no idea of getting angry,
but, so as to be prepared for anything, I lowered my
head with a guilty air and said with affected distress :

" Forgive me, Melle Kate, I was carried away ; my
feelings were too much for me."

And as she did not interrupt me I went on in a still
lower but at the same time passionate tone :

" You are so beautiful, Melle Kate."

The moment was favourable. Kate appeared to be
waiting for me to go on, but a sudden timidity seized me
and I only asked pleadingly, as I looked into her eyes :
" You're not really angry with me, are you ? Tell me.
. . . This tortures me so much."

" No, I'm not angry," Kate whispered, turning her
head away with a bashful and unconsciously pretty
movement.

Well now, the moment has come, I said to myself
encouragingly. Forward, forward ! One can't stop half
way in love. Be more daring.

But daring had decidedly left me, and this silence of
hers, after words that had been almost a confession, became

heavier and heavier. Probably, just because of this, Kate said good-bye to me, as we reached the end of the alley for the second time.

When she gave me her small, delicate, but firm hand, I kept it in my own and looked enquiringly into her eyes. I thought that I saw a silent consent in them. I began once more to kiss that dear little hand, as passionately as I had done on the terrace. At first, Kate resisted and called me disobedient, but the next moment I felt a deep warm breath on my hair, and my cheek was swiftly brushed by those fresh, charming little lips. In the same second—I hadn't even time to draw myself up—she slipped out of my hands, ran a few steps away and stopped only when she was at a safe distance.

" Kate, wait, Kate, for heaven's sake ! I have such a lot to say to you," I exclaimed as I approached her.

" Stay where you are and be silent," Kate ordered, frowning with her eyebrows and tapping her foot impatiently on the rustling leaves.

I stopped. Kate put her hand to her mouth and made of it a kind of speaking trumpet as, bending slightly forward, she whispered softly but clearly : " To-morrow, as soon as the moon is up ; wait for me on the wharf. I will slip out quietly. We'll go out on the lake and you shall tell me all you want to tell me. You understand ? You understand me ? "

After these words, she turned away quickly in the direction of the garden door without once glancing back. As for me, I stood there gazing after her, lost, deeply stirred, and happy.

Kate, dear Kate, if only your position and mine in the world were the same ! However, they say that love is higher than class distinctions or any prejudices. But no, no. I will remain strong and self-sacrificing.

Oh, my God, how swiftly they fly away, my poor, naïve, comic dreams ! As I write these lines, the captain is lying in his bed, playing on his guitar and singing hoarsely an old, old song.

Miserable little man, I say to myself; in order not to stuff your head with idle and unrealisable rubbish, sit down and, for your own punishment, write these lines :

A young army lieutenant
Began to make love to me,
And my heart throbbed for him
In strange and fatal passion.

My darling mother heard
That I was not against wedding,
And, smiling, said to me :
" Listen, my dearest daughter ;

The young army lieutenant
Wants to deceive you.
From his evil hand
It will be hard to escape."

The young army lieutenant
Shed torrents of tears.
Somehow, at early dawn,
He drove to the neighbouring town.

There, in the wooden chapel,
Under the icon of God,
Some pope or other, half drunk,
Wedded and yoked our hearts.

And then on a peasant's cart
He carried me home.
Ah, how the glamour has fled :
I moan through my tears.

There is no sugar, no tea,
There is neither wine nor beer ;
That is how I understand
That I am a lieutenant's wife.
That is how I understand
That I am a lieutenant's wife.

Yes, yes, shame on you, poor army lieutenant ! Tear your hair. Weep, weep through the stillness of the night. Thank you, Captain, for that wise lesson of yours.

September 24th.

Night, and love, and the moon, as Mme. Riabkova, the wife of the commander of the 2nd platoon, sings on our regimental guest nights. Never in my most daring dreams did I venture to imagine such intoxicating happiness. I even doubt if the whole evening was not a dream— a dear, magical, but deceptive dream. I don't even know myself how this almost imperceptible, but bitter, sediment of disillusion came into my soul.

I got down to the wharf late. Kate was waiting for me, seated on the high stone balustrade which borders the wharf.

" Well, shall we start ? " I asked. Kate pulled her wrap closely over her and shuddered nervously.

"" Oh no, it's too cold ; look what a fog there is on the water."

The dark surface of the lake, indeed, could be seen only for a distance of about five feet. Further off, uneven, fantastical tufts of grey fog swept over the water.

" Let us walk about the garden," Kate said.

We started. In this mysterious hour of a misty autumn night the deserted garden looked sad and strange, like a neglected cemetery. The moon shone pale. The shadows of the naked trees lay across the paths in black, deceptive silhouettes. The swish of the leaves beneath our feet startled us.

When we emerged from the dark, and seemingly damp-archway of acacias, I put my arm round Kate's waist and gently, but insistently, drew her to me. She made no resistance. Her light, supple, warm body only started slightly under the touch of my hand, that was burning, as if in fever. In another minute, her head was on my shoulder and I caught the sweet aroma of her loosened hair.

" Kate . . . I'm so happy . . . I love you so, Kate, I adore you."

We stopped. Kate's arms went round my neck. My

lips were moistened and burned by a kiss, so long, so passionate that the blood mounted to my head and I staggered. The moon was shining tenderly right into Kate's face, into that pale, almost blanched face. Her eyes had grown larger, had become enormous, and, at the same time, so dark, so deep under their long eyelashes, like mysterious abysses. And her moist lips were clamouring for still more of those insatiable torturing kisses.

" Kate, darling. . . . You are mine ? . . . quite mine ? "

" Yes . . . quite . . . quite."

" For ever ? "

" Yes, yes, my dear one."

" We will never part, Kate ? "

Her expression changed. " Why do you ask that ? Are you not happy with me just now ? "

" Oh, Kate ! "

" Well then, why ask about what will come later ? Live in the present, dear."

Time ceased. I could not realise how many minutes or hours had passed. Kate was the first to come back to reality and, as she slipped out of my arms, she said :

" It's late. They'll discover my absence. See me home, Alesha."

While we walked once more through the dark alley of acacias, she nestled against me, like a graceful kitten that dreads the cold.

" I should be frightened to be alone here, Alesha. How strong you are ! Put your arms round me. Again . . . tighter, tighter. . . . Take me up in your arms, Alesha . . . Carry me."

She was as light as a little feather. As I held her, I almost ran with her along the alley, and Kate's arms wound round my neck still more clingingly, still more nervously. Kissing my neck and temples, and enveloping my face with her quick, burning breath, she kept whispering :

" Faster, faster still. . . . Ah, how nice, how exquisite ! Alesha, faster ! "

At the garden door we said good-bye.

" What are you going to do now ? " she asked, while I, after bowing, began to kiss her hands one after the other.

" I'm going to write my diary," I answered.

" A diary ? " Her face expressed surprise, and—as it seemed to me—annoyed surprise. " Do you write a diary ? "

" Yes. Perhaps you don't like that ? "

She gave a forced laugh.

" It depends on how you do it. . . . Of course you'll show me this diary of yours, some time or other ? "

I tried to refuse, but Kate insisted so strongly that at last I had to promise.

" Now, understand," she said, as we parted and she held up her finger threateningly, " if I see even a single correction, look out ! "

When I got home, I banged the door and the captain woke up, grumbling.

" Where are you always gallivanting about like this, Lieutenant ? It's a rendezvous, I suppose ? Nobility and all that sort of thing. . . ."

I've just read over all the nonsense that I've been scribbling in this book from the very beginning of September. No, no, Kate shall not see my diary, or I should have to blush for myself every time that I remembered it. To-morrow I shall destroy it.

September 25th.

Once more night, once more moon, and again the strange and, for me, inexplicable mingling of the intoxication of love and the torture of wounded pride. It is no dream. Someone's footsteps are sounding under the window. . . .

Kate to Lydia.

September 28th.

MY ANGEL, LIDOTCHKA,

My little romance is coming to a peaceful end. To-morrow we leave Olkhovatka. I purposely did not tell Lapshine because—one never knows—he might turn up at the station. He is a very sensitive young man and, on the top of it all, he hasn't the faintest notion of controlling his feelings. I think he would be quite capable of bursting into tears at the station. Our romance turned out a very simple and, at the same time, a very original one. It was original because the man and woman had exchanged their conventional rôles. I was attacking ; he was defending himself. He was asking from me oaths of fidelity, almost beyond the tomb. At the end, he bored me a good deal. He is a man who does not belong to our circle. His manners and habits are not ours. His very language is different. At the same time, he is too exacting. To spare his feelings, I never even hinted to him how impossible it would have been for Papa to receive him, if he had presented himself in the light of a prospective son-in-law.

The foolish fellow ! He himself did not want to prolong these oppressive delights of unsatisfied love. There is something charming in them. To lose one's breath in tight embraces and burn slowly with passion—what can be better than this ? But then how do I know ? Perhaps there are caresses more daring, more languishing, of which I have no idea. Ah, if he had only had in him a touch of that daring, that inventiveness, and . . . that depravity which I have divined in many of my Petersburg acquaintances !

But he, instead of becoming every day more and more enterprising, whined, sighed, talked bitterly about the difference in our positions (as if I would ever consent to marry him !), hinted almost at suicide. As I said before, it was becoming almost intolerable. Only one, one solitary meeting has remained vividly in my memory—that was when he carried me in his arms along the garden, and he, at all events, was silent. Lidotchka, among other things, he blurted out to me that he keeps a diary. This frightened me. Heaven knows into whose hands this diary might fall later on. I insisted that he should give it to me. He promised, but he did not keep his word. Then (a few days ago), after a long night walk and after having said good-bye to him, I crept up to his window. I caught him in the very act. He was writing, and when I called out he was startled. His first movement was to conceal the paper, but, you understand, I ordered him to hand over all that was written. Well, my dear, it's so funny and touching, and there are so many pitiful words . . . . I'll keep this dairy for you.

Don't reproach me. I'm not afraid on his account —he won't shoot himself ; and I'm not afraid on my own account either : he will be solemnly silent all his life. Still, I confess, for some reason or other, I feel vaguely sad. . . . But all this will pass in Petersburg, like the impression of a bad dream.

I kiss you, my beloved one. Write to me in Petersburg.

Your K.

AUTUMN FLOWERS

MY DEAR ANGRY FRIEND,

I write "angry" because I can imagine first your stupefaction and then your anger when you receive this letter and learn by it that I have not kept my word, that I have deceived you and have suddenly left the town instead of waiting for you to-morrow evening in my hotel, as had been decided. My darling, I have simply run away from you, or rather from us both, have run away from that torturing, that awkward, and unnecessary tension which unfailingly would have sprung up between us again.

And don't hasten, with that caustic smile of yours, to accuse me of a saving wisdom, for you know, more than anyone on earth, how that leaves me when I am most in need of it. God is my witness that, up to the last minute, I did not know whether I should really go or not. Even now I am not at all sure that I shall resist to the end the intolerable temptation to have one more look at you, if only one more, even fugitively, even from a distance.

I don't even know that I shall keep myself sufficiently in hand not to jump out of this railway carriage after the third bell. That is why, when I have finished this letter (if I can only manage to finish it) I shall give it to a porter and tell him to post it at the very moment when the train starts. And I shall watch him from the window and feel, as if I were actually saying good-bye to you, that painful oppression of the heart.

Forgive me. All that I told you about lemons and sea air and doctors who wanted to send me here from

Petersburg, was untrue. I came here solely because I was irresistibly drawn to you, aching to recapture a poor little particle of that burning, dazzling happiness which sometimes we revelled in prodigally and carelessly, like czars in fairy tales.

From what I have told you, I think you must have gathered a rather clear picture of my mode of life in that gigantic Zoo which is called Petersburg society : visits, theatres, balls, my compulsory at home days, the charity bazaars, etc., etc., in all of which I must play the rôle of a decorative advertisement to my husband's career and business affairs. But please don't expect from me the usual tirade about the meanness, the emptiness, the flatness, the falsehood—I've forgotten how they put it in our society novels. I have been drawn into this life, with its comforts, its good manners, its novelties, its connections, its associations, and I should never have the force to tear myself away from it. But my heart has no share in it. Some sort of people flash before my eyes, repeat some sort of words, and I myself do things of some sort, talk about something, but neither the people nor the words reach my soul, and sometimes all this seems to be happening far, far away from me, as if in a book or a picture, as though it were all " arranged," as Domnoushka, my old nurse, used to say.

And suddenly, in this dull, indifferent life, I was caught up by a wave from our dear, sweet past. Did you ever happen to wake up from one of those strange dreams which are so joyous that, after them, one goes about the whole day in a state of blissful intoxication, and which are at the same time so feeble in themselves, that if you repeated them, not merely to a stranger, but to your dearest friend on earth, they would sound null and flat, almost grotesque ? " Dreamers often lie," says Shakespeare's Mercutio, and, my God, what a deep psychological truth there is in that.

Well then I, too, once woke up after such a dream.

I saw myself in a boat with you, somewhere far out to sea. You were holding the oars and I was lying in the stern, looking up at the blue sky. That was the whole dream. The boat was rocking slightly and the sky was so blue that sometimes I seemed to be looking into a bottomless abyss. And a kind of unattainable feeling of joy permeated my soul with such tenderness, such harmony, that I wanted to cry and laugh at the same moment from too much happiness. I woke up, but the dream remained in my soul as if it had taken root in it. With a little effort of imagination, I was often able to recall it and to recapture a pale shadow at least of my dream.

Sometimes it would come to me in the drawing-room, during some lifeless conversation, which one listens to without hearing, and then I would have to cover my eyes with my hand for a moment to hide their unexpected gleam. Oh, how powerfully, how inevitably, I was drawn to you ! How that captivating, magic tale of our love that flashed into my life six years ago under those caressing southern skies rises up before me, new-born in such moments. Everything comes back to me in a rush : our sudden quarrels, stupid jealousies, the comic suspicions and the joyous reconciliations, after which our kisses renewed their first fresh charm, the eagerly anticipated meetings, the feeling of sad emptiness in those minutes, after parting in the evening only to see each other again the next morning, when, again and again, we would turn at the same moment and our eyes would meet over the shoulders of the crowd that separated us, looking pink against the background of the dusky sunset. I remembered every atom of this illumined life, so full of strong, untrammelled happiness.

We couldn't remain in the same spot. We were drawn eagerly to fresh places and fresh impressions. How charming they were, our long trips in those antediluvian, stuffy diligences covered with dirty sail-cloth, in the company of gloomy Germans, with red, sinewy necks

93

and faces that looked as if they had been roughly carved out of wood ; and the lean, prim German women who stared at us with stupefied eyes, as they listened to our mad laughter. And those haphazard lunches " at some good old honest settler's," under the shade of the flower-laden acacia, hidden away in a clean yard, that was surrounded by a white wall and covered with sand from the sea-shore. Don't you remember them ? How ravenously we used to attack the stuffed mackerel and the rough wine of the country, indulging in thousands of funny, tender little *bêtises*, like that historic, impertinent ·kiss which made all the tourists turn their backs on us with indignation. And the warm July nights in the fishing villages ? Do you remember that extraordinary moonlight which was so bright that it seemed fantastic and unreal ; that calm, irradiated sea, with ripples of silvery moire and, on the lit-up background, the dark outlines of the fishermen as they drew in their nets, monotonously and rhythmically, all bending in the same direction ?

But sometimes we would be seized by a longing for the noise of town and the hurly-burly of strangers. Lost in an unknown crowd, we would wander, pressing against each other, and realising more than. ever our nearness each to each. Do you remember, my darling ? As for me, I remember every minute detail and feel it until it hurts. All that is mine ; it lives in me and will be with me always, to my death. I could never, even if I wanted to, get rid of it. . . . Do you understand ?— never. And yet it is not a reality. And I torture myself with the knowledge that I could never live it and feel it again because, God or Nature—I really don't know which—after giving man an almost God-like intelligence has, at the same time, invented for him two torturing traps : ignorance of the future and the impossibility of forgetting the past, with the equal impossibility of returning to it.

On receiving the little note that I sent you at once

from the hotel, you hastened to me. You were hurrying and you were agitated. I knew it at a distance by your quick, nervous step, and also because, before knocking at my door, you stood quite a long time in the corridor. At that moment, I was equally nervous myself realising that you were standing there behind the door, only two steps away from me, pale, pressing your hand tightly against your heart, and breathing deeply and even with difficulty. And for some reason or other, it seemed to me then impossible, unimaginable, that at once, in a few seconds, I should see you and hear your voice. I was in a mood such as one experiences when half asleep, when one sees things rather clearly, but, without waking up, one says to oneself : this is not real, it is only a dream.

You had changed during the years, you had become more manly ; you seemed to have grown. Your black jacket suits you much better than your student's tunic ; your manners have become more collected ; your eyes look at one with more assurance and more coldly ; that fashionable, pointed little beard of yours is decidedly becoming. You thought that I too had improved in looks, and I quite believe that you said it sincerely, all the more because I read it in your first, quick, slightly surprised glance. Every woman, unless she is hopelessly stupid, will realise unerringly the impression that her appearance has produced. . . .

All the way down here in the train, I was trying to imagine our meeting. I admit that I never thought it would turn out so strange, so strained, so awkward for both of us. We exchanged unimportant, common-place words about my journey, about Petersburg, about our health, but the eyes of each were searching the other's, jealously looking for what had been added by time and the strange life that was completely unknown to the other. . . . Conversation failed us. We began with " vous " in an artificial, affected tone, but both of us soon felt that every minute made it more difficult and more stupid to keep it up. There seemed to be between us some foreign, oppressive, cold obstacle, and we did not know how to remove it.

The spring evening was quietly fading. It grew dark in the room. I wanted to ring for lights, but you protested against it. Perhaps the darkness helped us in our decision to touch upon the past. We began to talk about it with that kindly condescending mockery with which grown-up people allude to the pranks of their childhood. But the odd part of it was that the more we tried to deceive each other and ourselves and appear gay and indifferent, the sadder grew our tone. At last, we became silent and sat for a long time—I in the corner of the sofa, you in the armchair—without moving, almost without breathing. Through the open window there came to us the indistinct drone of the large town, the noise of wheels, the hoarse shrieks of the tramway hooters, the jerky bicycle bells and, as always on spring evenings, these sounds reached us softened into a melancholy that was almost tender. Through the window one could see a narrow strip of the sky—pale as faded bronze—and, against it, the dark silhouette of a roof with chimneys and a watch-tower that shimmered faintly. In the darkness I could not distinguish your figure, but I could see the shining of your eyes, fixed on the window, and I thought there were tears in them.

Do you know what comparison occurred to me while we silently reviewed our dear, touching memories? It was as though we had met, after years of separation, at the tomb of someone whom we had both at one time loved with equal fondness. A quiet cemetery . . . spring . . . young grass all round ; the lilacs are blossoming, and we are standing beside the familiar tomb, unable to go, unable to shake off the sad, confused, and endlessly dear phantoms that have claimed us. This dead being—it is our old love, my darling.

Suddenly you broke the silence, jumping up and pushing your chair sharply away.

"No," you exclaimed, "this is impossible, this is becoming torment." I could hear how painfully your voice shook. "For God's sake, let us get out into the fresh air, or I shall break down or go mad."

We went out. The transparent, soft, tawny darkness of the spring evening was already in the air, enveloping with amazing lightness, delicacy, and distinctness the angles of buildings, the branches of trees, and the contours of human figures. When we had passed the boulevards you called a cab, and I knew already where you wished to take me.

There everything is as it once was. The long stretch of yellow sand, carefully pounded down, the bright blue lights of hanging electric lanterns, the playful, exhilarating sounds of the military orchestra, the long rows of little marble tables, occupied by men and women, the indistinct and monotonous talk of the crowd, the hastily darting waiters, the never-changing, stimulating environment of an expensive restaurant. Heavens, how quickly, how ceaselessly the human being changes, and how permanent and immovable are the places and things that surround him. In this contrast, there is always something infinitely sad and mysterious. You know, it has sometimes been my lot to stumble on bad lodgings, not merely bad, but disgusting, utterly impossible, and, in addition to this, to encounter a whole series of unpleasant incidents, disappointments, illness. When you change lodgings like those, you really think that you have entered the zone of heaven. But a week or so later it is enough to pass by chance that very house and glance up at the empty windows with the white placards stuck on them, for your soul to become oppressed by a painful, languid regret. It is true that everything there was odious, distressing, but, all the same, you seem to have left there a whole strip of your life, a strip that you cannot recover.

Just as before, girls with baskets of flowers were standing at the doors of the restaurant. Do you remember

97

how you used always to choose for me two roses, one dark crimson and the other tea-coloured ? As we were driving past, I noticed, by a sudden movement of your hand, that you wanted to do the same, but you pulled yourself up in time. How grateful I was to you for this, my dear one !

Under hundreds of curious eyes, we made our way to the same little arbour that juts out so impertinently over the sea-front at a fearful height, so that, when you look down, leaning over the railing, you cannot see the shore and you seem to be swimming in the air. Beneath our feet, the sea was clamouring ; at this height it looked so dark and terrible. Not far from the shore, large black, angular rocks emerged from the water. The waves were constantly rushing at them, breaking themselves against them and covering them with mounds of white foam. When the waves retreated, the wet, polished flanks of the rocks shone as if they had been varnished and reflected the lights of the electric globes. Sometimes a gentle little breeze would blow up, saturated with such a strong, healthy smell of seaweed, fish, and salt ozone, that one's lungs expanded from it, of their own accord, and one's nostrils dilated.

But something bad, dull, and constraining was more and more surely chaining us down. . . .

When champagne was brought in, you filled my glass and you said with gloomy gaiety :

" Well, let us try to get a little artificial life. ' Let us drink this good, brave wine,' as the fiery French say."

No, in any case, " the good, brave wine " would not have helped us. You grasped that yourself, for you added immediately, with a long sigh :

" Do you remember how we used to be, both of us, from morning till night, drunk without wine merely from our love and the joy of life ? "

Below, on the sea, near the rocks, a skiff appeared, its large white stately sails swinging prettily as it dipped and rose through the waves. In the skiff, one could hear a woman's laugh, and someone, probably a foreigner, was whistling, quite in tune with the orchestra, the melodies of the Waldteufel waltz.

You too were following the sails with your eyes, and, still looking at it, you said dreamily :

" It would be nice to get into a little boat like that and go far out to sea, out of sight of land. . . . Do you remember how we used to do it in the old days ? "

" Yes, our old days are dead. . . ."

It slipped from me unintentionally, in answer to my thoughts, and immediately I was frightened by the unexpected effect that the words produced on you. You grew suddenly so white and threw yourself back in your chair so quickly that I thought you were fainting. A minute later, you began to speak in a strangled voice that seemed suddenly to have become hoarse :

" How oddly our thoughts have met. I was just thinking the same. It seems to me fantastic, unreal, impossible that it was really we, not two other people, quite strangers to us, who, six years ago, loved each other so madly and revelled in life so fully, so beautifully. Those two have long ceased to belong to this world. They have died . . . died. . . ."

We returned to the town. The road ran through cluster after cluster of villas built by the local millionaires. We passed impressive cast-iron railings and high stone walls behind which the thick green of platanes hung down over the road ; enormous gateways carved like lace work ; gardens with wreaths of many-coloured lanterns ; magnificent verandahs, brilliantly illuminated ; exotic plants in the flower gardens in front of villas which seemed like magic palaces. The white acacias had such a strong odour, that the aroma of their luscious sweetness could be felt, even on one's lips. Sometimes we experienced, for a second, a damp chilliness, but immediately afterwards we passed once more into the perfumed warmth of the quiet spring night.

The horses were running fast, their hoof-beats falling loudly in even time. We swayed gently on the carriage springs, as we sat silent. When we were nearing the town, I felt your arm cautiously, slowly, winding round my waist and quietly but insistently it drew me to you. I made no resistance, but did not yield to this embrace. And you understood, and you were ashamed. You withdrew your arm and I groped in the dark for your hand, gratefully pressing it, and it answered me with a friendly, apologetic pressure.

But I knew that your wounded male pride would assert itself all the same. And I was not wrong. Just before we parted, at the entrance to the hotel, you asked permission to come to see me. I fixed a day, and then— forgive me—I stealthily ran away from you. My darling ! If not to-morrow, then in another two days, in a week perhaps, there would have flamed up in us merely sensuality. against which honour and will and mind are powerless. We would have robbed those two dead people by substituting for our love of the past a false and ludicrous make-believe. And the dead people would have cruelly avenged themselves by creating between us quarrels, distrust, coldness, and—what is more terrible than all the rest—a ceaseless jealous comparison of the present with the past.

Good-bye. In the heat of writing I have not noticed how I have passed on to the old " tu " of lovers. I am sure that in a few days, when the first ache of your wounded pride has passed, you will share my opinion and will stop being angry at my escape.

The first bell has just sounded. But I am sure now that I shall resist temptation and shall not jump out of the train.

All the same, our brief meeting is beginning, in my imagination, to clothe itself in a little cloud of smoke, a kind of tender, quiet, poetic, submissive sadness. Do you remember that beautiful verse of Pouchkine :

" Autumn flowers are dearer than the beautiful newborn ones of the fields. . . . So, sometimes the hour of parting is more vivid than the meeting itself . . . " ?

Yes, my darling, these very autumn flowers. Have you ever been out in a garden late in autumn on a wet, morose morning ? The almost naked trees are threadbare and swing to and fro ; the fallen leaves rot on the paths ; on all sides is death and desolation. And only in the flower-beds, above the drooping yellow stalks of the other flowers, the autumn asters and dahlias bloom brightly. Do you remember their sharp, grassy odour ? You are standing, perhaps in a strange listlessness, near the flower-beds, shivering with cold ; you smell this melancholy, purely autumnal odour and you are distressed. There is everything in this distress ; regret for the summer that has fled so quickly, expectation of the cold winter, with its snow, and the wind howling through the chimneys, and regret for one's own summer that has so swiftly rushed away. My dearest one, my only one ! Exactly that feeling has taken hold of my soul at this moment. In a little time, your recollection of our meeting will become for you just as tender, sweet, sad, and poignant. Good-bye, then. I kiss you on your clever, beautiful eyes.

Your Z——.

EMERALD

" I dedicate this story to the memory of that incomparable
piebald race-horse, Kholstomer."

EMERALD, the four-year-old, a full-grown race-
horse of American breed, of a uniform grey,
steel-like colour, woke up as usual at about midnight in his loose box. The other horses, his neighbours
on the left and right and opposite on the other side of
the passage, were chewing hay with quick regularity,
as though they were keeping time, crunching it with relish
between their teeth and, every now and then, sniffing on
account of the dust. On a heap of hay in a corner, slept
the stable-boy on duty. Emerald knew by the sequence
of days and by the particular snore that it was Vassili,
a lad whom the horses disliked, because he smoked a reeking
tobacco in the stables, frequently came in drunk, pounded
their bellies with his knees, shook his fists in their eyes,
tugged their halters roughly, and always addressed them
in an unnatural, hoarse, threatening voice.

Emerald went up to the railed entrance opposite which,
facing him in her stable, stood a young black, not yet
full-grown, mare, named Chegolikha. Emerald could
not see her body in the dark, but every time that she left
off munching the hay and turned her head, her large eyes
would gleam for a few seconds with a pretty purple fire.
Emerald drew a long breath with his delicate dilated nostrils

as he took in the scarcely noticeable, but insistent, agitating, odour of her skin and gave a short neigh.

The mare turned round quickly and answered with a light, trembling, and playful neighing.

From the box, immediately on his right, Emerald heard a jealous, angry breathing. It came from old Onieguine, a vicious chestnut, who still appeared from time to time in the town races.

The two horses were separated by a light board partition and could not see each other, but, by placing his nose on the rail, Emerald could catch easily the warm odour of the chewed hay as it came from the panting nostrils of the chestnut. In this way, for some little time, the two horses sniffed at each other in the darkness, their ears flat on their heads, their necks arched as they grew more and more angry. Then, all of a sudden, each of them gave tongue to his rage, stamping fiercely at the same moment.

" Stop that nonsense, you devils," the stable-boy shouted at them sleepily, but with the familiar threat in his voice.

The horses sprang back from the rails and pricked up their ears. Their hostility towards each other was of long standing, but only three days before this there had been brought into this very stable that graceful black mare, a quite unusual occurrence, due to lack of space just before the races. And now not a day passed without a quarrel between them. In the stables, on the racetrack, and when they were taken to water, they would provoke each other to fight. But in his soul Emerald felt a certain fear of this long, self-assertive chestnut, a fear of that pungent smell of an angry horse, his rough, camel-like Adam's apple, his gloomy, sunken eyes, and particularly of his strong, stone-like frame, hardened by years of training and previous combats.

Pretending to himself that he was not in the least afraid, and that nothing at all had happened, Emerald turned, bent his head into the manger, and rummaged the hay with his soft, mobile, elastic lips. At first he just nibbled capriciously at separate morsels, but soon the gusto of chewing came over him and he really plunged into feeding. And at the same time slow indifferent thoughts were leaking into his head, linking together memories of shapes and perfumes and sounds, and then losing themselves finally in that dark abyss which lay before and behind everything except the passing moment.

Hay was the floating thought just now and he recalled the old stable-man, Nazar, who distributed the hay in the evening. That good old Nazar ! he always has such a cosy smell of black bread and just a slight sniff of wine ; his movements are gentle and unhurried ; on his days the oats and hay taste better, and it is nice to listen to him, for, when grooming you, he talks to you in whispers, with just a tender reproach, and all the time he is wheezing to himself. But for all that, he lacks the main thing, the horse touch, and when he has you between the shafts you can feel, through the reins, that his hands are fumbling and inexact.

Vassili has not got that horseman feel either, and, though he shouts and strikes, all the horses know that he is a coward and they are not afraid of him. And he, too, is unable to drive—he pulls at you and gets nervous. The third stable-man, the squint-eyed one, is better than these two, but he has no love for horses and is cruel and impatient ; besides, his hands are heavy as if they were made of wood. And the fourth, Andriashka, is still quite a boy and plays with the horses just like a sucking colt, stealthily kissing them on the upper lip, between the nostrils, which isn't particularly agreeable, but rather funny.

But that other one, the tall, thin, clean-shaven one with the stoop and the gold-rimmed glasses—oh, he's quite another affair. He's like some extraordinary horse wise and strong and fearless. He never gets angry, never, uses the whip, never even threatens, but, all the same, when he's up in the American buggy, it is so nice, so terrifyingly pleasant, to obey every hint of his strong, clever, all-comprehending fingers. He alone can produce in Emerald that state of joyous harmony in which the whole force of the body lends itself to the rush of the race and makes one feel so light and merry.

And at once, Emerald saw in imagination the short track to the hippodrome, saw almost every house, every kerbstone, saw the sand of the hippodrome itself, the tribune, the other horses, the green of the grass and the yellow of the track. Then suddenly he recalled the dark bay three-year-old who had recently twisted his foot on the track and had begun to limp. And thinking of him Emerald tried, mentally, to go lame himself just a little.

One bit of hay which Emerald had in his mouth had a peculiarly delicate taste. The colt chewed it for some time, and long after he had swallowed it, he retained in his mouth the fine perfume of faded flowers and dry, odorous grass. Then a dim quite formless, far-off memory slid into the horse's brain. This is just what happens sometimes with smokers when the chance inhaling of a cigarette brings back suddenly for an irresistible second the memory of a dark corridor with old wall-paper and a solitary candle on the buffet ; or else a long journey through the night with the regular tinkling of sledge bells and the sensation of languid sleepiness ; or else the dark blue wood, not too far off, the snow dazzling one's eyes, the noise of an approaching battue, the passionate impatience that makes one's knees tremble—all in a moment such bygone, forgotten, touching, but no longer translatable, feelings slide into one's soul with a sombre and dim caress.

Meanwhile the little black window above the manger, invisible until now, began to get grey and to become faintly outlined in the darkness. The horses chewed more lazily and sighed one after the other deeply and softly. In the yard the cock sounded his familiar call, sonorous, bold, and sharp like a trumpet. And far away in the distance, other cocks, each in turn, spread the summons of the morning

With his head bent in the manger, Emerald was still trying to keep in his mouth and get back with renewed force that strange taste that had aroused in him the echo of an exquisite, almost physical, but incomprehensible memory. But he could not revive it and, before he knew where he was, he began to doze.

II

His feet and body were perfectly built ; that is why he always slept standing, scarcely swinging either backwards or forwards. Sometimes, though, he would give a start and then his deep sleep would pass for a few seconds into a light slumber. But the short intervals of sleep were so profound that the muscles, nerves, and skin of the horse were rested and refreshed.

It was just at dawn that he was dreaming of an early spring morning, a reddish streak suffusing the earth, and a low-lying sweet-scented meadow. The grass was thick and luscious, green as in some charming fairy-tale, but tinged by the dawn with a delicate pink just as human beings and animals see it in early childhood, the dew gleaming all over it like trembling fires. In the pure, rarefied air every sort of perfume comes to one with peculiar intensity. One catches, through the freshness of the morning, the smell of the blue and transparent smoke that curls over the village chimneys ; every flower in the meadow has a distinct scent ; on the moist broken road that leads into the town innumerable scents are mingled with the smell of human beings, of tar, of horse-dung, of dust, and of cow's milk, fresh from a passing herd, of aromatic gum that drips from the pine trees over the hedge.

Emerald, a seven-months' stallion (his mane and tail

107

cut short) is running aimlessly through the meadow,
bending his neck and kicking out his hind legs. He
seems to be made of air, and is not in the least conscious
of the weight of his body. The white, perfumed camomile
flowers keep running backwards under his feet. He
whisks away straight on to the sun. The wet grass swishes
against his feet, his knees, making them feel cold and
dull just for the moment. The blue sky, the green grass,
the golden sun, the exquisite air, the drunken ecstasy of
youth, of strength and speed !

But just then he hears a short, restless, tender, and
appealing neighing, so familiar to him that he can recog-
nise it at a distance among thousands of neighs. He
stops short in his full gallop, listens for an instant, his
head raised, his delicate ears moving and his broom-
shaped, short downy tail shaking as he answers with a
long-drawn call, with which the whole of his fine, thinnish,
long-legged body vibrates. And then he speeds to his
mother.

She—-a quiet, bony old mare—raises her wet muzzle
from the grass, smells over the colt quickly and attentively and then resumes her chewing as though she were
in a hurry to finish a pressing business. Bending his
flexible neck under her with upturned muzzle, the colt
from habit thrusts his lips between her hind legs, to find
a warm elastic nipple full of sweet, scarcely sourish, milk
that flows, in hot little ripples, into his mouth. On and on
he drinks and cannot tear himself from it. The brood mare
shakes herself free at last and pretends to bite his groin.

It is quite light now in the stable. An old smelling,
bearded goat who lives with the horses has approached
the stable doors (that had been strengthened inside with
beams) and commenced to bleat, looking backwards
at the stable-boy. Vassili, bare-footed, scratching his
woolly head, got up to open them for him. The day
was a regular autumn one, bluish and cold. The square,

in front of the open doors, was covered at once by the warm vapour that steamed out from the stables, while the aroma of the white frost and the fallen leaves penetrated delicately into the horses' stalls.

They knew well that oats were going to be served out to them and they were giving impatient grunts near their railings. The greedy and capricious Onieguine was stamping with his hoofs and was exhibiting his old bad habit of champing with his upper teeth against the chewed iron-bound brim of the manger, swallowing and belching out the morning air. Emerald, for his part, contented himself with rubbing his muzzle against the railing.

The other stable-men—there were four altogether—came in and began to distribute the oats in iron bins. While Nazar was heaping up the heavy rustling oats in Emerald's manger, the colt, his warm nostrils trembling, did his best to get at it, first over the old man's shoulder and then under his arm. The stableman, who liked this impatience of a quiet horse, loitered purposely, barricaded the manger with his elbows and grumbled out in his rough kindly way, " Now, you glutton . . . there's lots of time. . . . Punch me again with your nose, and I'll be punching you to-night."

From the little window, above the manger, rose a square joyous sun-beam in which millions of golden fragments of dust, divided by long shadows from the window-panes, were whirling downwards.

III

Emerald had just finished his oats when they came to take him out into the yard. It was warmer now and the ground had become softer, but the stable walls were still white with frost. From the manure heaps, just taken out of the stables, rose a thick vapour, and the sparrows were swarming on them, chirruping excitedly as though they were quarrelling. Emerald bent his neck under the doorway and crossed the threshold carefully. Then he drank in joyfully deep draughts of the delicious air, shook the full length of his body and gave a sonorous sneeze. " Good health to you," observed Nazar quite gravely. Emerald would not keep still. He wanted vigorous movements, the tickling feeling of the air rushing into one's eyes and nostrils, the burning heart-beats and the long, deep breathing. Tied with a halter, he was neighing, dancing on his hind legs and curving his neck sideways to get a backward glimpse of the black mare, with one of his large rolling eyes, the whites of which were ribbed with little red veins.

Breathless from exertion, Nazar lifted high up above his head a pail of water, and dashed it upon the colt's back from crest to tail. This was a familiar sensation to Emerald, vigorous, pleasant, and always a little startling. Nazar brought more water and sprinkled his flanks, chest, feet, and tail with it. And each time that he soused him, his horny palm would pass over the horse's coat to mop off the water. Glancing backwards, Emerald could see his own sloping haunches suddenly darkened and then shining again, as with a varnish in the sun.

It was race day. Emerald knew that by the way the stablemen hurried and bustled about the horses, some of whom had usually to wear horse-shoes ; others had to wear leather pads on their knees ; others had their hind legs bandaged with linen belts up to the knees, or their chests protected with fur-bordered coats that reached to the forelegs. From the coach-house they pulled out the two-wheeled American buggies with high seats ; their metal spokes shone merrily and their red rims and large red curved shafts glowed under a new coat of varnish.

Emerald was already quite dry, brushed, rubbed and

groomed, when the head stableman, an Englishman, came in. Every man and horse in the stable had an equal respect for, and dread of, this tall, thin, long-handed man with the slight stoop. His clean-shaven face was sunburnt and his strong, thin lips were set in a mocking curve. He wore gold-rimmed glasses through which his light blue eyes looked straight out on the world with stubborn calmness. He watched the preparations, standing with his long legs wide apart in his high boots, his hands buried in his trouser pockets as he munched his cigar first at one corner of his mouth and then at the other. He wore a grey jacket with a fur collar and a narrow black cap with a long square peak. From time to time he made curt remarks in a jerky, careless tone and immediately all the stablemen and workmen turned their heads in his direction, while the horses pricked up their ears.

He paid particular attention to the harnessing of Emerald and examined the horse minutely from crest to hoof. And as Emerald felt the sure attentive glance he lifted his head proudly, slightly arched his supple neck, and raised his delicate, almost transparent, ears. The English-man tested the girth, slipping his finger between it and the horse's belly. Then they threw over the horses grey linen horse-cloths with red borders, red circles round the eyes, and red monograms low down on their hind legs. Two stable-boys, Nazar and the squint-eyed one, took a rein on each side of Emerald and led him to the hippodrome along the well-known road between two rows of scattered, large stone buildings. It was scarcely four versts to the racecourse.

There were already several horses in the enclosure ; they were taken round the circle all in the same direc- tion as in the actual race, that is to say, in the opposite direction of the hands of a watch. In the enclosure they were leading medium-sized strong-legged horses, with docked tails, among whom Emerald quickly recog- nised the little white colt who always raced near him.

111

Both horses greeted each other with a quiet and kindly neigh.

IV

A bell was rung. The stable-men removed Emerald's horse-cloth. The Englishman, his eyes blinking under his spectacles owing to the sun, was showing his long yellow horse-like teeth as he came up with a whip under his arm, buttoning his gloves on his way. One of the stable-men picked up Emerald's fluffy tail that reached almost to the back of his knees and placed it carefully on the seat of the racing buggy so that its light-coloured tip stuck out at the back. The shafts gave like elastic under the driver's weight. Emerald took a peep round and saw him sitting almost over his haunches, his feet stretched wide apart on the shafts. Without any hurry, the driver took up the reins, then he shouted a brief order to the stable-men, who at once let go of the reins. Rejoicing at the coming race, Emerald at first plunged forward, but, reined in by those strong hands, he merely reared on his hind legs, shook his neck, and ran through the enclosure gate to the hippodrome at a strong restrained trot.

Along the wooden fence that formed an ellipse of a verst, ran a large racing track, covered with yellow sand that was compact and slightly moist, thus at once yielding to and responding to the pressure of hoofs. The sharp hoof-marks and the straight stripes from the gutta-percha tyres furrowed it.

They ran past the tribune, a high wooden building with a frontage of two hundred horse-lengths at least, where, like a mountain extending to the very roof, which was itself supported by thin pillars, a black human crowd buzzed and swayed. Through a slight, scarcely perceptible, motion of the reins Emerald understood that he might increase his pace, and snorted gratefully in response.

He was trotting deliberately, hardly moving his back and keeping his neck stretched forward, but a little to the left, his muzzle lifted firm and high. Thanks to a restrained, though unusually long, pace his running produced from a distance no impression of speed. It seemed that the racer measured the road without hurrying, his forelegs, straight as a compass, scarcely touching the ground with the tips of the hoofs. It was the result of real American training in which everything combined to sustain the horse's wind and diminish to the utmost extent the resistance of the air. Under this régime all movements unnecessary to running are held to waste unproductively the horse's strength, and beauty of form is sacrificed to that lightness, dryness, long wind, and energy which transform the horse into a faultless living machine.

Now in this interlude between races the walking of the horses, so necessary to a trotter's lungs, was taking place. Many were running in the outer circle in the same direction as Emerald and in the inner in the opposite direction. A big dapple-grey, with a white muzzle, of the pure Orloff breed, with a high short neck, and a tail like piping, the whole resembling a ginger-bread horse at a fair, ran past Emerald ; his heaving flanks and large fat chest were steaming and darkened by sweat as he ran, throwing his forelegs sideways from the knees, while, at every pace, there rang from his spleen a sharp sound.

Then came behind him a stately, long-bodied, brown half-bred mare with a thin dark mane. She was beautifully trained on the same American system as Emerald ; her short, well-cared-for coat was so glossy that it revealed the play of the muscles under the skin. While the drivers were talking over something or other, the two horses ran for a little side by side. Emerald sniffed at the mare, quite prepared to make friends on the way, but the Englishman did not permit this and Emerald submitted.

Then there met them at full trot an enormous black

113

colt swathed in bandages, knee-caps, and pads. His left shaft stretched out a yard and a half longer than the right and a bearing rein clasped on the top and on both sides through a ring the nervous muzzle of the horse in its steel grip. As the mare glanced at him simultaneously each of them instantly recognised a racer of wonderful strength, speed, and endurance, but curiously stubborn and bad-tempered, conceited and very touchy. Just behind the black horse ran a pale grey colt, very spruce but ludicrously small. Looking at him sideways one would have thought he was whisking away at a terrific rate, so often did he throw out his feet, so high did he raise his knees and arch his short neck, while his small pretty head had such an earnest, business-like expression. Emerald merely squinted at him contemptuously and moved one ear in his direction.

The other driver stopped talking, with a short, loud laugh, like a neigh, and gave the mare her head. Quietly, without any effort, as if her speed had nothing to do with her, the mare shot ahead of Emerald, her shining back smooth and regular, with a scarcely noticeable little strap outlining her spine.

But a red fire-like racer with a large white spot on his muzzle caught up Emerald and her and soon left both behind. He galloped with long bounds, now stretching himself and almost stooping to the ground, and now almost joining his fore and hind legs in the air. His driver was lying, rather than sitting, on the box, his body thrown backwards as he hung on to the taut reins. Emerald got excited and lurched sideways, but the invisible English-man pulled on the reins and, all of a sudden, those hands, so supple and so sensitive to every movement of a horse, became like iron. Near the tribune the red colt, after another gallop round the ring, caught up to Emerald once more. Till then he had been galloping and he was already in a lather, with bloodshot eyes and panting breath. His driver, leaning forward, was lashing him

114

along the back with all his might. At last the stable-man managed to bar his course and seized the reins close to his muzzle, after which he was led away from the ring wet, wheezing, trembling, grown thin in a minute. Emerald did another half lap at a full trot, then turned on to the path which cut across the racecourse, and made his way back through the gate into the yard.

V

A bell rang several times on the hippodrome. Beyond the open gate the racehorses were running like lightning from time to time, while the people on the Grand Stand shouted and applauded. Emerald, lined up with the other horses, was stepping out beside Nazar, shaking his bent head and moving his ears in their linen cases. After his exercise his blood ran merry and hot in his veins ; his breathing grew deeper and freer as his body became more rested and cooler, while in every muscle he could feel the renewed longing for the race.

Half an hour went by. Another bell sounded on the hippodrome. Now the driver sat on the racing buggy without his gloves. His hands were large, white, magical, and inspired Emerald with both devotion and fear.

The Englishman drove out unhurriedly to the race track, from which horses were filing out on their way to the yard after finishing their walk. In the enclosure only Emerald and the enormous black colt whom he had met on that preliminary drive were left. The stands, from top to bottom, were black with a dense human crowd, and from this black mass emerged, gaily and untidily, countless white faces and hands, variegated umbrellas, women's hats, and airily swung programmes. Gradually quickening his pace, as he passed the stands, Emerald felt thousands of eyes following him fixedly. And he realised clearly that these eyes expected from him swiftness, the full tension of his strength, the full beating of his heart—and this understanding communicated to his muscles a joyous lightness and a coquettish precision of movement. A white horse of his acquaintance, ridden by a boy, was going at a hand gallop to his right.

With a regular measured trot, bending his body slightly to the left, Emerald traced an angular turn and moved up to the post with the red disc. A bell rang out curtly on the hippodrome. The Englishman imperceptibly straightened himself on the box seat and his hands became suddenly firmer. " Now go, but nurse your strength. It's too soon now." Emerald understood, and, to show his comprehension, he lowered for a second and then straightened his fine sensitive ears. The white colt was galloping regularly at his side and a little behind. Emerald could feel close to his crest the horse's fresh, even breath.

The red post flew behind him ; another sharp turn, the path straightens itself and the second stand comes nearer, blackens, becomes variegated with its buzzing crowd and grows larger with every step. " Faster," the driver permits—" faster, faster." Emerald grows a little excited and wants to throw into the race all his strength. " May I ? " he thinks to himself. " No, it's still too soon, don't be excited," answer the soothing, magic hands ; " afterwards."

The two colts pass the winning-posts at the same second but from opposite sides of the diameter linking the two stands. The slight resistance of the thread and the sense of its being broken made Emerald prick his ears, but he instantly forgot about it, so absorbed was he by those marvellous hands. " A little faster, but don't get excited. Go evenly," his driver orders. The black rocking tribune swims past him ; another hundred yards or so, and all four of them—Emerald, the young white colt, the Englishman and the boy who, standing on his short stirrups, was almost over the horse's mane—merge themselves in one close, rushing mass of speed, animated by one will, one

116

beauty of powerful movement, one rhythm resonant as music. " Rat-tat-tat," exactly and regularly, Emerald beats out with his hoofs. " Tra-ta-tra-ta," curtly and sharply the hoofs of the white horse reply. Another turn and the second stand rushes towards them. " Shall I force the pace ? " Emerald asks. " Yes," reply the hands, " but coolly."

The second stand flies swiftly by. The people are shouting out something. It distracts Emerald. He gets excited, loses the feeling of the reins, loses his step for a second, and gives four capricious beats with his right hoof. But the reins immediately become hard, tear his mouth, wring his neck downwards and force his head to the right. Now he can't gallop with the right feet. Emerald grows angry and refuses to change his feet, but the driver, seizing his moment, coolly and authoritatively pulls him into a trot. The stand is now far behind them. Emerald gets back into his pace and the hands become friendly and soft once more. Emerald feels that he has done wrong and wants to double his pace. " But oh no, it's too soon yet," the hands observe kindly. " We'll have time to make up for this. Don't worry."

And so they pass in perfect harmony without any change of pace a full round and a half. But the black colt is in perfect form to-day ; while Emerald had been out of step, he had had time to outdistance him by six lengths. Emerald, however, makes up for the lost time and, at the last post but one, he is three seconds and a quarter ahead. " Now you can do it. Go," the driver orders. Emerald draws back his ears and gives one quick glance behind him. The Englishman's face burns with a sharp, decisive expression ; his clean-shaven lips have wrinkled into an impatient grimace, exposing his long yellow clenched teeth. " Now for the last ounce ! " the reins in the high uplifted hands order ; " faster, faster." Suddenly the Englishman shouts in a loud vibrating voice that rises like a siren : " Oh—eh, eh—eh ! "

117

"There, there, there, there," the boy behind them shouts shrilly in tune.

The rhythm has now reached its highest pitch and the tension hangs on a single hair, almost ready to snap. "Ta-ta-ta," regularly stamp out on the ground Emerald's feet. "Trra, trra, trra," one hears ahead the gallop of the white colt spurring Emerald on. The elastic shafts swing in time with the race, and the boy, almost lying on his horse's neck, rises in his saddle to the rhythm of the gallop.

The air, rushing to meet one, whistles in one's ears and tickles the nostrils, from which great streams of steam emerge. It becomes more difficult to breathe and one's skin burns. Emerald takes the last turn, all his body swerving in the middle of it. The stand becomes alive with the roar from a thousand throats, frightening, troubling, and gladdening Emerald all at once. He can trot no longer but wants to gallop, only those astonishing hands behind him implore and order and soothe: "Don't gallop, my dear. Whatever you do, don't gallop; that's it, that's it, just like that; that's it." And Emerald, rushing past the post, breaks the control thread, without even noticing it. Shouts, laughter, a torrent of applause is hurled down from the stand. The white leaves of the race-programme, umbrellas, sticks, hats turn and flash amid a sea of hands and faces. The Englishman throws the reins aside gently. "It s all over, my dear, thanks," this movement says to Emerald, as he, with difficulty, recovers from the impetus of the race and slows down to a walk. At this moment the black colt is just arriving at his post, seven seconds later, on the opposite side.

The Englishman raises his stiff legs with difficulty, jumps heavily from the buggy, takes off the padded seat, and goes with it to the weighing. Stable-men run up to fling a horsecloth over Emerald's hot back and take him to the yard. He is followed by the rumbling of the crowd and the loud bell of the members' pavilion. A slight yellowish froth falls from the horse's mouth on the ground and on the stable-man's hands.

A few minutes later Emerald, already harnessed, is brought back to the judge's box. A tall man, with a long coat and a new shining hat, whom Emerald has often seen in his stable, pats him on the neck and thrusts a lump of sugar straight into his mouth. The English-man is standing there in the crowd, smiling, wrinkling his face, as he grins with his long teeth. The horse-cloth is removed from Emerald and he is put in front of a box, standing on three feet and covered with a black cloth, under which a man in grey is hiding himself, busy with something or other.

But already people are swarming down from the grand stand in a black, serried mass. They come close to the horse on all sides, shouting, waving their hands, stretching out close to one another their red, sweating faces, with gleaming eyes. They are dissatisfied about something. They thrust their fingers in the feet, the head, the flanks of Emerald, rumple his hair on the left flank where there is a brand, and roar out altogether, " A false trotter ! A fake ! A swindle ! Money back ! " Emerald listens to this without understanding the words and moves his ears anxiously. " What's it all about ? " he thinks with surprise, " when I've been running so well ! " Then for a second the Englishman's face leaps before his eyes. Usually so calm, slightly mocking and firm, it is now burning with anger. And all of a sudden the Englishman shouts something in a high guttural voice, swings his arm quickly, and the sound of a blow cuts drily through the general turmoil.

VI

Emerald was taken home and three hours later he was given oats. In the evening, when he was watered at the well, he could see the large yellow moon rising behind the edge of a cloud and this inspired him with a dark dread.

Then began the dull days.

He was not taken out any more either for exercise or walks or to races. But every day strangers, crowds of people, came, and for their benefit Emerald was dragged out into the yard, where they examined him and felt him all over, their hands crawling into his mouth, scrubbing his coat with pumice-stone, all shouting at each other together.

Afterwards, he remembered, he was once taken out of the stable, late in the evening, and led for a long time through stony, empty streets, past houses and lit-up windows. Then came the station, a dark shaky horse-box, his feet trembling from fatigue after a long journey, the whistles of the engines, the rattle of the rails, the stifling smell of smoke, the dull light of the swinging lantern. At one station he was dumped out of the horse-box and led along an endless unknown road that ran between huge bare autumn fields, past villages until he reached an unfamiliar stable, where he was shut up alone away from the other horses.

At the beginning he would still recall the races and think about his Englishman and Vassili and Nazar and Onieguine, often dreaming about them, but gradually he began to forget them all. He was hidden away for some reason or other, and his beautiful young body was pining and grieving and growing weak from inaction. And new strangers were constantly arriving, crowding round Emerald, prodding him, pulling him about and angrily abusing each other.

Sometimes Emerald could catch glimpses, through the open door, of other horses walking and running about in freedom. Then he would shout to them in protest and complaint. But the door was instantly closed again, and time would crawl once more, dull and lonely, for Emerald.

The head of this stable was a large-headed, sleepy man with small black eyes and a thin black moustache on his fat face. He seemed to be quite indifferent to Emerald, but the horse felt an incomprehensible fear of him. And then once, early in the morning, while all the stablemen were still asleep, this man came noiselessly up to Emerald on tip-toe, poured oats into his manger, and left the stable. Emerald was a little surprised, but began immediately to eat. The oats were nice, just a little bitter, but pleasant to the taste for all that. " It's odd," thought Emerald, " I never tasted such oats before."

Then, all of a sudden, he became conscious of a slight colic. Pain came, it stopped, then came back stronger than ever, and grew sharper every minute. At last it became intolerable. Emerald began to moan dully. Wheels of fire were dancing before his eyes ; all his body was wet and flabby from this sudden weakness. His feet shivered, bent under him, and the colt fell heavily on the floor. He tried to get up again, but could only raise himself on his forelegs, and once more slipped on his side. A buzzing turmoil whirled through his head ; the Englishman swam by with his horse-like grin from the long teeth ; Onieguine ran by, neighing loudly, with his camel-like Adam's apple projecting beneath his jaw. Some force or other was dragging Emerald mercilessly and ruthlessly deep down into a dark, cold hole. Already he was unable to move.

Suddenly convulsions passed over his feet and neck and arched his back. The horse's skin began to tremble in small swift ripples and became covered with a froth that had a pungent smell.

The moving yellow light of the lantern played straight into his eyes for a second and then died away with his failing eyesight. His ear caught once more a coarse human shout, but already he was unable to feel himself pushed in the side by someone's heel. Then everything disappeared—for ever.

HAPPINESS

A Fairy-Tale

A GREAT tzar ordered the poets and sages of his country to be brought before him. And he asked them this question :

" In what does happiness consist ? "

" In this," answered the first hastily : " to be able to see always the illumination of thy God-like face and feel for ever . . . "

" Have his eyes put out," said the tzar indifferently. " Next."

" Happiness is power. Thou, tzar, art happy," exclaimed the next.

But the tzar answered with a bitter smile :

" All the same, I suffer in my body and have no power to cure it. Tear out his nostrils, the scoundrel. Next."

" Happiness is wealth," said the next, hesitatingly.

But the tzar answered :

" I am rich and yet it is I who ask the question. Will a wedge of gold the weight of thy head content thee ? "

" O, tzar ! "

" Thou shalt have it. Fasten on his neck a wedge of gold the weight of his head and cast this beggar into the sea."

And the tzar shouted impatiently : " The fourth."

Then a man in rags with feverish eyes crept on his stomach and stammered out :

" O, most wise one ! I want very little. I am hungry. Give me satiety and I shall be happy and will glorify thy name throughout the whole universe."

123

" Feed him," said the tzar in disgust. " And when he dies of overeating, let me know about it."

And there came two others : One, a powerful athlete with a rosy body and a low forehead. He said with a sign :

" Happiness lies in creation."

The other was a thin, pale poet on whose cheeks were burning two bright spots, and he said :

" Happiness lies in health."

But the tzar smiled bitterly and observed :

" If it were in my power to change your destinies, then thou, oh poet, wouldst beg for inspiration in a month, and thou, image of Hercules, wouldst be running to doctors for pills to reduce thy weight. Go both in peace. Who else is there ? "

" A mere mortal," exclaimed proudly the seventh, decorated with narcissus flowers : " Happiness lies in non-existence."

" Cut off his head," the sovereign pronounced lazily.

" Tzar, tzar, be merciful ! " lisped the condemned man, and he became paler than the petals of the narcissus. " I did not mean that."

But the tzar waved his hand wearily, yawned, and said gently :

" Take him away. Cut off his head. The tzar's word is hard as agate."

Many others came. One of them said only two words :

" Women's love."

" Very well," the tzar acquiesced. " Give him a hundred of the most beautiful women and girls of my country. But give him also a goblet of poison. And when the time has arrived let me know and I will come to look at his corpse."

And another said :

" Happiness consists in having each of my wishes fulfilled immediately."

" And what does thou want now ? " the tzar asked cunningly.

" I ? "

" Yes, thou."

" Tzar . . . the question is too unexpected."

" Bury him alive. Ah, and still another wise man ? Well, well, come a little nearer, perhaps thou knowest in what happiness consists ? "

The wise man—for he was a real wise man—answered :

" Happiness lies in the charm of human thought."

The tzar's eyebrows contracted and he shouted in wrath :

" Ah ! Human thought ! What is human thought ? "

But the wise man—for he was a real wise man—only smiled compassionately and did not answer at all.

Then the tzar ordered him to be hurled into an underground prison where there was perpetual darkness and where no sound from outside could be heard. And when, a year later, they brought to him the prisoner who had become blind and deaf, and could scarcely stand on his feet, he answered quietly to the tzar's question, " Well, art thou still happy now ? " in these words :

" Yes, I am happy. While in prison I was a tzar, and a rich man, and in love, and with my fill of food, and hungry—all this was given to me by my thought."

" What, then, is thought ? " exclaimed the tzar impatiently. " Remember that in another five minutes I will have thee hanged and will spit in thine accursed face. Will thy thought console thee then ? And where will then be thy thoughts, which thou didst lavish on this earth ? "

The wise man answered quietly, for he was a real wise man :

" Fool, thought is immortal."

HOW I BECAME AN ACTOR

THIS sad and funny story—more sad than funny—
was told me by a friend of mine who had led the
oddest sort of life. He had been what we Russians
call " on the horse and under the horse," but he had not,
in the least, lost, under the lash of destiny, his kindness of
heart and his alertness of mind. Only this particular
experience produced a rather curious effect on him—he
gave up going to the theatre after it and, until the present
moment, nothing will drag him into one.

I shall try to transmit my friend's story, though I am
afraid that I shall be unable to reproduce the simplicity,
the soft and melancholy mockery, which he put into it.

I

Well, it's like this. Can you picture for yourself a
wretched little southern country town ? In the middle of
it there is a sort of monstrous shallow pit where the Ukrainians of the neighbourhood, up to their waists in mud, sell
cucumbers and potatoes from their carts. This is the
bazaar. On one side is the cathedral, and naturally the
cathedral street, on the other the town square, on the third
the market stone stalls, the yellow plaster of which has
peeled off ; pigeons are perching on the roof and cornices ;
finally, on the fourth side, stretches the main street, with a
branch of some bank or other, a post office, a solicitor, and

127

the barber Theodore from Moscow. In the outskirts of
the town an infantry regiment was then billeted, and in
the town itself a regiment of dragoons. In the town square
stood the summer theatre. And that's all.

Still one must add that the town itself, with its Duma
and secondary school, to say nothing of the square, the
theatre, the paving of the main street—all this exists,
thanks to the liberality of the local millionaire and sugar
manufacturer, Kharitonenko.

II

How I stumbled into the place is a long story, but I'll
tell it briefly. In this little town I was to meet a friend,
a real, true friend (God rest his soul), but he had a wife
who, as is usual with the wives of our *true* friends, could not
bear me. He and I each had several thousands put by
through hard work : he, you see, had worked for many
years as a pedagogue and as an assurance inspector at
the same time, while I had been lucky at cards for a whole
year. Suddenly we stumbled on a very advantageous
enterprise in southern skins and decided to try our luck at it.
I started at once, and he was to rejoin me two or three days
later. As my carelessness was an old story, our little
capital was kept by him, but in a separate bundle, for my
friend was a man of German carefulness.

And then began the hail of misfortunes. At the station
of Kharkoff, while I was eating some cold sturgeon, sauce
Provençale, I was robbed of my pocket-book. I arrive at
C. (this very little town of my story) with the small change
left in my purse and a lanky, but good reddish-yellow
English portmanteau. I put up at an hotel—naturally
the Petersburg Hotel—and began to send telegram after
telegram. Silence of the grave. Yes, yes, literally of the
grave, because at the very moment when the thief was

128

stealing my pocket-book—what tricks fate plays !—at that very moment my friend and companion died in a cab from paralysis of the heart. All his things, including his money, were sealed and for some idiotic reason or other the wrestling with officials lasted a month and a half. Did the widow, deeply lamenting, know about my money, or did she not ? I can't answer that question myself. However, she received all my telegrams, every one of them, but remained stubbornly silent—silent from petty, jealous, silly, feminine revenge. All the same, these telegrams were of great use to me later on. After removing the seals, an advocate, a complete stranger to me, who was looking after the widow's inheritance, came across them quite by accident, made the widow ashamed of herself, and, at his own risk, transferred five hundred roubles to me at the theatre. But I must add the fact that they were not mere telegrams but tragic lamentations of twenty or thirty words each.

III

I had been at the Petersburg Hotel for ten days already. My tragic lamentations had quite exhausted my purse. The hotel proprietor—a gloomy, sleepy, hairy Ukrainian, with the face of an assassin—had long ago ceased to believe in my word. I showed him certain letters and papers by which he could have, etc., etc., but all he did was to turn his face scornfully away and snort. Finally, they served me with dinner as though I were Gogol's Khlestakov : " The proprietor has said that this is for the last time."

And then came the day when there was left in my pocket a single, orphan, greenish silver twenty kopek-piece. That morning the proprietor said insolently that he was not going to feed me or keep me any longer, but was going to report me to the police inspector. By his tone I could see that he would stop at nothing.

I left the hotel and wandered about the town. I remember entering a transport office and another place to look for work. Naturally it was refused me at the very first words. Sometimes I would sit down on one of the green benches that lay all along the main street between the high pyramid-like poplars. My head swam; I felt sick from hunger. But not for a moment did the idea of suicide enter my mind. How many, many times in my tangled life have I been on the border of these thoughts, but then a year would pass, sometimes a month, or even simply ten minutes, and suddenly everything would be changed, everything would be going luckily again, gaily, nicely. And all through that day, as I wandered about the hot, dull town, all I kept saying to myself was : " Ye-es, my dear Pavel Andreevitch, you've got into a nice mess."

I wanted to eat. But through some sort of mysterious presentiment I clung to my twenty kopeks. Dusk was already falling when I saw on the hoardings a red poster. In any case I had nothing to do. So I mechanically approached it and read that they were giving that day in the town gardens Goutzkov's tragedy, " Uriel Akosta," in which so-and-so and so-and-so were to appear. Two names were printed in large black letters : An artist from the Petersburg theatres, Madame Androssova, and the well-known artist from Kharkoff, M. Lara-Larsky ; the other names were in small print. Last of all, in the smallest letters, came : Petrov, Serguiev, Ivanov, Sidorov, Grigoriev, Nikolaev, and others. Stage-manager, M. Samoilenko. Managing director, M. Valerianov.

A sudden desperate inspiration seized me. I rushed across to the barber, Theodore from Moscow, and, with my last twenty kopeks, had my moustache and short pointed beard shaved off. Good Lord ! What a morose, naked face glanced at me from the looking-glass ! I could scarcely believe my own eyes. Instead of a man of thirty, not too good-looking, but at all events of decent appearance, there in the looking-glass in front of me, swathed up to his throat in a barber's sheet, sat an old, burned-out, inveterate, provincial comic with traces of all sorts of vice in his face and apparently not quite sober.

" You are going to work in our theatre ? " asked the barber's assistant as he shook off the sheet.

" Yes," I answered proudly. " Here you are."

IV

On my way to the town gardens, I thought to myself : There's no misfortune without some good in it. I shall be taken at once for an old and experienced sparrow. In these little summer theatres every useless man is useful. I shall be modest at the beginning . . . about fifty roubles . . . say forty a month. The future will show . . . I'll ask for an advance of about twenty roubles . . . no, that's too much . . . say, ten roubles. The first thing I'll do with it will be to send a hair-raising telegram . . . five times five— twenty-five and a nought—two roubles fifty kopeks, and fifteen extra charge—that's two roubles and sixty-five kopeks. On the remainder I'll get through somehow or other until Ilia arrives. If they want to test me . . . well, what about it ? I shall recite something—why not the monologue of Pimen in " Boris Goudounov " ?

And I began aloud, in a deep, pompous, strangled tone :

" And yet ano—other fa—arewell word."

A passer-by jumped away from me quite frightened. I felt ashamed and cleared my throat. But I was already getting near the town gardens. A military band was playing ; slim young ladies of the district, dressed in pink and sky blue, were walking about without their hats and behind them stalked, laughing aloud, their hands thrust in their jackets, their white caps rakishly on one side, the local scribes, the telegraph and excise clerks.

The doors were wide open. I went in. Someone asked me to take a ticket from the cash desk, but I said carelessly : " Where is the manager, M. Valerianov ? " Two clean-shaven young men, sitting on a bench not far from the entrance, were at once pointed out to me. I approached them and halted two steps away.

They were engrossed in their conversation and took no notice of me, so I had time to examine them. One of them, in a light Panama hat and a light flannel suit with little blue stripes, had an air of sham nobility and the haughty profile of a principal lover. He was playing negligently with his walking-stick. The other, in a greyish suit, was extraordinarily long-legged and long-armed ; his legs seemed to begin at the middle of his chest, and his arms probably extended below his knees. Owing to this, when sitting, he had the appearance of an odd, broken line, which, however, one had better describe as a folding measure. His head was very small, his face was freckled, and he had animated dark eyes.

I coughed modestly. They both turned towards me.

" Can I see M. Valerianov ? " I asked amiably.

" I am he," the freckled one answered. " What do you want ? "

" You see, I wanted . . . "—something tickled my throat—" I wanted to offer you my services, as . . . as . . . well, as a second comic, or . . . well . . . third clown. Also character parts."

The principal lover rose and went off whistling and brandishing his stick. .

" What previous experience have you had ? " Valerianov asked.

I had only been once on the stage, when I took the part of Makarka at some amateur theatricals, but I drew convulsively on my imagination and replied :

" As a matter of fact, I haven't taken part in any important enterprise, like yours, for example, up till now. But I have occasionally acted in small troupes in the South-

West. They came to grief as quickly as they were organised . . . for instance, Marinitch . . . Sokolovsky . . . . and there were others too."

" Look here, you don't drink, do you ? " Valerianov asked disconcertingly.

" No," I replied without hesitation. " Sometimes at dinner, or with my friends, but quite moderately."

M. Valerianov looked down at the sand, blinking with his dark eyes, thought for a few seconds, and then said :

" Well, all right, I'll take you on. Twenty-five roubles a month to begin with and then we'll see. You might be wanted even to-day. Go to the stage and ask for the manager's assistant, Doukhovski. He will introduce you to the stage-manager."

On my way I thought to myself : Why didn't he ask me for my stage name ? Probably he forgot. Perhaps he guessed that I had none. And in case of an emergency I then and there invented a name—not particularly sonorous, a nice simple name—Ossinine.

V

Behind the scenes I found Doukhovskoi, a nimble fellow with a thievish, tipsy face. He at once introduced me to the stage-manager, Samoilenko, who that day was acting in some kind of heroic part and for this reason sported golden armour, hessian boots, and the make-up of a young lover. However, through this disguise I could distinguish that Samoilenko was fat, and his face was quite round, and two small cunning eyes and a mouth folded in a perpetual sheep's smile. He received me haughtily, without even offering his hand. I was inclined to move away from him, when he said :

" Wait a minute ; what's your name ? I didn't make it out."

" Vassiliev." Doukhovskoi rushed up with the information.

I felt confused, wished to correct the mistake, but already it was too late.

" Here you are, Vassiliev. Don't leave the place to-day. Doukhovskoi, tell the tailor to give Vassiliev his get-up."

Thus from Ossinine I became Vassiliev, and I remained Vassiliev together with Pstrov, Ivanov, Nikolaev, Grigoriev, and Sidorov and others to the very end of my stage career. Inexperienced actor as I was, it was only after a week that I realised that, among all those sonorous names, mine alone covered a human being. The accursed series of names ruined me !

The tailor came, a thin, lame man, wrapped me up in a long, black calico shroud with sleeves, and tacked it on to me from head to foot. Then came the coiffeur, in whom I recognised Theodore's assistant who had just shaved me, and we exchanged a friendly smile. He put a black wig with love-locks on my head. Doukhovskoi rushed into the dressing-room and shouted :

" I say, Vassiliev, make yourself up."

I stuck my finger into some kind of paint, but my left-hand neighbour, a severe man with the forehead of a deep thinker, stopped me :

" Can't you see that you're using a private box ? Here's the box for general use."

I saw a large case with divisions full of dirty paint all mixed together ; I felt dazed. It was easy enough for Doukhovskoi to shout out : " Make yourself up," but how was it to be done ? I manfully put a white dash along my nose and looked immediately like a clown. I traced cruel eyebrows. I made blue marks under my eyes. Then I reflected : What else could I do ? I blinked and managed to insert between my eyebrows two vertical wrinkles. Now I resembled a Red Indian chief.

" Vassiliev, get ready," someone shouted from the top of the stairs.

I went up and came to the threadbare cloth doors of the back wall. Doukhovskoi was waiting for me.

" You are to go on at once. Devil take it, what on earth do you look like ? As soon as they say : ' No, he will come back,' go on. Go on and say—he gave some kind of proper name which I've forgotten—' So-and-so is asking for an interview,' and then exit. You understand ? "

" Yes."

" No, he will come back," I hear, and pushing past Doukhovskoi I rush on to the stage. What the deuce was the name of that man ? A second, another second of silence. The house is like a black, moving abyss. Straight in front of me, on the stage, are strange, roughly-painted faces, brightly lit up by the lamps. Everyone looks at me expectantly. Doukhovskoi whispers something at the back, but I can't make it out. Then suddenly I fire off in a voice of solemn reproach :

" Yes, he has come back."

Past me like a hurricane rushed Samoilenko in his golden coat of mail. Thank God ! I disappear behind the curtain.

I appeared twice more in that show. In the scene when Akosta gives the familiar thundering against the Jews and then falls. I was supposed to catch him in my arms and drag him behind the curtain. In this business I was helped by a fireman, got up in a black shroud like my own. (How is one to know ? Perhaps the public thought he was Sidorov.) Uriel Akosta appeared to be the actor who had been sitting with Valerianov on the bench ; he was, too, the well-known artist from Kharkoff, Lara-Larsky. We took him a little awkwardly—he was a heavy muscular man—but luckily we didn't drop him. He said to us in a whisper : " Devil take you, you louts." We dragged him with equal luck through the narrow doors, though afterwards the black wall of the ancient temple shook and swayed for a long time.

My third appearance was without words at the judgment of Akosta. A little incident, hardly worth mentioning, occurred. It was simply that when Ben-Akib came in everyone rose, but, thanks to my habit of gaping about, I continued sitting. Someone, however, pinched me painfully above the elbow and hissed out :

" Are you crazy ? It's Ben-Akib. Get up ! "

I rose hurriedly. On my honour I didn't know that it was Ben-Akib. I thought it was just a little old man.

At the end of the performance Samoilenko said to me :

" Vassiliev, rehearsal to-morrow at eleven."

I went back to the hotel, but on recognising my voice the proprietor banged the door in my face. I spent the night on one of the little green benches between the poplars. It was warm sleeping there and I dreamed of glory. But the cold morning dew and the feeling of hunger woke me up rather early.

VI

Exactly at half-past ten I arrived at the theatre. There was no one there as yet. Here and there in the gardens sleepy waiters from the summer restaurant were wandering about in their white aprons. In a summer-house of green trellis-work interwoven with wild vines they were preparing someone's breakfast or morning coffee.

I learned later on that the manager, M. Valerianov, and the elderly ex-actress Mme. Boulatova-Tchernogorskaya, a lady of about sixty-five who financed the theatre, and the manager himself, breakfasted there every morning in the fresh air.

The table was laid for two with a white glistening cloth and two little piles of sliced white and brown bread rose on a plate . . .

Here comes the ticklish part of my story. For the first and last time in my life, I became a thief. Glancing round quickly, I dived into the arbour and seized several slices of bread in my open hand ; it was so soft, so exquisite. But as soon as I was outside again I ran up against the waiter. I don't know where he came from ; probably I hadn't noticed him behind the arbour. He was carrying a cruet-stand with mustard, pepper, and vinegar. He looked hard at me, then at the bread in my hand, and said quietly :

" What does this mean ? "

A sort of burning, scornful pride welled up in me. Looking right into the pupils of his eyes, I answered as quietly :

" It means . . . that since four o'clock the day before yesterday I have had positively nothing to eat."

He spun suddenly round, without uttering a word, and ran off somewhere. I hid the bread in my pocket and waited. I had a feeling at once of dread and joy. That's excellent, I was thinking. Now the proprietor will rush up, the waiters will gather round, they will whistle for the police . . . there will be a row, insults, a fight. Oh, how magnificently I shall smash these very plates and cruets over their heads. I'll bite them till I draw blood.

But then, what do I see ? My waiter is running back to me by himself. He was a little out of breath. He came up to me sideways, without looking at me. I, too, averted my eyes. And then suddenly, from under his apron, he pushed into my hand a piece of yesterday's cold meat, carefully salted, and whispered entreatingly :

" Please, do eat, I beg of you."

I took the meat roughly from him, went with it behind the scenes, chose a corner—a rather dark one—and then, sitting among the old stage properties, I tore the meat greedily with my teeth and shed happy tears.

Later on I saw that man often, almost every day. His name was Serguei. When there were no customers, he used to look at me from a distance kindly with faithful, hospitable eyes. But I had no wish to spoil, either for myself or for him, that first sympathetic impression, though I confess I was sometimes as hungry as a wolf in the winter.

He was a small, rather fat, rather bald man, with black cockroach-like moustaches and kind eyes, shaped like narrow radiant semi-circles. He was always in a hurry and gave the impression of hopping along. When I received my money at last and my theatrical slavery remained only a dream, and all these rotten people were lapping up my champagne and flattering me, how I did miss you you dear, funny, pathetic Serguei ! Of course I should neve r have dared to offer him money—can one possibly estimate in money such kindness and human affection ? I merely wanted to give him some little present before going away . . . a little trifle . . . or else something for his wife or his kids—he had a whole swarm of them, and in the morning sometimes they used to run up to him, agitated and clamorous like young sparrows.

But a week before my marvellous transformation Serguei was dismissed, and I know the reason. Captain von Bradke had been served a beefsteak not to his taste. He bawled out :

" What's this you're giving me, you rascal ? Don't you know that I like it red ? "

Serguei ventured to remark that it was not his fault, but the cook's, and that he would go and change it at once. He even added timidly :

" Excuse me, Mister."

This apology maddened the officer. He struck Serguei with his beefsteak on the cheek, and turning purple, he yelled out :

" Wha-at ! I am a mister to you, am I ? I am not a mister to you, I am staff captain of cavalry to my emperor ! Where's the proprietor ? Call the proprietor. Ivan Lukian- ytch, I want this idiot cleaned out of here to-day. I don't want a trace of him here. If there is, I'll never set foot in your pothouse again."

The staff captain of cavalry, von Bradke, was a man of big sprees and for this reason Serguei was dismissed that very day. The proprietor spent the whole evening in calming the officer. I myself, when I came out between the acts for a breath of fresh air in the gardens, heard for a long time the enraged, bellowing voice issuing from the arbour.

" What a scoundrel the fellow is ! Mister ! If it hadn't been for the ladies I would have shown him the meaning of mister ! "

VII

In the meantime the actors had gradually drifted in and at half-past twelve the rehearsal, due at eleven, began. They were giving a play entitled " The New World," a kind of insipid side-show transformation of Senkevicz's novel " Quo Vadis ? " Doukhovskoi gave me a type-written sheet of paper containing my lines. I had the part of the Centurion in the division of Mark the Magnificent. They were pompous, loud lines, as, for example : " Thy orders, O Mark the Magnificent, have been punctually obeyed," or " She will wait for thee at the pedestal of the statue of Pompeii, O Mark the Magnificent." I liked the part, and I was already preparing a manly voice of a sort of old swashbuckler, stern and faithful.

But as the rehearsal proceeded, an odd thing happened to me ; to my surprise I began to get divided and multiplied. For instance, at the end of the Matron Veronica's speech, Samoilenko, who followed the play with the full text in front of him, claps his hands and shouts :

" A slave comes in."

No one comes in.

" But who is the slave ? Doukhovskoi, see who is the slave."

Doukhovskoi rummages hastily through some sheets of paper. " There is no slave ! "

" Cut him out, what about it ! " lazily advises Boev,

the argumentative person with a forehead of a thinker, into whose paint-box I had stuck my fingers the day before.

But Mark the Magnificent (Lara-Larsky) suddenly takes offence at this :

" No, that won't do, please. I have an effective entrance here . . . I don't play this scene without a slave."

Samoilenko's eyes gallop round the stage and halt at me.

" There you are, I mean . . . I mean . . . Vassiliev, are you on in this act ? "

I consult my copybook.

" Yes, at the very end."

" Then here's another part for you—Veronica's slave. Read it from the book." He claps his hands. " A little less noise, gentlemen, please. Enter the slave. . . . 'Noble dame.' . . . Speak up, speak up, one couldn't· hear you from the first row."

A few minutes later they couldn't find a slave for the divine Marcia (in Senkevicz's text she is Ligia), and this part is dumped on to me. Then some kind of house steward is missing. Me again ! In this way, by the end of the rehearsal, I had, without counting the Centurion, five additional parts.

It wouldn't go at all at the beginning. I come out and pronounce my first words :

" O Mark the Magnificent . . ."

Then Samoilenko stretches his legs wide apart, bends forward, and puts his hands to his ears :

" Wha-at ! What's that you're mumbling ? I understand nothing."

" O Mark the Magnificent . . ."

" What's that ? I can hear nothing . . . Louder ! " He comes quite close to me. " This is the way to do it," and in a guttural goat's voice he shouts out loud enough to be heard all over the gardens :

" ' O Mark the Magnificent, thy order ' . . . That's

how it's got to be done. Remember, young man, the immortal apothegm of one of the greatest of our Russian artists : ' On the stage one doesn't speak, one declaims ; one doesn't walk, one struts.' '' He looked round with a self-satisfied air. '' Repeat.''

I repeated, but it was still worse. Then, one after the other, they began to coach me, and positively the whole lot of them instructed me to the very end of the rehearsal : Lara-Larsky with a careless and disgusted manner ; the old, swollen, noble father Gontcharov, whose flabby red-veined cheeks were hanging down below his chin ; the argumentative Boev ; the idiot Akimenko, who was made up as a sort of Ivan the Simpleton. I was getting like a worried, steaming horse, around whom a street crowd of advisers had gathered, or a new boy who had fallen from his safe family nest into a circle of cunning, experienced, and merciless schoolboys.

At this rehearsal I made a petty, but persistent, enemy who afterwards poisoned every day of my existence. It happened like this :

I was repeating endlessly : '' O Mark the Magnificent,'' when suddenly Samoilenko rushed up to me.

'' Allow me, allow me, my friend ; allow me, allow me. Not like that, not like that. Think whom you're addressing —Mark the Magnificent himself. Well, you haven't got the faintest notion how subordinates in ancient Rome addressed their supreme chief. Watch me ; here's the gesture.''

He shot his right leg forward half a pace, bent his trunk at a right angle, and hung down his right arm, after manipulating his palm into the shape of a little boat.

'' Do you see what the gesture is ? Do you understand ? Repeat.''

I repeated, but with me the gesture proved so stupid and ugly that I decided on a timid objection :

'' I beg your pardon, but it seems to me that military training . . . it generally avoids somehow the bent

position . . . and, apart from that, there's a stage direction
. . . . he comes out in his armour . . . and you will
admit that in armour . . ."

" Kindly be quiet ! " Samoilenko shouted angrily ;
he had become purple. " If the manager orders you to
stand on one foot with your tongue out, you must obey
in absolute silence. Kindly repeat."

I repeated and the effect was still more grotesque.
But at this point Lara-Larsky came to my rescue.

" Leave it alone, Boris," he said weariedly to Samoilenko. " Can't you see that he isn't up to it ? And
apart from this, as you know yourself, history gives us
no direct indications. The question . . . hum . . . is
debatable."

Samoilenko left me in peace about his classical gesture.
But after that he never missed a chance of knifing me,
stinging me, and generally insulting me. He followed
all my blunders jealously. He hated me so much that
I'm sure he dreamed of me every night. For my part,
even now, after ten years, this very day, as soon as I
remember this man, rage surges up in me and chokes
my throat. It is true that before my departure . . .
however, I'll tell about that later on, otherwise it will
spoil the harmony of the story.

Towards the very end of the rehearsal, there suddenly
appeared on the stage a tall, thin, long-nosed man, with
a bowler hat and a moustache. He staggered slightly,
knocking against the wings, and his eyes were exactly
like a pair of pewter buttons. Everyone looked at him
with disgust, but no one passed any remark.

" Who is he ? " I asked Doukhovskoi in a whisper.

" Eh ! A drunkard," he answered casually. " Nelioubov-Olguine, our scene-painter. He's a clever fellow,
acts sometimes when he's sober, but he's a perfectly hopeless
drunkard. Still, there's no one to take his place ; he's
cheap and paints scenes very quickly."

142

VIII

The rehearsal ended. People were going away. The actors were joking, playing on words : Mercia-Commercia. Lara-Larsky was telling Boev meaningly to come " there." I caught up with Valerianov in one of the alleys and, scarcely able to keep pace with his long strides, I said :

" Victor Victorovitch . . . I want very much to ask you for some money . . . if only a little."

He stopped and seemed quite stupefied.

" What ? What money ? Why money ? For whom ?"

I began to explain my position to him, but, without hearing me to the end, he turned his back on me and went on. Then suddenly he stopped and called out :

" I say, you there . . . what's your name ? . . . Vassiliev. You'd better go to that man, your proprietor, and tell him to come and enquire for me here. I shall remain at the box-office for another half-hour. I'll have a word with him."

I didn't go to the hotel, I flew to it. The Ukrainian listened with gloomy distrust ; however, he put on his brown jacket and crawled slowly to the theatre. I waited for him. A quarter of an hour later he returned. His face was like a stormy cloud, and a bundle of theatre passes was sticking out of his right hand. He shoved them right under my nose and said in a muffled bass :

" There you are ! I thought he'd give me coins and he gives me bits of paper. What good are they to me ? "

I stood confused. However, the bits of paper had a certain utility. After long exhortations, the proprietor consented to share my belongings : he kept as a deposit my beautiful new English leather portmanteau and I took my underclothes, my passport and, what was more precious to me than anything else, my travelling note-books. By way of good-bye, the Ukrainian asked me :

" What—are you, too, going to play the fool over there ? "

" Yes, I, too," I said with dignity.

" Ho, ho, you be careful. As soon as I set eyes on you on the stage, I'll shout out : ' What about my twenty roubles ? ' "

For the next three days, I didn't venture to trouble Valerianov, and slept on the little green bench with my small parcel of underclothes under my head as a pillow. Two nights, thank God, were warm ; I even felt, as I lay on the bench, a dry heat mounting up from the pavement that had been well warmed during the day. But on the third night there was a fine, continuous rain and I took shelter on a doorstep and was unable to sleep till the morning. The town gardens were open at eight. I stole in behind the scenes, lay down on an old curtain, and slept soundly for two hours. Of course I came under Samoilenko's eyes and he, at great length and stingingly, informed me that a theatre was the temple of art and not at all a dormitory or a boudoir or a doss-house. Then I decided to overtake the manager again in the alley and ask him for some money, however little, as I had nowhere to sleep.

" I beg your pardon," he said waving his arms apart, " What has it got to do with me ? You're not a child, are you ? And in any case I'm not your nurse."

I kept silent. His half-closed eyes wandered over the bright, sunny sand of the footpath and then he said thoughtfully :

" Suppose . . . look here . . . suppose you spend the nights in the theatre. I suggested that to the night watch, but the fool was afraid."

I thanked him.

" But only on one condition. No smoking in the theatre. If you want to smoke, go out into the gardens."

After that I was guaranteed a sleeping place under a roof. Sometimes, in the daytime, I would go some three miles along the river and wash my clothes in a modest little corner and dry them on the branches of the willows. My linen was of great help to me. From time to time I would go to the bazaar and sell there a shirt or something. On the twenty or thirty kopecks acquired in this way I would feed myself for two whole days. Things were taking visibly a favourable turn for me. Once I even managed, in a happy moment, to get a rouble out of Valerianov and immediately I dispatched a telegram to Ilia :

" Dying from hunger. Wire money C. Theatre.— Leontovitch."

IX

The second rehearsal was the full-dress one. In this, by the way, I was stuck for two new rôles : that of an ancient Christian and that of Tigellius. I accepted them without a murmur.

Our tragedian, Timofeev-Soumskoi, took part in this. He was a broad-shouldered man, about five feet high, no longer young, with red curly hair, the whites of his eyes sticking out, and with a pock-marked face—a regular butcher, or rather an executioner. He had an enormous voice and he acted in an old-fashioned, hectoring manner.

He didn't know his lines at all (he was taking the part of Nero), and he had difficulty even in reading it from his copy-book with the aid of his powerful spectacles. When people said to him : " You ought to study your part just a little, Fedot Pamfylytch," he would reply in a low octavo :

" Oh, let it go. It'll do. I'll stand near the prompter. It isn't the first time. In any case the public understands nothing. The public's a fool."

He was constantly having trouble with my name. He simply couldn't pronounce " Tigellius," but called me either Tigelini or Tinegil.   Every time that he was corrected, he would bark out :

" Let it go.   Rot.   I'm not going to fill my brain with rubbish."

If he had a difficult phrase or several foreign words coming together, he would simply cross it out in pencil in his book and declare :

" I'm cutting that."

However, everyone used to cut. From the soup of our play there remained only the thickness.   Out of the long rôle of Tigellius there survived in the end only one reply.

Nero asks :

" Tigellius, in what state are the lions ? "

And I answer on my knees :

" Divine Cæsar, Rome has never seen such wild beasts. They are ravenous and ferocious."

That was all.

The opening night arrived.   The theatre was crammed. Outside, round the barriers, the crowd of the non-paying public was thick and black.   I was nervous.

My God, how horribly they all acted !   Just as if they had all acquiesced in Timofeev's verdict, " The public's a fool."   Every word, every gesture, recalled something old-fashioned, which has become stale through the repetition of generations.   These servants of art seemed to me to have at their disposal altogether about two dozen intonations, learned by heart, and about three dozen gestures, also learned by heart, as, for example, the one that Samoilenko fruitlessly tried to teach me.   And I was wondering how it was, through what moral fall had these people become so lost to all shame of their faces, of their bodies, of their movements !

Timofeev-Soumskoi was magnificent. Leaning over the right side of the throne, during which process his extended left leg protruded right into the middle of the stage, his fool's crown all awry, he was fixing the mobile whites of his eyes on the prompter's box and yelling in such a way that the little urchins behind the barriers shrieked with delight. Naturally he didn't remember my name. He simply bawled at me like a Russian merchant at the Russian baths :

" Teliantin ! Bring along my lions and tigers. Qui-ick ! "

I submissively swallowed my reply and went. Of course, the worst of the lot was Mark the Magnificent, Lara-Larsky, because he was more shameless, careless, trivial, and self-confident than the others. Instead of pathos he gave shrieks, instead of tenderness, sickliness. Through the authoritative speeches of a Roman patrician there peeped out the chief of a Russian fire-brigade. But then Adrossova was really beautiful. Everything about her was charming : her inspired face, delightful arms, her elastic, musical voice, even her long wavy hair which, in the last scene, she let loose over her shoulders. She acted just as simply, naturally, and beautifully as a bird sings.

With real artistic delight, sometimes even with tears, I followed her through the small holes in the cloth background of the stage. But I did not foresee that a few minutes later she would touch me, not artistically but in a quite different manner.

In this play I was so multi-figured that really the management might have added, in their advertisement list, to the names of Petrov, Sidorov, Grigoriev, Ivanov and Vassiliev, the names of Dmitriev and Alexandrov. In the first act, I appeared first of all as an old man with a white robe and with a hood on my head ; then I ran behind the scenes, threw off my things and came on again as a centurion with armour and a helmet, my feet naked ; then I disappeared again and crawled out as the ancient Christian. In the second act, I was a centurion and a slave. In the third act, two new slaves. In the fourth, a centurion and someone else's two new slaves. I was also a steward and a new slave. Then I was Tigellius and, finally, a voiceless knight who with an imperative gesture indicates to Marcia and Mark the way to the arena where they are going to be eaten by lions.

Even the simpleton, Akimenko, tapped me on the shoulder and said amiably :

" Devil take it, you are a quick-change artist and no mistake ! "

But I earned this praise at too great cost. I could scarcely stand on my feet.

The performance was over. The caretaker was putting out the lights. I was walking about the stage waiting for the last actors to remove their make-up so that I might be able to lie down on my old threadbare sofa. I was also thinking of that morsel of fried liver which was hanging in my little corner between the property room and the general dressing-room. (For since the rats robbed me of a piece of bacon I used to hang all eatables on a string.) Suddenly I heard a voice behind me :

" Good-night, Vassiliev."

I turned round. Androssova was standing with her hand stretched out ; her delightful face looked tired.

I must say that in the whole troupe she alone, not counting the insignificant ones, Doukhovskoi and Nelieubov-Olguine, used to shake hands with me (the others despised me). And even to this day I can recall the open, kindly, genuine way in which she shook hands like a woman and a comrade at the same time.

I took her hand. She looked at me attentively and said :

" Listen. Aren't you ill ? You look bad." And she added in a lower tone : " Perhaps you're in need of money ?
. . . eh ? . . . may I lend it ? . . ."

" Oh no, no, thank you," I interrupted her with feeling. And suddenly, yielding to the rush of emotion with which her acting had thrilled me, I exclaimed with fire :

148

" How beautiful you were to-night ! "

Probably the compliment, by its sincerity, was a little unusual. She blushed with pleasure, lowered her eyes, and said laughingly :

" I'm so glad that I gave you pleasure."

I kissed her hand respectfully. But at that instant a woman's voice shouted :

" Androssova ! Where are you ? Come along, we're waiting for you for supper."

" Good-night, Vassiliev," she said simply and kindly. Then she shook her head, and just as she was leaving, murmured scarcely audibly : " Ah, you poor one, you poor one . . ."

No, I didn't feel at all poor at that moment. But it seemed to me that if, in saying good-bye, she had brushed my forehead with her lips, I should have died from happiness.

X

I wasn't long in taking the measure of the whole troupe. I confess that even before my involuntary actor's career I never had a high opinion of the provincial stage. But, thanks to Ostrovsky, my idea of acting folk was that, though rough in externals, they were kindly and large in their hearts, happy-go-lucky people, but devoted to art in their way and full of *esprit de corps*. But now I perceived that the stage was held quite simply by a band of shameless men and women.

They were all heartless, treacherous, and envious of each other, without the slightest respect for beauty and creative power—in a word, base, insensitive souls. And, on the top of it all, they were people of dumbfounding ignorance and deep indifference, hysterical hypocrites, cold liars, with crocodile tears and theatrical sobs, stubbornly stunted slaves—always ready to crawl before their superiors and patrons. It was not without point that Tchekhov said once : " There is only one person more hysterical than the actor—it is the constable. See how they both stand in front of a buffet on a bank holiday, make speeches and weep."

But theatrical traditions were kept up immovably among us. Someone or other, before going on the stage, had the habit of making the sign of the cross. The story of this spread. And each of our principals, before his entrance, would not fail to go through the same perform-ance, looking round sideways while he was doing it to see if anyone was watching him or not. And if they are watching he imagine them to be saying to themselves : " How superstitious he is ! What an original creature ! "

One of these prostitutes of art, with a goat's voice and fat thighs, once beat the tailor and, on another occasion, the barber. This also became an established tradition. I have often watched Lara-Larsky throwing himself about the stage with bloodshot eyes, foaming at the mouth, and shouting hoarsely :

" Give me this tailor. I will kill him, this tailor."

And then, after having struck the tailor and, deep down in his soul, expecting and fearing a return blow, he would stretch his hands out backwards and roar :

" Hold me, hold me, or I shall become in reality a murderer ! "

But then how profoundly they would discuss " the holy art " and the theatre ! I remember one clear, green July day. Our rehearsal had not commenced. It was rather dark and cool on the stage. Of the principals, Lara-Larsky and his theatrical wife, Medvedieva, had arrived before the others. A few girls and schoolboys were sitting in the pit. Lara-Larsky walked backwards and forwards across the stage. He seemed preoccupied. Apparently he was thinking out some profound new type. Suddenly his wife addressed him :

" Sasha, please whistle that motif that we heard in
' Paillasse ' yesterday."

He stopped short, looked her up and down from head
to foot, and said in the actor's velvety baritone, glancing
sideways at the pit :

" Whistle ?   On   the   stage ?   Ha-ha-ha ! "   (He
laughed the actor's bitter laugh.) " And it's you who
tell me to do this ? But you don't know that the stage
is a temple, an altar on which we lay all our best thoughts
and hopes ? And then suddenly to whistle ! Ha-ha-ha."

All the same, to this very altar, in the ladies' dressing-
rooms, the local cavalry officers and the rich, idle, landed
proprietors used to come exactly as they would come to
rooms in a *maison de tolérance.* Of course we weren't
touchy about this sort of thing. How often have I seen
something like this : Inside the vineyard arbour a light
would be burning, a woman's laugh could be heard, the
click of spurs, the tinkling of champagne glasses, while
the theatrical husband, like a sentry on patrol, would be
walking backwards and forwards on the path near the
entrance, waiting in the darkness, and wondering if he
would or would not be invited. And the waiter, bringing
in the fish *au gratin* on a highly-lifted tray, would jog
against him with his elbow and say dryly :

" Step aside, sir."

And when he is invited, he will fuss and drink vodka
and beer and vinegar while he tells dirty anecdotes about
Jewish life.

But all the same, they used to talk hotly and proudly
about art. Timofeev-Soumskoi, more than once, lectured
us on the lost " classic gesture of exit."

" The classic gesture is lost," he would say gloomily.
" This is how an actor would leave the stage in the past.
Like this." Timofeev would stretch himself out at full
length and raise his right hand with his fist clenched
except for the index finger, which would stick out like a
hook. " Do you see ? " And with slow, enormous

151

strides he would move to the door. " That is what was called ' the classical gesture of exit.' And now? One just puts one's hands in one's trouser-pockets and off one goes home. That's about it now, my friends."

Sometimes they took a fancy for innovations on their own account. Lara-Larsky would interpret his rôle of Gogol's Khlestakov like this :

" No, allow me. I interpret this scene with the town bailiff in this way. The town bailiff says that the room is rather dark. And I answer, ' Yes, if you want to read something, *for example, Maxim Gorky*, it's impossible. It is da-ark, da-arkish.' And that always gets a round."

It was good to listen sometimes to the old ones, when they were a little drunk ; for instance, Timofeev-Soumskoi talking with Gontcharov.

" Yes, old pal, we don't get the same kind of actor nowadays. No, no, it isn't the same."

" It's a fact, my boy, it isn't the same. Do you remember Tcharsky and Lioubovsky ? . . . Eh ? "

" The old traditions are lost."

" It's the fault of Petersburg. It isn't the same. They don't respect any longer the sacredness of art. All the same, you and I, we were priests in the temple, but these others . . . Eh ? . . . let's drink, old man."

" And do you remember Ivan Kozlovsky ? "

" Ah, let it alone, don't revive an old sore. Let's drink. What can they do, the people of to-day ? "

" Yes, what can they do ? "

" Wha-at can they do ? "

And there, in the midst of this mixture of triviality, stupidity, swindling, mannerisms, bragging, ignorance, and depravity, Androssova alone truthfully served art. Androssova—clean, charming, beautiful, and talented. Now that I am older, I understand that she was no more conscious of this filth than the white, beautiful corolla of a flower is conscious that its roots are being fed by the slime of a marsh.

XI

The plays were produced at express speed. Short dramas and comedies would be given one rehearsal. " The Death of Ivan the Terrible " and " The New World " would be given two. " Ismael," the composition of M. Boukharine, required three rehearsals, thanks only to the fact that about forty supers from the local commands, the garrison, the army transport, and the fire brigade took part in it.

I remember particularly well the performance of " The Death of Ivan the Terrible," because of a stupid and amusing incident. Timofeev-Soumskoi was taking the part of Ivan. In his long brocade robe and his pointed dogskin hat he looked like a moving obelisk. In order to give the terrible tzar a little more ferocity, he kept protruding his lower jaw and dropping his thick underlip, rolling his eyes about, and bellowing as he had never bellowed before. Of course he knew nothing about his part and read it in such verse that even the actors, who were long inured to the fact that the public is a fool and understands nothing, were startled. But he particularly distinguished himself in the scene where Ivan, in an attack of repentance, kneels and confesses before the boyards : " My mind has clouded," etc.

And when he came to the words, " like a reeking cur . . ." it goes without saying that his eyes were all the time on the prompter's box. In the hearing of the whole house he said, " like—— " and then stopped.

" Like a reeking cur," whispered the prompter.

" Like," roared Timofeev.

" Like a cur . . ."

" Like . . ."

" Like a reeking cur . . ."

In the end he succeeded in getting through the text, but he showed not the slightest confusion or shame. But as for me—I was standing near the throne at the time—

I was seized with an irresistible attack of laughter. It always happens like this ; when you know that you *must not* laugh, it will be exactly then that you will be mastered by this convulsive, wretched laughing. I realised quickly that the best thing to do was to hide at the back of the throne and there laugh it out to my heart's content. I turned round and walked in a solemn, boyard-like manner, hardly able to keep my face straight. I got round the throne and there . . . I saw two of the actresses pressing against the back of it, shaken and choking with suppressed laughter. This was more than I could endure. I ran behind the scenes, fell on the stage sofa—*my* sofa—and began to roll on it. . . . Samoilenko, who always jealously followed me, docked me five roubles for that.

On the whole, this performance was rich in incidents. I forgot to say that we had an actor named Romanov, a tall, very handsome, representative young fellow, for the loud and majestic secondary parts. But, unfortunately, he was so extremely short-sighted that he had to wear glasses of a quite special kind. Without his pince-nez he would be everlastingly knocking against something on the stage, upsetting the columns, the vases, and the armchairs, getting entangled in the carpets and falling down. He was already famous for the fact that, in another town and in another strolling company, when acting the knight in " La Princesse Lointaine," he fell down and rolled in his tin armour, rattling like an enormous samovar, into the footlights. In " The Death of Ivan the Terrible " Romanov surpassed himself. He broke into the house of Shuisky, where the plotters had gathered, with such impetuosity that he upset a long bench on which the boyards were all sitting.

These boyards were delightful. They were all recruited from the young Karaim Jews who were employed at the local tobacco factory. I ushered them on to the stage. I am not tall, but the tallest of them was only up to my shoulder. One half of these illustrious boyards was dressed in Caucasian costumes with kaftans, and the other half in long jackets which had been hired from a local choir. On their youthful faces were fastened black beards, their black eyes shone, their mouths were enthusiastically open, their movements awkward and shy. The audience neighed heartily at our solemn entrance.

Owing to the fact that we produced a fresh play every day, our theatre was rather well patronised. The officers and the landed proprietors came for the actresses. Apart from them, a box ticket was sent every day to Kharitonenko. He himself came seldom, not more than twice during the whole season, but on each occasion he sent a hundred roubles. On the whole, the theatre wasn't doing so badly. And if the young actors received no salary, it was thanks to the delicate calculations of Valerianov. The manager was like the coachman who used to dangle a wisp of hay in front of his hungry jade's muzzle to make him run faster.

XII

On one occasion — I don't remember why — there was no performance. The weather was bad. At ten o'clock that night I was already on my sofa, listening in the dark to the drumming of the rain on the wooden roof.

Suddenly I heard a rustling somewhere behind the scenes, then steps, then the crash of falling chairs. I lit a candle-end and went out to investigate the sounds, only to see the drunken Nelioubov-Olguine who was helplessly groping between the scenery and the wall of the theatre. On catching sight of me, he was not alarmed, but expressed a tranquil surprise.

" Wh—at the d—d—evil are you doing here ? "

I explained to him in a few words. He thrust his hand

into his pockets, nodded with his long nose, and swayed from his heels to the tips of his toes for some time. Then he suddenly lost his balance, but recovered it, moved a few steps forward and said :

" And why not come with me ? "

" We scarcely know each other . . ."

" Rubbish ! Come along."

He took my arm and we went off together. From that hour to the very end of my career as an actor I shared with him his dark, tiny room which he rented from the ex-police inspector of C——. This notorious drunkard, the object of the whole troupe's hypocritical scorn, showed himself to be a kind, quiet man, a true comrade, possessed of much inner delicacy of feeling. But he had in his heart a kind of sickly, incurable wound—the work of a woman. I could never get at the reality of his romance. When drunk, he would often drag out from his travelling basket the portrait of a woman, not very beautiful, but not ugly either, slightly squint-eyed, with a turned-up, provoking little nose. She looked to me a provincial. He would either kiss this photograph or fling it on the floor, press it to his heart or spit on it, place it against the icons in the corner or pour candle-grease over it. I could never make out which of them had thrown the other over, or who the children were of whom he spoke, his, hers, or someone else's.

Neither he nor I had any money. Long ago he had obtained from Valerianov a rather large sum to send *her*, and now he was in a condition of bond-service which simple honour prevented him from evading. Occasionally he would earn a few kopecks from the local signboard artist. But this source of increment was a great secret from the rest of the troupe ; how would Lara-Larsky have tolerated such an insult to art ?

Our landlord, the retired police inspector, a fat, red-cheeked man, with a moustache and a double chin, was a very benevolent person. Every morning and evening, after they had finished tea in his house, a newly-filled samovar, a tea-pot, with the tea previously used, and as much black bread as we wished, was sent to us. We used to be quite satisfied.

The retired police inspector would take a nap after dinner and then come out in his dressing-gown with his pipe and sit on the steps. Before going to the theatre, we would sit near him. The conversation was invariably the same : his misfortunes in the service, the injustice of his superiors, and the base intrigues of his enemies. He always asked us for advice as to how he was to write a letter to the principal newspapers, so that his innocence might triumph and the governor, and the vice-governor, with the present district inspector, and that scoundrel the inspector of the second section, who was the main cause of all his misfortunes, might be hounded from their posts. We would make different suggestions, but he would only sigh, frown, shake his head, and repeat :

" Eh, not that . . . not that, not that. There, if I could find a man with a pen ; it's a pen that I must find. I wouldn't spare any money."

And he, the rascal, had money. Once on entering his room I found him sorting his securities. He was slightly confused, rose from his chair, and hid the papers behind him with the help of his open dressing-gown. I am quite convinced that during his period of service there were many things to his credit : acceptance of bribes, extortions, the misuse of power, and other deeds of the sort.

At night, after the performance, Nelioubov and I would often wander about the gardens. In the quiet, lit-up gardens there were everywhere little white tables on which the candles burned unwaveringly in their glass shades. Men and women, somehow or other in a festive atmosphere, smiled and leaned towards each other significantly. and coquettishly. The sand rustled under the light steps of women.

"What about landing a little fish," Nelioubov would sometimes say in his hoarse bass voice, looking sideways at me slyly.

That sort of thing annoyed me at first. I always hated this eager, noble readiness of garden actors to paste themselves on to the dinners and lunches of strangers, these kind, moist, hungry dog's eyes, these baritones at table with their unnaturally detached manners, their universal knowledge of gastronomy, their forced attentiveness, their habitual authoritative familiarity with the waiters. But afterwards, when I got to know Nelioubov better, I understood that he was only joking. This odd fellow was proud and extremely touchy in his way.

But a funny and slightly discreditable incident happened which caught my friend and me in a culinary net. It happened like this :

We were the last to leave the dressing-room after the performance when suddenly, from somewhere behind the scenes, there jumped out on to the stage a certain Altshiller, a local Rothschild, a Jew, still young but already fat, with very airy manners—a rosy-cheeked man, of the sensual type, covered with rings and chains and trinkets. He threw himself at us.

"Good gracious ! I've been running about for the last half hour. I'm dead beat. Tell me, for Heaven's sake, if you've seen Volkova and Bogoutcharskaia ? "

As a matter of fact, immediately after the performance, we had seen these actresses drive off with some dragoon officers, and we amiably imparted the news to Altshiller. He caught his head between his hands and threw himself about the stage :

"But this is shameful ! I've ordered the supper. No, this is really the limit ! To give one's word, to promise and . . . What do you call that gentlemen, I ask you ? "

We were silent .

He made a few more contortions on the stage, then

stopped, hesitated, scratched his head nervously, smacked his lips thoughtfully, and said suddenly, in a decided manner :

" Gentlemen, may I ask you to have supper with me ? "

We refused.

But he would take no refusal. He stuck to us like glue. He threw himself first at Nelioubov and then at me, shook our hands, looked appealingly into our eyes, and assured us with warmth that he was devoted to art. Nelioubóv was the first to give way.

" Oh, the devil ! Let's go, what about it ! "

Maecenas led us to the main platform and began bustling about. He chose the most conspicuous place, got us seated, and kept jumping up, running after the waiters, waving his arms and, after drinking a glass of kümmel, pretended to be a desperate debauchee. His bowler hat was all on one side, to give him an air of wickedness.

" Try a little cucumber ! How does one put it in Russian ? Isn't it that without a little cucumber no festivity is possible ? Try a little vodka. Do eat. Go ahead, I beg of you. And perhaps you'd like some Bœuf à la Stroganof ? It's excellent at this place. Here, waiter ! "

From a large piece of hot roast beef I became drunk as though from wine. My eyes were closing. The verandah with its lights, the blue tobacco smoke, and the fantastic gallop of talk, kept flowing past me, and I could hear as in a dream :

" Please eat a little more, gentlemen. . . . Don't be on ceremony. Really, I don't know what to do with myself, I am so devoted to art."

XIII

But the dénouement was near at hand. My fare of black bread and tea was undermining my health. I became irritable, and often, in order to keep myself in hand, I would run away from the rehearsal to some remote corner in the gardens. Besides, I had long ago exhausted my stock of underclothes.

Samoilenko continued to torment me. You know how it is sometimes at a boarding school, when a master, for no reason at all, suddenly gets his knife into some poor little wretch of a pupil. He will hate him for the pallor of his face, because his ears stick out, because he shrugs his shoulders unpleasantly, and this hate will last for years. This is exactly how Samoilenko behaved towards me. He had already managed to find me fifteen roubles altogether, and during rehearsals he would speak to me as though he were the head of a prison addressing a convict. Sometimes, as I listened to his insolent remarks, I would lower my eyelids and would then see fiery circles in front of my eyes. As for Valerianov, he had stopped speaking to me at all, and when we met he would bolt like an ostrich. I had been with him a month and a half already and had received exactly one rouble.

One morning I woke up with a headache, with a metallic taste in my mouth, and in my soul a black, heavy, unreasoned anger. In this frame of mind I went to the rehearsal.

I don't remember what we were acting, but I remember well that there was a thick rolled up copy-book in my hand. I knew my part, as usual, perfectly. It contained the words : " I have deserved this."

And when the play got to this passage I said :

" I have deserved this."

But Samoilenko ran up to me and bawled out :

" Who speaks Russian like this ? Whoever speaks like this ? ' I have deserved this ! ' One says : ' I have deserved for this.' Mediocrity ! "

Growing white I stretched the copy-book out to him with these words :

" Kindly look at the text."

But he shouted out in a guttural voice :

" To hell with your text ! I myself am your text. If you don't want to keep your job here, you may go to the devil."

I quickly raised my eyes to his. Suddenly he understood everything, became as pale as I was, and moved back quickly two steps. But it was already too late. With the heavy rolled copy-book I struck him heavily and loudly on the left cheek and on the right, then again on the left, and then on the right again, and again, and again. He made no resistance, did not even duck, did not even try to run away, but, at each blow, only switched his head to left and right, like a clown who plays at being surprised. Finally I flung the copy-book in his face and left the stage for the gardens. Nobody stopped me.

And then the miracle happened. The first person that I saw in the gardens was a little messenger-boy from the local branch of the Volga-Kama bank. He was asking for Leontovitch and handed me a notification of five hundred roubles, that were waiting for me at the bank.

An hour later Nelioubov and I were already in the gardens ordering a gigantic lunch, and two hours later the whole troupe was drinking my health in champagne and congratulating me. On my honour, it wasn't I but Nelioubov who had spread the news that I had come in for sixty thousand roubles. I didn't contradict it. A little later Valerianov swore to me that business was going to the dogs and I made him a present of a hundred roubles.

At five o'clock that evening I was at the station. In my pocket, apart from my ticket to Moscow, I had only seventy roubles, but I felt like an emperor. When, after the second bell, I was getting into my compartment, Samoilenko, who, up to now, had kept his distance, came up to me.

" Forgive ; I was hot-headed," he said theatrically.

161

I pressed his outstretched hand and answered amiably :
" Forgive, I too was hot headed."

They gave me a farewell cheer. I exchanged the last
kindly glance with Nelioubov. The train started and
everything receded never to return. And when the last
of the little blue huts of the outskirts began to disappear
and the mournful, yellow, burnt-out steppe stretched
itself endlessly—a strange sadness tugged at my heart,
as if there, in that scene of my misfortunes, sufferings,
hunger, and humiliations, had remained for ever a particle
of my soul.

« ALLEZ ! »

THIS jerky, exclamatory order was Melle Nora's earliest memory from the dark monotony of her erring childhood. This word " Allez " was the very first that her weak, childish little tongue ever framed, and always, even in her dreams, this cry reproduced itself in Nora's memory, evoking in its five letters the chill of the unheated circus ring, the smell of stables, the heavy gallop of the horse, the dry crackling of the long whip and the burning pain of its lash, suddenly deadening the momentary hesitation of fear. . . .

" Allez ! . . ."

In the empty circus it is cold and dark. Here and there, the wintry sunlight, scarcely piercing the glass cupolas, lies in pale spots over the raspberry-coloured velvet and the gilt of the boxes, over the shields with the horses' heads, over the flags that decorate the pillars ; it plays on the dim glasses of the electric globes, gliding over the steel of the tourniquets and trapezes, up there at a tremendous height amid the entanglement of the machines and the ropes, from which one can scarcely distinguish the first rows of the stalls, and the seats behind and the gallery are completely drowned in darkness.

The day's routine is in full swing. Five or six of the performers, in great-coats and fur caps, are smoking rank cigars at the end of the first row of armchairs near the entrance from the stables. In the middle of the ring stands a square-built, short-legged man, with a tall hat

163

perched on the back of his head, and a black moustache, carefully twisted to a fine point at the ends. He is tying a long string round the waist of a tiny little five-year-old girl, who is standing in front of him shivering from fright and cold. The big white horse, which a stable-man leads round the ring, snorts loudly, shaking its arched neck as the white steam gushes from its nostrils. Every time that it passes the man in the tall hat, the horse looks askance at the whip that sticks out under his arm, snorts with agitation, and, plodding round, drags the tugging stable-boy behind it. Little Nora can hear behind her back its nervous plunges, and she shivers still more.

Two powerful hands seize her round the waist and lightly toss her on to the large leather mattress on the horse's back. Almost at the same instant, the chairs, the white pillars, the tent cloth hangings at the entrance —all this is merged in the bizarre circle which spins round to meet the horse. In vain her numb hands clutch convulsively at the rough wave of mane as her eyes close tightly, blinded by the devilish flash of the seething circle. The man in the tall hat walks in the centre of the ring, holding in front of the horse's head the end of his long whip, which he cracks deafeningly. . . .

" Allez ! . . ."

And again she is in her short gauze skirt, with her bare, thin, half-childish arms, standing in the electric light, beneath the very cupola of the circus on a well-balanced trapeze. From this, at the little girl's feet, there is hanging, head downwards, his knees clutching the upright post, another square-built man, in pink tights, with gold spangles and fringe, curled, pomaded, and cruel. Now he has raised his lowered hands, spread them out, and, fixing Nora's eyes with that penetrating, meaning look—the hypnotising glance of the acrobat—he claps his hands. Nora makes a quick forward movement with the intention of hurling herself straight down into those strong, pitiless hands. (*What* a thrill it will give the hundreds of spec-

tators !)   But all of a sudden, her heart grows cold, seems
to stop from terror, and she only squeezes more tightly
the thin ropes of the trapeze.   Up go once more the cruel
bent hands, and the acrobat's glance becomes still more
intense. . . . Beneath her feet the space seems that of
an abyss.

" Allez ! . . ."

Again she balances, scarcely able to breathe, on the
very apex of the " Living Pyramid."   She glides, wriggling
with her body, supple as a serpent's, between the cross-
beams of the long white ladder which a man is holding
on his head.   She turns a somersault in the air, thrown
up by the feet of the jongleur, strong and terrible, like
steel springs.   Again at a great height, she walks on thin,
trembling wire which cuts her feet unbearably. . . .
And everywhere are the same dim, beautiful faces, the
pomaded heads, the puffed curls, the moustaches upturned, the reek of cigars and perspiration, and always
that inevitable fatal cry, the same for human beings, for
horses, and for performing dogs :

" Allez ! . . ."

She was just sixteen, and a very pretty girl when, during
a performance, she fell from the airy tourniquet past
the net on to the sand of the ring.   She was picked up
unconscious and taken behind the scenes, where, in accordance with circus traditions, they began to shake her
by the shoulders with all their might to bring her back
to herself.   She awoke to consciousness, groaning with
pain from her crushed hand.

" The audience is getting restless and beginning to
go," they were saying around her.   " Come, show yourself to the public."

Obediently her lips framed the usual smile, the smile
of the " graceful horsewoman," but after walking two
steps the pain became unbearable and she cried out and
staggered.   Then dozens of hands laid hold of her and
pushed her forcibly in front of the public.

" Allez ! "

During this season there was " working " in the circus a certain star clown named Menotti. He was not the ordinary pauper clown who rolls in the sand to the rhythm of slaps in the face and who manages, on a quite empty stomach, to amuse the public for a whole evening with inexhaustible jokes. Menotti was a clown celebrity, the first solo-clown and imitator on the planet, a world-known trainer who had received innumerable honours and prizes. He wore on his breast a heavy chain of gold medals, received two hundred roubles for a single turn, and boasted of the fact that for the last five years he had worn nothing but moire costumes. After the performance, he invariably felt " done up " and, with a high-falutin bitterness, would say of himself : " Yes, we are buffoons, we must amuse the *well-fed* public." In the arena he would sing, pretentiously and out of tune, old couplets, or recite verses of his own composition, or make gags on the Duma or the drainage, which usually produced on the public, drawn to the circus by reckless advertising, the impression of insistent, dull, and unnecessary contortions. In private life, he had a languidly patronising manner, and he loved with a mysterious and negligent air, to insinuate his conquests of extraordinarily beautiful, extraordinarily rich, but utterly tiresome countesses.

At her first appearance at the morning rehearsal, after her sprain had been cured, Menotti came up to her, held her hand in his, made moist tired eyes at her, and asked in a weakened voice about her health. She became confused, blushed, and took her hand away. That moment decided her fate.

A week later, as he escorted Nora back from the evening performance, Menotti asked her to have supper with him at the magnificent hotel where the world-famous first solo-clown always stopped.

The *cabinets particuliers* are on the first floor, and as

she made her way up, Nora stopped for a minute, partly from fatigue, partly from the emotion of the last virginal hesitation. But Menotti squeezed her elbow tightly. In his voice there rang fierce animal passion and with it the cruel order of the old acrobat as he whispered :

" Allez ! "

And she went. . . . She saw in him an extraordinary, a superior being, almost a god. . . . She would have gone into fire if it had occurred to him to order it.

For a year she followed him from town to town. She took care of Menotti's brilliants and jewels during his appearances, put on and took off for him his tricot, attended to his wardrobe, helped him to train rats and pigs, rubbed his face with cold cream and—what was most important of all—believed with idolising intensity in his world-fame. When they were alone he had nothing to say to her, and he accepted her passionate caresses with the exaggerated boredom of a man who, though thoroughly satiated, mercifully permits women to adore him.

After a year he had had enough of her. His attention was diverted to one of the Sisters Wilson who were executing " Airy Flights." He did not stand on ceremony with Nora now, and often in the dressing-room, right in front of the performers and stable-men, he would box her ears for a missing button. She bore all this with the humility of an old, clever and devoted dog who accepts the blows of his master.

Finally, one night after a performance in which the first trainer in the world had been hissed for whipping a dog really too savagely, Menotti told Nora straight out to go immediately to the devil. She left him, but stopped at the very door of the room and glanced back with a begging look in her eyes. Then Menotti rushed to the door, flung it open furiously and shouted :

" Allez ! "

But only two days later, like a dog who has been beaten

and turned out, she was drawn back again to the master. A blackness came to her eyes when a waiter of the hotel said to her with an insolent grin :

" You cannot go up ; he is in a *cabinet particulier* with a lady."

But Nora went up and stopped unerringly before the door of the very room where she had been with Menotti a year ago. Yes, he was there. She recognised the languid voice of the overworked celebrity, interrupted from time to time by the happy laugh of the red-haired Englishwoman. Nora opened the door abruptly.

The purple and gold tapestries, the dazzling light of the two candelabras, the glistening of crystals, the pyramid of fruit and the bottles in silver buckets, Menotti lying on the sofa in his shirt-sleeves, and Wilson with her corsage loosened, the reek of scent, wine, cigars, powder—all this, at first, stupefied her ; then she rushed at Wilson and struck her again and again in the face with her clenched fist. Wilson shrieked and the fight began. . . .

When Menotti had succeeded with difficulty in separating them, Nora threw herself on her knees, covered his boots with kisses and begged him to come back to her. Menotti could scarcely push her away from him as he said, squeezing her neck tightly with his strong fingers :

" If you don't go at once, I'll have you thrown out of the place by the waiter."

Almost stifled, she rose to her feet and whispered :

" Aɪ—ah . . . in that case . . . in that case. . . ."

Her eyes fell on the open window. Quickly and lightly, like the experienced gymnast she was, she bounded on to the sill and bent forward, her hands grasping on each side the framework of the window.

Far down beneath her, the carriages rattled, seeming from that height mere small, strange animals. The pavements glistened after the rain, and the reflections of the street lamps danced about in the pools of water.

Nora's fingers grew cold and her heart stopped beating

168

for a second of terror . . . Then, closing her eyes and
breathing heavily, she raised her hands above her head
and, fighting down, as usual, her old weakness, she cried
out, as if in the circus :

" Allez ! "   . . .

BLACK FOG

A Petersburg Case

I REMEMBER perfectly his first arrival in Petersburg from his hot, lazy, sensual south. There emanated from him the very atmosphere of black earth-force, the odour of dry, sun-baked feather-grass, the simple poetry of quiet sunsets, gradually fading away behind the cherry trees of little orchards. He had the inexhaustible health of the steppe and he was so vivid in his fresh naïveté.

He came straight from the station into the furnished rooms where I was living. It was winter, eight o'clock in the morning, when, in the Petersburg streets, the lamps are still lit and the tired horses are dragging the sleeping night-cabmen to their homes. He would take no refusal. He wouldn't listen to any of the maid's arguments, and said in his sonorous voice that rang through the corridor :

" What are you talking about ? As if I didn't know him ! Why, he's more to me than my own brother. What next ? Show me in to him."

We had been at school together in the South, where, incidentally, he had not finished his course. I was fond of him, not more than of a real brother—he exaggerated this in his hurry—but, all the same, I was sincerely attached to him. However, though I immediately recognised his voice with its soft and yet guttural southern " g " and its provincial breadth of diapason, I cannot say that in the first minute I was particularly pleased. You know what

it is when a man has been gallivanting all over the place
through the night, goes to bed with his head not quite clear
and, on the top of it all, is faced with serious, timed work
for the next day . . . In a word, I cursed under my blankets
and firmly decided, if he came in, to pretend that I was
asleep or dead, like a beetle that had been placed on the
palm of a hand.

Easier said than done. He burst in like a hurricane,
threw himself at me, dragged me out of bed as if I were a
child, shook me and pulled me about. It was impossible
to be angry with him. The frost had given him a delightful
emanation of apples and something else—healthy and
vigorous ; his moustache and beard were thawing, his
face was burning brightly, his eyes were shining.

" Well, well, how long are you going to wallow in those
blankets ? Get up," he roared ; " get up or I'll smash you
into little bits."

" Listen, you poor, benighted provincial "—I was trying
to make him feel ashamed—" here in Petersburg no one
gets up before eleven. Lie down on the sofa or ask for
some tea, or send someone to fetch newspapers and read,
but let me doze, if only for half an hour."

No, nothing had any effect on him. He was bursting
with stories of the past and plans for the future, so filled
with new impressions that he seemed ready to blow up
under their pressure if I hadn't acted as a sort of safety-
valve. First came the greetings : it appears that, up to
the present, they all remembered me, are quite fond of me
and read with pleasure my articles on economics. I was
flattered and pretended not to have forgotten a single one
of all those extraordinary names, all those Gouzikovs, Lia-
doushenkos, Tchernysh, and so many other old acquaintances. Secondly, Petersburg had utterly stupefied him.

" Deuce take it, what an enormous town ! What do
you think ? At the station there were nothing but swagger
cabs, not a single ordinary one."

" Swagger cabs ? " I repeated doubtfully.

" On my honour, yes. I didn't grasp it at first and I was in one of them before I saw that it was on tyres. Well, I've let myself in, I thought. I wanted to crawl out of it, but I was ashamed to do that, and a policeman was hurrying them all. I was lucky to get out of it so cheaply—a rouble and a half altogether.! "

" At the very most you ought to have paid fifty kopecks," I put in.

" There you're talking nonsense. What ! give a cab on tyres fifty kopecks for such a distance ! Oh, and what streets you have here ! And the people—oh, Lord ! it's worse than the ferry-boats at home. They're all over the place. And on one of the bridges there is a statue of four horses. Have you seen it ? It's a sight. . . You live well here, I can see that."

The whole time he kept saying " at home " and " you people here "—drawing a line between the two as all provincials do. He was greatly struck by the fires lit at cross-streets on account of the severe frost.

" What's that for ? " he asked with naïve curiosity.

I answered quite seriously :

" It's an idea of the town council to heat the streets so as to spend less on fuel in Government offices."

His eyes grew round, and so did his mouth, from astonishment, and all he could pronounce was :

" Oh ! "

The next minute he saw it and burst out laughing— laughed in long, deafening, youthful peals. I had to remind him that all the other lodgers were still asleep, that the partitions were made of *papier maché* and that I didn't want to get into trouble with my landlady.

Irisha came in with the samovar. She looked sideways at Boris with an expression of distrust and agitation, as though a horse had been received into the room. She was a regular Petersburg maid, sensitive and not without understanding.

At five o'clock we dined at the Nevsky in an enormous

and bad restaurant. The room, with its colours, the Rumanians, the plush furniture, the electric lights, the mirrors, the monumental head waiter, and particularly the spectacle of the heavy, impudent, frock-coated waiters, with their enormous moustaches—all this overwhelmed my country friend. During the whole meal, he sat bewildered, awkward, winding his feet round the front legs of his chair, and it was only when we were having coffee that he said with a sigh, shaking his head slowly :

" Ye-e-es, a restaurant ! They wouldn't have believed it at home. It's a regular temple of Baal with his priests. You'd better take me to a place where it's simpler. Here I see only the aristocracy. Probably they're all princes and counts."

But in the evening in my rooms, he brightened up again. I asked him for the first time seriously what he intended to do with himself. Up to this, we had only touched on this question in a hurried, rather diffuse way.

He puffed himself out like a young bantam and answered proudly :

" I have come to conquer Petersburg."

These very words are often uttered by the young heroes of French novelists, who, just arrived in Paris, are looking out at it from the heights of some garret. I smiled sceptically. He noticed it and began with special warmth, the comic side of which was heightened by his southern accent, to convince me of the fact that he represented the gifted, large, provincial South which was going to be victorious over the anæmic, untemperamental, dry, capital-like North. It was the inevitable law of struggle between two temperaments, and its result is always easily guessed. Oh, one can cite any number of names : ministers, writers, painters, barristers. Beware, withered, cold, pale, dull Petersburg. The South is coming !

I wished to believe him, or rather I didn't wish to disillusion him. We dreamt a little together. He produced

174

from his basket-trunk a bottle of good old, home-made plum liqueur which we began to drink in friendly fashion.

" Eh, what ? Eh, what ? Do they make in Petersburg here such old plum liqueur ? " he kept asking proudly ; and then scornfully : " There you are ! And you still discuss . . ."

Little by little, he settled down. I established him in furnished rooms next my own, for the time being on credit, in anticipation of the trophies to be won in victories over the withered North. It is extraordinary how at once he won the general good-will of the establishment, pushing into the background the former favourite—a poet with red curly hair who looked like a deacon in a picture. The landlady (everyone knows the Petersburg landlady of furnished rooms : a lady of full figure, forty-five years old, with corkscrew curls on her forehead, always in black and very tightly laced)—the landlady used often to invite him to her apartments in the morning, to have coffee, a high honour to which many, even of the old lodgers, never dared to aspire. In return for this amiability, he would give her the contents of the morning papers, as well as business advice in her innumerable pettifogging transactions (" Everyone wants to get the better of a poor widow ").

Deuce take it ! like a true Southern Russian, for all his apparent simplicity, he was a very adroit and practical fellow, with a quick comprehension and a certain benevolent shrewdness. Even Irisha got used to him and regarded him, I believe, with a sort of—well, I don't want to gossip. All I will say is that in those days he was very good-looking : tall, strong, with dark, melancholy eyes and young laughing red lips under his Ukrainian moustache.

He was nearer the truth than I was, I, the old Petersburg sceptic. The luck was with him ; probably because a bold, self-confident man can control destiny though destiny whirls and scatters in different directions perplexed and weak people. Perhaps, too, he was assisted by those original traits of character which he brought with him from the heart of his provincial South : shrewdness, observation, a tranquil and open manner of speech, an innate tendency to humour, strong nerves that refused to be troubled by the chaos of life in the capital. It may have been this or that, but in any case the South, as represented by him, obviously and successfully conquered the North.

My friend, quickly, in three or four days, found work for himself in connection with one of the largest railways and, a month later, had attracted the attention of the authorities. He was entrusted with the revision of some plans of railway traffic, or something of the sort. The whole thing might have been easily finished in a week or two, but, for some reason or other, Boris got particularly interested in it in his stubbornly insistent way. He took it into his head to frequent the public library, dragged home enormous reference books, stuffed with figures, and devoted his evenings to mysterious mathematical calculations. The result of all this was that he presented the authorities with a scheme of passenger and goods trains that combined simplicity and obviousness with many other practical signs of efficiency. He was praised, and attracted special attention. Six months later, he was already in receipt of a hundred and fifty roubles a month and was employed on independent work.

But apart from this, he gave frequent music lessons— he was an excellent musician—wrote articles for the newspapers and technical articles on railway questions, and sang on Saturdays and Sundays in a well-known church choir as well as sometimes in opera and light opera choruses. He was capable of an amazing amount of work, but without strain, without any effort ; it came to him somehow naturally, easily, as though he were wading through it, as though it were all a joke, with that externally lazy manner of his. And always, with his shrewd little smile, he would be observing something, keeping his eye on something, as though, after all, he were only playing

176

with the present, merely testing his untouched force while, at the same time, vigilantly and patiently waiting for his real opening. For some mysterious, remote object, known only to himself, he was studying, through the self-teaching methods of Toussaint, and Langestedt, French, German, and English. I could hear him sometimes at the other side of the partition repeating, with his terrifying pro-nunciation : *L'abeille bourdonne, la mouche vole.* When I asked him why all this was necessary he would answer with his sly benevolence : " Oh, it's like this—I've nothing to do."

All the same, he knew how to enjoy himself. Some-where on Vassilief island, he had unearthed some of his fellow-countrymen. Ukrainians from Poltava, who wore embroidered shirts, with little ribbons instead of ties, and enormously wide trousers tucked into their top boots. They used to smoke long pipes, would ostentatiously spit through the corners of their lips on to the floor, and had nothing but contempt for all our town cultivation. I went once or twice to their little evenings. They drank " gorilka," not our vodka, but a special brand brought from " down there," ate slices of pork and enormous sausages so long that one had to coil them on one's plate in ten or fifteen circles. There was singing, too, wonderful singing, extraordinarily sad and stately. I can still remember, as if it were yesterday, Boris passing his hand nervously over his long, beautiful, wavy hair as he started the couplet of an old Cossack song.

His voice was warm, tender, slightly vibrating, and every time that I listened to him I experienced a tickling and throbbing in my chest and I felt like crying without any reason.

And afterwards one drank gorilka again and, at the end, one danced the " gopak," one of the national Ukrainian dances. Boris' jacket would fly away from his immense shoulders to a corner of the room and he himself would soar from end to end, rapping out the time with his heels whistling in tune and slyly raising and lowering his dark eyebrows.

He became the head of this dear Ukrainian farm village, tucked away among the severe parallel streets of Petersburg, There was something about him attractive, charming, irresistible. And everything seemed to come to him as a joke, as if it were merely by the way. I believed now definitely in his victory over the North, but something inexplicable, something perturbing, would never leave my soul when I thought of him.

It began in the spring. Soon after Easter, which was late that year, we drove together to the islands. It was a clear, pensive, gentle evening. The quiet waters of the rivers and canals dozed peacefully beside their banks, reflecting the pink and mauve colours of the deadened sky. The young, greyish foliage of the black, century-old lime trees on the banks looked at itself in the water so naïvely, so joyfully. For a long time we were silent. At last, under the charm of this exquisite evening, I said slowly :

" How delightful ! For the sake of an evening like this one can fall in love with Petersburg."

He didn't answer. I looked at him stealthily, side-ways. His face was gloomy and he had an angry expression.

" Don't you like it ? " I asked.

Boris made a slight gesture of annoyance.

" It's scenery," he said with disgust. " It's the same as at the opera. You call this Nature ? "

A strange, dreamy expression had come suddenly into his dark eyes and he began in a low, jerky, troubled voice :

" There now, in Little Russia, there is the real spring. Wild berries, white hazel trees are blossoming. The frogs are croaking in the creeks, the nightingales are singing. When it is night there, it is real night, dark with dread, with mysterious passion. And what days there are there now ! What sun, what sky ! What is

178

this Finland of yours ? A mixture of rain and snow . . ."

He turned away and became silent. But I understood instinctively that there was something wrong, something unhealthy at work in my friend's heart.

And, in fact, from that very evening, Boris began to fret and seemed to wilt. I could hear no longer behind the partition his melodious purring ; he no longer projected himself like a bomb into my room in the mornings ; his usual talkativeness had disappeared. Only when conversation turned on Ukrainia would he grow animated, and then his eyes became dreamy, beautiful and pitiful, and he seemed to be looking into the distance, hundreds of miles away.

" I'll go there for the summer," he would say decidedly. " Damn it, at all events I'll get a rest from the cursed Peter."

But in the end, he didn't succeed in going " there." His office kept him. In the middle of the summer we said good-bye to each other—I had to go abroad on business. I left him sad, irritated, tired out at last by the white nights, which brought him sleeplessness and a distress bordering on despair. He saw me off at the Warsaw station.

I returned in the very middle of a nasty, wet, foggy Petersburg autumn. Oh, how well I recall those first dismal, irritating impressions : dirty pavements, thin, endless rain, a sort of grey, slimy sky and in the background of the picture rough dvorniks with their brooms, hunted-looking cabmen with their rumpled clothes, women with hideous sheepskin goloshes, the hems of their skirts all wet, bilious, angry people with perpetually swollen faces, coughs and spleen. But I was still more struck and saddened by the change that had taken place in Boris.

When I came in, he was lying dressed on his bed, which had not been made. His hands were folded under his head and he didn't rise when he saw me.

" How are you, Boris ? " I said, seized already by a

feeling of presentiment, and I met with a cold, estranged glance.

Afterwards he apparently decided to greet me, for he rose as if it were a matter of duty, welcomed me and lay down again on the bed. With great difficulty, I managed to persuade him to dine with me that night at a restaurant. On the way he was silent, walked with a stoop, had an air of indifference, as though he were being led on a string, and I had to repeat every question I asked.

" Listen ; what in the world is the matter with you ? Have they changed you ? " I said, touching his shoulder.

He shook my hand off.

" Nothing. . . . Only boredom with everything. . . ."

For some time we walked on side by side without a word.

I remembered his musty, neglected room, its untidiness, the dry bits of bread on the table, the cigarette ends on the saucers, and I said decidedly and with real anxiety :

" I'll tell you what it is, my dear friend ; in my opinion you are quite simply ill. . . . No, don't wave your hands, but listen to what I'm going to say. These things can't be neglected. . . . Have you got any money ? "

A plan for curing my downhearted friend had quickly ripened in my mind. It was truly a rather ancient, rather trivial and, if you like, a rather ignoble plan. I had merely decided to take him to one of those equivocal places where one sings and dances, where people don't know themselves what they are doing, but are sure that they are enjoying themselves and through this conviction infect other people with the same illusion.

Having dined somewhere or other, we turned towards the Aquarium at about eleven o'clock so as to get the atmosphere of a spree. I took a " swagger cab " which whirled us past the insults of the cabmen, past the pedestrians all slobbered over with mud.

I was supporting the shattered, thinned back of Boris ; he was as stubbornly silent as ever, only once asking discontentedly :

" Where are we hurrying off to like this ? "

The dense crowd, the smoke, the rattle of the orchestra, the naked shoulders of the women with their made-up eyes, the white splashes of the tables, the red, brutalised faces of the men—all this pandemonium of tipsy gaiety had a quite different effect on Boris from what I was expecting. At my invitation he was drinking, but he was not getting drunk and his expression was becoming more and more distressed. A bulky, powdered woman, with an ostrich boa round her fat, naked neck, sat down for a minute at our table, tried to start a conversation with Boris, then looked at him in dismay and silently hurried off into the crowd, from which once more she glanced back towards us. And at this glance dread came to me, as if I had become stricken by something deadly, as if someone, black and silent, were standing close beside us.

" Let's drink, Boris," I shouted above the noise of the orchestra and the din of the crockery.

With his face puckered up as though from toothache, he formed an unspoken sentence on his lips, which I guessed to be :

" Let's get out of this. . . ."

I insisted on driving from the Aquarium to another place from which we emerged at dawn in the cold, dark blue twilight of Petersburg. The street in which we were walking was long and narrow, like a corridor. From the sleepy five-storied stone blocks there emanated the cold of the night. The sleepy dvorniks were plying their brooms while the chilled night-cabmen shivered and swore hoarsely. Stumbling as they strained on the cords round their chests, small boys were dragging their loaded stalls through the middle of the streets. At the doors of the butchers' shops hung the red, open carcasses of repulsive-looking meat. Boris was walking dejectedly, when suddenly he caught me by the arm and, pointing to the end of the street, cried out :

" There it is, there. . . ."

181

" What is it ? " I asked in consternation.

" You see . . . the fog."

The fifth stories were drowning in the mist which, like the drooping belly of a black serpent, was descending into the corridor-like street, had stopped halfway and, hugging itself, was peering down as if getting ready to spring at someone. . . .

Boris shook my arm and said, with eyes blazing, in a sudden anger :

" Do you understand what this is ? Do you understand ? It is the town that is breathing ; this is not fog, it is the breath from these stones with holes. There is here the reeking dampness from the laundries, the smoke from the coal ; there is here the sin of the people, their anger, their hatred, the emanations from their mattresses, the reek of their sweat and their putrescent mouths. . . . My curse upon you ! anathema, monster, monster—I loathe you ! "

Boris' voice broke and rang alternately, as he shook his bony fists in the air.

" Cool down," I said, taking him by the shoulders. " Come, cool down ; can't you see that you're startling people ? "

Boris choked and coughed for a long time.

" Look," he exclaimed, his face contracted by his cough, and he showed me a handkerchief which he had pressed against his lips, on the whiteness of which I saw a large stain of blood.

" It is he who has eaten me up . . . the fog. . . ."

We walked back to his lodgings in silence.

In April, before Easter, I looked in at Boris one day. The weather was extraordinarily warm. There was a smell of melted snow, of earth, and the sun was shining bashfully and timidly, as a woman smiles when she is making friends again after tears. He was standing by the opening of the double window, breathing in the spring air. As I entered the room he turned round slowly and on his face there was a kind of tranquil, appeased, childish expression.

"It is nice now at home in the Government of Poltava," he said, smiling, by way of a greeting.

And suddenly it came home to me that this man would die soon, perhaps even that very month.

"It is nice," he went on thoughtfully and, getting suddenly animated, he hurried towards me, seized my hands and said :

"Sachenka, dear, take me down to my home . . . take me, old man. Won't you do it ? "

"But am I refusing ? Of course we'll go."

And so just before Easter we started on our journey. When we left Petersburg it was a damp, cold day and over the town a thick black fog was hovering, that same black fog which had poisoned the soul and eaten the body of my poor friend.

But the nearer we came to the South, the more excited and joyful my poor Boris became. The spring seemed rushing to meet us. And when we caught our first glimpse of the white dabbed little huts of Ukraine, it was already in full bloom. Boris could not tear himself from the window. All along the line, large simple flowers, bearing the poetical name of " dreams," blossomed in blue patches. Boris told me with ecstasy that in Little Russia one dyes Easter eggs with these flowers.

At his home, under the blue caressing sky, under the full but not yet hot rays of the sun, Boris began to revive quickly, as if he were recovering with his soul from some low, clutching, icy nightmare.

But bodily he grew weaker every day. The black fog had killed in him something vital, something that gave life and the desire to live.

A fortnight after his arrival, he was confined to his bed.

All the time he had no doubt that he would soon die, and he died bravely and simply.

I was with him the day before his death. He pressed my hand hard with his dry, hot, emaciated fingers, smiled caressingly and sadly, and said :

" Do you remember our conversation about the North and the South ? It's long ago now ; do you remember it ? Don't imagine that I'm eating my words. Well, I admit it, I have not withstood the struggle, I have perished. . . . But after me others are coming—hundreds, thousands of others. Understand, they must win the victory, they cannot fail to conquer. Because over there the black fog is in the streets, in the hearts and in the' heads of the people, and we come from the exulting South with joyous songs, with the dear bright sun in our souls. My friend, people cannot live without the sun."

I looked at him attentively. He had just washed and had combed his hair flat back over his head after moistening it with water. It was still moist, and this gave his face a pitiable and innocent and festive expression behind which one detected all the more clearly the proximity of death. I remember, too, that he kept looking attentively and in apparent astonishment at his nails and the palms of his hands as though they were strange to him.

The next day I was called hastily to his bedside to find—not my friend, but only his body, which was passing unconsciously in a swift death agony.

Early that morning he had asked to have his window opened and it remained open. Into the room, from the old garden, crept in branches of white lilac with their fresh, elastic, odorous flowers. The sun was shining. The blackbirds sang out their madness of delight.

Boris was becoming quiet. But in the very last minute he suddenly lifted himself up and sat on his bed ; an insane awe showed itself in his wide-open eyes. And when he fell again against the pillows and after a deep sigh stretched himself out with all his body, as if he wanted to stretch himself before a long, deep sleep, this expression of awe did not leave his face for a long time.

What had he seen in that last minute ? Perhaps to the eyes of his soul there had outlined itself that bottomless, perpetual black fog which, inevitably and pitilessly, absorbs people, and animals, and the grass, and the stars and whole worlds ? . . .

When they were laying him out I could not bear to see his terrible yellow feet and I left the room. But when I came back he was already lying on the table and the mysterious little smile of death lurked peacefully round his eyes and lips. The window was still open. I broke off a small branch of lilac—wet and heavy under its white clusters—and placed it on Boris' breast.

The sun shone joyfully, at once tender and indifferent. . . . In the garden the blackbirds were singing. . . . On the other side of the river the bells were ringing for the late church service.

THE MURDERER

THEY were talking over current events, executions, people being shot, burnt alive, women being violated, old men and children killed, gentle, liberty-loving souls disfigured for ever, trampled into the mud by the loathsome force of violence.

The master of the house said : " It is terrible to think how the scale of life has altered. Was it long ago ?— no, only about five years ago—when our whole Russian society was distressed and shocked over any solitary instance of violence. The police had beaten a Tchinovnik in prison, some rural authority had arrested a newly-arrived student for disrespect. And now . . . a crowd has been fired on without warning ; a man has been executed through error, having been mistaken for his namesake ; nowadays, people are shot casually, out of mere idleness, just to let off a round or two. An intellectual young man is seized in the middle of the street and whipped with knouts, whipped for no reason at all, just as a gratuitous distraction for the soldiers and officers. And already this sort of thing provokes no astonishment, no alarm. Everything goes on as though nothing at all had happened."

Someone moved nervously in the corner of the sofa. Everyone turned towards him, feeling, though they could not see him, that he was going to talk. And he did begin in a low, exaggeratedly even tone, but with so many pauses between the words and such curious shudders in his voice that he was clearly keeping back, only with the greatest difficulty, his inner emotion and sorrow.

" Yes, . . . that is what I want to get at. . . . In my opinion . . . it is not true that one can . . . become used to this. I can understand . . . murder out of revenge—there is a kind of terrific . . . wild beast pleasure in that. I understand murder in anger, in the blindness of passion, from jealousy. Murder in a duel, that's comprehensible. . . . But when people set about it mechanically . . . without irritation, without fear of any sort of responsibility . . . and without anticipating even self-defence . . . no, that is for me as savage, dreadful, and incomprehensible as the psychology of the executioner. . . . When I read or think about pogroms, about pacifying expeditions or about the way prisoners are finished off in war, so as not to overload a detachment, I lose my head. I seem to be standing over a kind of black fetid abyss into which the human soul is sometimes capable of falling. . . . But I understand nothing . . . I feel dread and disgust . . . a nausea. . . . But . . . a strange torturing sick curiosity chains me to this dread . . . to all the immensity of this fall."

He remained silent for a few seconds, breathing jerkily, and when he continued one could divine by his changed voice, which had become suddenly deadened, that he had covered his face with his hands.

" Well, . . . never mind . . . I must tell you this. . . . On my soul, too, lies this old blood-madness. . . . About ten years ago I committed a murder . . . I never told anybody about it until now. . . . But . . . never mind. . . . In one of the isbas on my estate, you see, there lived a cat, such a small, thin, starved little thing —more like a kitten than a cat—meant to be white, but as she always lived under the stove, she had become a dirty grey, a sort of pale blue. It all happened in the winter . . . yes, late in the winter. It was a gorgeous morning, quiet and windless. The sun was shining and it was already warm. One simply could not look at the snow, it was so glittering. It was, too, extraordinarily thick that year and we all walked on skis. And so I put my skis on and went that morning to look at an orchard that had been damaged by hares during the night. I was moving quietly past the regular rows of young apple trees— I can see it all at this moment—the snow seemed to be pink and the shadows of the little trees lay quite still, so exquisite they looked that one felt like kneeling close to them and burying one's face in the fleecy snow.

"Then I happened to meet an old workman, Iazykant; it wasn't his real name, but just a nickname. He was on skis, too, and we went on together side by side, talking about one thing or another. All of a sudden, he said with a laugh:

"'That little cat of ours has lost a leg, Master.'

"'How did that happen?' I asked.

"'Most likely she fell into the wolf trap. Half her leg's clean gone.'

"I thought I'd have a look at her and so we went on towards the servants' quarters. Our road was soon crossed by a very thin track of red spots, which led to a mound beside which the wounded cat was sitting. As soon as she saw us, she crinkled up her eyes, opened her mouth pitifully and gave a long 'mi-aow.' Her little muzzle was extraordinarily thin and dirty. The right fore-leg was bitten clean through, above the knee-joint, and was projecting in front curiously, just like a wounded hand. The blood dropped at long intervals, accentuating the whiteness of the poor thin bone.

"I said to Iazykant: 'Go to my bedroom and bring me my rifle. It is hanging over the bed.'

"'But what will happen to her? She will lick it up all right,' the workman pleaded.

"I insisted on having my own way. I wished to end the torture of the mutilated animal. Besides, I was sure that the wound would suppurate and the cat would die in any case from blood-poisoning.

" Iazykant brought the rifle. One barrel was loaded with small shot for woodcock and the other with buck-shot. I coaxed the cat, calling ' Puss, Puss, Puss.' She mewed quietly and came a few steps towards me. Then I turned to the right, so that she would be on my left, took aim, and fired. I was only some six or seven paces from the animal and, immediately after the shot, I thought that there was a black hole in her side, as large as my two fists. I hadn't killed her. She shrieked and ran away from me with extraordinary speed and without limping. I watched her run across a stretch of about one hundred and fifty yards and then dive into a shed. I felt horribly ashamed and disgusted, but I followed her. On the way, one of my feet slipped out of the ski fastening and I fell on my side in the snow. I rose with difficulty. My movements had become laboured, snow had caught in the sleeve of my coat and my hand shook.

" I got into the shed, where it was dark. I wanted to call the cat but, for some reason or other, I felt ashamed. Suddenly I heard a low, angry grumbling above my head. I looked up and saw just two eyes—two green burning spots.

" I fired at random into those spots, almost without taking aim. The cat spat, shrieked, threw herself about and then became still once more. . . . I wanted to go away, when I heard again from the stove that long angry grumbling sound. I looked round. Two green lights were shining in the dark with an expression of such devilish hatred that my hair rose and my scalp felt cold.

" I hurried home ; my stock of cartridges for the rifle had run out, but I had a revolver from Smith and Wesson and a full box of revolver cartridges. I loaded the six chambers and returned to the shed.

" Even at a distance, the cat's dreadful grumbling greeted me. I emptied the six chambers into her, went back, reloaded and again fired six rounds. And each time there was the same diabolical spitting, scratching and

tossing about on the stove, the same tortured shrieks, and then the two green fires and the long-drawn furious grumbling.

" At this stage, I was no longer sorry for her, but, on the other hand, I felt no irritation. A kind of stupid feeling mastered me and the cold, heavy, insatiable necessity of murder controlled my hands, my feet, my every movement. But my conscience was asleep, covered up, as it were, in a sort of dirty wrapper. I felt cold inside and there was a sickening, tickling sensation of faintness in my heart and stomach. But I could not stop.

" I remembered, too, how the sweet, clear winter morning had, somehow or other, strangely changed and darkened. The snow had become yellow, the sky grey, and in me myself there was a dull wooden indifference to everything, to the sky, to the sun, even to the trees with their clean blue shadows.

" I was returning to the shed for the third time, and once more with a loaded revolver. But Iazykant came out of the shed, holding by the hind legs something red, torn to pieces, the intestines falling out, but something that was still shrieking.

" Seeing me, he said, almost roughly : ' That's enough ! . . . Don't ! go ! I'll do it myself.'

" He tried not to look into my eyes, but I caught clearly an expression of utter disgust round his mouth and I knew that this disgust was at me.

" He went round the corner and banged the cat's head with all his might on a log. And it was over."

The speaker paused ; one could hear him clearing his throat and moving on the sofa. Then he continued in a tone that had become still more restrained, but with a touch of anguish and perplexity in his voice :

" Well, then . . . this sanguinary dream did not get out of my head the whole of that day. At night I could not sleep, and kept on thinking of the dirty white kitten. Again and again I saw myself going to the shed and hearing that suffering, angry grumbling and seeing those green spots full of terror and hate, and still shooting, shooting into them endlessly. . . . I must confess, ladies and gentlemen, that this is the most sinister and repulsive impression of my whole life. . . . I'm not at all sorry for that scurvy white cat. . . . No . . . I've shot elks and bears. Three years ago I shot a horse at the races. Besides, I've been at the war, deuce take it ! . . . No, it's not that. But to my last hour I shall remember how all of a sudden, from the depths of my soul, a sort of dark, evil, but, at the same time, invincible, unknown, and awful force took possession of it, blinding it, over-flowing from it. Ah, that miasmic fog of blood, that woodening, stifling indifference, that quiet lust of murder ! ''

Again he was silent and then from a far corner someone's low voice said : '' Yes, it's true . . . what a dreadful memory ! ''

But the other interrupted with emotion : '' No, no, for God's sake think of those unhappy ones who have gone to kill, kill, kill. It is my belief that for them the day has been always black as night. It is my belief that they have been sick with blood, but, for all that, they had to go on. They could still sleep, eat, drink—even talk, even laugh—but it was not they themselves who did these things, but the devil who possessed them, with his murky eyes and viscous skin. . . . I call them ' unhappy ' because I imagine them, not as they are now, but years later, when they are old men. Never, never will they forget the disgust and terror which, in these days, have mutilated and defiled their souls for ever. And I imagine the long sleepless nights of these old men— their horrible dreams. All through the nights they will dream that they are going along dismal roads under a dark sky with disarmed, bound people standing, in an endless chain, on both sides of them, and that they strike these people, fire on them, smash their heads with the butt-ends of their rifles. And in these murderers there is neither anger nor sorrow nor repentance, only they cannot stop for the filthy delirium of blood has taken hold of their brains. And they will wake in terror, trembling at the sight of their reflections in the glass. They will cry out and blaspheme and they will envy those whose lives had been cut off by an avenging hand in the flower of their youth. But the devil who has drunk of their souls will never leave them. Even in their death-agony, their eyes will see the blood that they have shed."

MEASLES

I

IT was before dinner and Dr. Iliashenko had just
finished bathing with a student named Voskresenski. The warm, south-east wind had whipped
the sea into eddies. Close to the shore, the water was
murky and had a sharp smell of fish and sea-plants. The
hot, swinging waves did not cool and refresh one's body,
but on the contrary, fatigued and unnerved it still more.

" Come on out, my colleague," the doctor exclaimed
as he splashed a handful of water over his own large white
stomach. " We shall get faint if we go on bathing like
this."

From the bathing-machine, they had to climb up the
mountain along a narrow path which was laid in friable
black slate, zig-zag fashion, covered with small rough
oak and pale green sea-cole heads. Voskresenski climbed
up easily, his long muscular legs moving in spacious strides.
But the fat doctor, who wore a wet towel instead of a hat,
succumbed to the heat and to his asthma. He came to a
dead stop at last with his hand on his heart, shaking his
head and breathing laboriously.

" Phew ! I can't stick it any longer. I'd almost
rather be back in the water. Let's stop for a minute."

They halted in a flat circle between two joints of the
path, and both of them turned round to face the sea.

Flogged by the wind, now· dazzlingly lit up by the
sun, now shadowed by clouds—it was a medley of patches
of colour. By the shore, the white foam melted into a

large fringe of tulle lace on the sand ; further out ran a dirty ribbon of light chocolate colour still further lay a miserable green band, all wrinkled up and furrowed by the crests of the waves, and last of all—the powerful, tranquil bluishness of the deep sea with those fantastically bright spots—sometimes of deep purple, sometimes of a tender malachite colour, with unexpected shining pieces like ice covered with snow. The whole of this living mosaic seemed to be belted at the horizon by the black, quiet, motionless ribbon of the shoreless distance.

" All the same, it's good, isn't it ? " said the doctor. " It's a beauty, isn't it ? Eh ? "

He stretched out his short arm, fat like an infant's, and with widespread fingers theatrically stroked, as it were, the course of the sea.

" Oh, it's all right," Voskresenski answered with a half-affected yawn, " but one soon gets sick of it. It's just decoration."

" Yes, yes, we've eaten it. There's a yarn about that sort of thing," Iliashenko explained. " A soldier came home to his village after the war. Well, of course, he lies like an elephant and the village folk were naturally wonder-struck : ' We went,' says he, ' to the Balkans, that is to say, into the very clouds, right into the middle of them.' ' Oh, dear, have you really been in the clouds ? ' The soldier answered indifferently : ' Well, what are the clouds to us ? We ate them the same as jelly.' "

Dr. Iliashensko loved telling stories, particularly those from the life of the people and from Jewish life. Deep down in his heart, he thought that it was only through a caprice of destiny that he had not become an actor. At home he would madden his wife and children with Ostrovski, and, when paying his patients a visit, he liked to recite Nikitine's " The Driver," for which he would unfailingly rise to his feet, turn a chair round, and lean on its back with his hands turned outwards. He read in the most unnatural, internal voice, as though he were

196

a ventriloquist, under the. impression that this was how a Russian moujik would speak.

After telling the story about the soldier he immediately burst out into a free, boisterous laugh. Voskresenski forced himself to smile.

" You see, doctor, the south . . . " he began in his jaded way, as though he had difficulty in choosing his words. " I'm not fond of the south. Here everything . . . somehow or other . . . is oily . . . somehow . . . I don't know . . . excessive. Look at that magnolia . . . but forgive me for asking, is it a plant ? It seems as if it had been made up out of cardboard, painted green, and varnished at the top. Then look at Nature here. The sun goes up from the sea, we have the heat, in the evening it goes over the mountains and it is night at once. No birds ! Nothing of our northern dawn with the smell of young grass in it, nothing of the poetry, of twilight with the beetles, the nightingales, the stamp of cattle trotting in the dust. It's all opera scenery, but it isn't Nature."

" In your hou . . . se," the doctor sang in a hoarse little tenor. " Of course you are a Moscow town bird."

" And these moonlit nights, deuce take them ! " Voskresenski continued, as old thoughts which, up till now, he had kept to himself, stirred in him with new force. " It's a perfect torment. The sea is glossy, the stones are glossy, the trees are glossy. It's a regular oleography ; the stupid cicadas squall ; you can't hide from the moon. It's sickening, and somehow or other you get agitated as if someone were tickling you in the nose with a straw."

" What a barbarian you are ! Why, in that Moscow of yours they're having twenty-five degrees of frost, and even the policemen are almost frozen, while here the roses are in full bloom and one can bathe."

" And I don't like the southern people either," the student went on, following stubbornly his own thoughts. " Rotten little people, lazy, sensual, with narrow fore-

197

heads, sly, dirty ; they gobble up any sort of filth. Even their poetry is somehow or other oily and mawkish ; in a word, I can't bear them."

The doctor pulled up again, swung his arms and made round, stupefied eyes.

" Tu-tu-tu," he went in a long whistle. " Et tu, Brute ? I catch in your words the spirit of our honoured patron. The Russian song, the Russian shirt, eh ? The Russian God, and the Russian largeness ? The Jews, the Sheenies, the Poles, and the other poor devils, eh ? "

" That's enough, Ivan Nikolaevitch. Stop that," Voskresenski said curtly. His face had grown suddenly pale and wrinkled as though from toothache. " There is nothing to laugh at in this. You know my point of view very well. If I haven't run away from this parrot, this fool, up till now, it is only because one must eat, but it's all much more saddening than funny. It's enough that for twenty-five roubles a month I deny myself every day the delight of expressing what suffocates me—strangles my very throat, what lowers all my thoughts."

" First rate ; but why get so hot about it ? "

" Oh, I'd like to tell him many things," the student exclaimed, furiously shaking his strong fist, which was whitened by the tension of the muscles. " I'd like to— Oh, this buffoon . . . Well, never mind—we're not strapped to each other for a century."

Suddenly the doctor's eyes narrowed and glittered. He took hold of Voskresenski's arm and, leaning his head playfully against his shoulder, whispered : " Listen, my boy ; why boil up like this ? What sense is there in insulting Zavalishine ? It will only mean a row in a noble house, as one says, just that. You had much better combine the sweetness of vengeance with the delights of love. What about Anna Georgievna—eh ? Or has that come off already ? "

The student remained silent and tried to free his arm from the doctor's hand. But the other pressed it still more tightly and continued to whisper, his laughing eyes playing all the time :

" You queer fellow, you've no notion of taste. The woman is thirty-five years old, in full bloom, all fire— and her figure ! Haven't you had enough of playing Joseph ? She looks at you the way a cat looks at cream. Why be too scrupulous in your own country ? Remember the aphorism : A woman with experience is like a cherry picked by a sparrow—it's all the sweeter. Ah, where is my youth ? " he began theatrically in a high-pitched, bleating, throaty voice. " Where is my youth ? Where is my thick crop of hair, my thirty-two teeth in my mouth, my—— "

Voskresenski managed at last to free himself from the doctor's clutch, but he did this so roughly that they both felt awkward.

" Forgive me, Ivan Nikolaevitch, but I simply can't listen to such meanness. It isn't bashfulness, it isn't chastity, but it merely feels dirty, and—speaking generally —I don't like it. I can't—— "

The doctor threw up his arms mockingly and slapped his thighs : " My dear fellow, you mean that you can't take a joke ? Personally, I have the greatest respect for other people's convictions and, honestly, I rejoice to see among the youth of to-day so many who look on these matters cleanly and honestly. But why can't one joke a little without your spreading your tail like a peacock immediately ? Why ? "

" Forgive me," the student said, in a muffled voice.

" Ah, my dear fellow, that's not why I am saying all this. The fact is, you've got into a twitching state, the whole lot of you young fellows. Look at you, a strong man with a big chest and shoulders—why, your nerves are like a schoolgirl's. By the bye, look here," the doctor went on in a business-like tone, " you oughtn't to bathe quite so often, particularly in such a hot spell. Not being used to it, you know, you might bathe yourself into a serious illness. One of my patients contracted a nervous. eczema through overdoses of sea-bathing."

They were now walking along the last open stretch of the path, which had become practically smooth. To their right, the mountain rose almost to a perpendicular, while behind them, in the distance, the boiling sea seethed endlessly. To their left, bushes of dog-roses, covered with tender pink blossoms, clung to the slope, projecting above the reddish-yellow earth and the grey corked stones that resembled the backs of recumbent animals. The student was glancing at the ground between his feet with a look of angry confusion.

" It has turned out so badly," he thought with a frown. " Yes, somehow it has turned out stupidly. As a matter of fact, the doctor's a good sort, always attentive, patient, even-tempered. It's true that he's sometimes a bit of a clown, a chatterbox, reads nothing, uses bad language and has got slack, thanks to his easy-going practice at a health resort. . . . But all the same, he's a good fellow and I've been brusque and rude to him—— "

In the meanwhile, Iliashenko was carelessly knocking off with his walking-stick the little thin white flowers that smelt like bitter almonds, while he sang to himself in an undertone :

> "In your hou . . . se I knew fi . . . rst
> The sweetness of a pure and tender love."

II

They turned out on to the road. Over a high white wall, as massive as that of a fortress, rose a villa, ingeniously and stridently built after the pattern of a stylish Russian gynæceum, with sea-horses and dragons on the roof, the shutters ornamented with variegated flowers and herbs, and carved doorways, with twisted little bottle-shaped colonnades on the balconies. This pretentious, ginger-bread-like construction produced a ponderous and incoherent impression in the full blaze of the Crimean sky, against the background of the aerial grey-bluish mountains, amid the dark, pensive, elegant cypresses and powerful plane-trees, covered from top to bottom with blush-like moss, in proximity to the beautiful joyous sea. But the owner of the villa, Pavel Arkadievitch Zavalishine—an ex-cornet of cavalry, afterwards an estate-agent, later on an attorney in a big port town in the south, and now a well-known dealer in naphtha, a shipowner, and the president of the stock exchange committee—was conscious of no incongruity.

"I am a Russian, and I have the right to despise all those renaissances, rococos, and gothics," he would shout sometimes, striking his chest. "We're not bound by what they think abroad. We've had enough of that in the past. We've bowed down to them enough. We have our own strong, original, creative power, and for a Russian gentleman like me there is only one thing to do, and that is to spit on all this foreignness."

The table was already laid on the enormous lower balcony. They were waiting for Zavalishine, who had just arrived from town and was changing his clothes in his bedroom. Anna Georgievna was leaning languidly back in a rocking-chair, overcome with the heat. She wore a light peignoir of Moldavian stuff, gold-embroidered with large sleeves slit up underneath almost to the shoulders. She was still very handsome, with a heavy, assured, superb beauty—the beauty of a plump, well-preserved brunette of the southern type.

"Good-morning, Doctor," she said in a deep voice, and with a slight burr. "Why didn't you guess that we wanted you yesterday? I had such a migraine."

Without raising herself from the armchair, she lazily stretched out her hand to Ivan Nikolaevitch, while her drooping sleeve revealed her round, full shoulder with its white vaccination mark, the small blue veins in the inner curve of the elbow, and a dark, pretty little mole slightly higher up the arm. Anna Georgievna (she insisted for some reason or other on being called " Nina " instead of Anna) knew the value of her hands and liked to show them.

The doctor leaned over the outstretched hand so respectfully that she had to pull it away by force.

" You see what a gallant doctor we have," she said as she glanced at Voskresenski with laughing, caressing eyes. " You never kiss ladies' hands. What a bear you are ! Come here, and I'll make your tie for you. You dress goodness knows how."

The student came up awkwardly and, as he leaned over her, he caught through the strong aroma of her perfume the smell of her hair as the light agile fingers ran round his neck.

Voskresenski was chaste in the straightforward, healthy meaning of the word. Naturally, from the time that he entered his Lycée, he could not help learning everything about the most intimate relations of the sexes, but he never dreamed of doing what his comrades boasted of openly. The tranquil, healthy blood of an old Church family showed itself in him. For all that, he had no sanctimonious, hypocritical anathemas for the " shameless men." He would listen indifferently to what was said on the subject and he would make no protest against those little anecdotes without which no conversation is possible in Russian intellectual society.

He knew well what Anna Georgievna's constant playfulness really meant. When saying " good-morning " or " good-bye," she would keep his hand lingeringly in her soft, feminine and, at the same time, strong, fingers. Under the mask of playfulness, she liked to ruffle his hair, sometimes called him patronisingly by the diminutive of his name, and would say in front of him risky things with a double meaning. If by any chance they were looking over an album together or happened to be leaning side by side over the balcony watching a steamer out at sea, she would always press against him with her large bust and he would feel her hot breath on his neck, while the curls of her hard hair tickled his cheek.

And she roused in the student a medley of strange, mixed feelings—fear, shame, passionate desire and disgust. When he thought about her she seemed to him just as exaggerated and unnatural as southern Nature. Her eyes seemed much too expressive and liquid, her hair much too dark, her lips unnaturally bright. The lazy, backward, unprincipled, sensual southern woman could be detected in every one of her movements, in every smile. If she came too close to him he could even detect, through her clothes, the warmth oozing up from her large, over-developed body.

Two schoolboys, Voskresenski's pupils, and three little girls were seated at the table dangling their feet. Voskresenski glanced at them sideways as he stooped, and suddenly he felt ashamed of himself, ashamed for them and particularly for their mother's warm bare hands which were moving so close to his lips. Unexpectedly he drew himself up and said with a red face and a hoarse voice :

" Excuse me, I'll tie it myself."

Zavalishine was now on the balcony dressed in a fantastic national costume, a silk kaftan with a blue silk Russian shirt and high patent leather boots. This costume, which he always wore at home, made him resemble one of those provincial contractors who are so willing to exploit to the merchant-class their large Russian nature and their clothes in the Russian style. The likeness was completed by a heavy gold chain across his stomach which tinkled with dozens of trinkets.

Zavalishine came towards the group with a quick, heavy step, carrying his head high and smoothing picturesquely each side of his fluffy beard, which was turning slightly grey. As he came, the children jumped up from the table. Anna Georgievna rose slowly from her rocking-chair.

"Good-morning, Ivan Nikolaevitch. Good-morning, Cicero," said Zavalishine, as he stretched out his hand carelessly to the doctor and the student. "I have kept you waiting, perhaps? Boris, grace."

Boris, with a frightened expression, jabbered out: "Our Father, which art in Heaven."

"Now, gentlemen," said Zavalishine, waving towards the table. "Doctor, some vodka?"

The *hors-d'œuvre* were laid on a small side table. The doctor approached it, walking like a buffoon, stooping a little, bowing, clicking his heels together and rubbing his hands.

"A man was once offered some vodka," he began, as usual trying to be funny, "and he answered 'No, thank you; firstly, I don't drink, secondly, it's too early, and thirdly, I've had a drink already.'"

"Twentieth edition," observed Zavalishine. "Have some caviare."

He pushed over to the doctor a large wooden bucket in which a silver fish-basin of caviare was standing in ice.

"How can you drink vokda in such heat?" Anna Georgievna exclaimed, with a grimace.

Her husband looked at her solemnly, as he held to his lips a silver embossed goblet.

"There's no harm in vodka for a Russian man," he replied imposingly.

And the doctor, having finished his glass, quacked loudly and added in the bass voice of a deacon:

"This was in time, anyhow. Well, Pavel Arkadie-vitch? Does Father Meleti order a third one?"

A man in a dress suit was serving at table. Formerly he used to wear something like a coachman's sleeveless coat, but one fine day Anna Georgievna discovered that it was improper for masters and servants to deck them-selves out almost in the same costumes, and she insisted on a European dress for the footmen. On the other hand, all the dining-room furniture and ornaments displayed that restless, racking style which is called Russian decadence. Instead of a table, there was a long chest, closed on every side, and as one sat in front of it it was impossible to move one's feet forward. One had to keep them cramped all the time, while one's knees would be painfully knocking against the protuberances of the carved ornaments and one had to stretch to reach one's plate. The heavy, low chairs, with high backs and wide-spread arms, were hard and uncomfortable, like wooden stage thrones. The wooden cans for kvass, the water-jugs and the wine ewers were of such monstrous dimensions and of such absurd shapes that one had to stand up to pour out from them. And all these things were carved, burnished, and adorned with multi-coloured peacocks, fish, flowers, and the inevitable cock.

" One eats nowhere as one does in Russia," Zaval-ishine began in a juicy voice, arranging his napkin in his collar with his white hairy hands. " Yes, Mr. Student, I know you don't like to hear that, but unfortunately, that's how it is. Take fish, to begin with. Where in the whole world will you find another Astrakan caviare ? And the sterlets from Kama, the sturgeons, the salmon from the Dvina, the fish from Belozer ? 'Be kind enough to tell me if you can find in France anything to match the Ladoga fish or the Gatchina trout. I'd just like you to find them ! I beg you to do it with all my heart. Now take game : we have everything you can wish for and everything in abundance : wood-hens, heath-hens, duck, snipe, pheasants from the Caucasus, woodcocks. Then just think of our Tcherkass meat, Rostov sucking-pig, the Nijni cucumber, the Moscow milk-calf. In a word, we've got everything . . . Serguei, give me some more botvinia soup."

Pavel Arkadievitch ate a great deal in an unpleasant and gluttonly way. He must have had hungry days in his youth, thought the student, looking at him sideways. Sometimes, in the middle of a sentence, Zavalishine would put too large a morsel into his mouth and then there would be a long torturing pause, during which he would chew with objectionable haste while he looked at his interlocutor with his eyes starting out of his head, grunting, moving his eyebrows and impatiently shaking his head and even his whole body. During such pauses, Voskresenski would lower his eyes so as to conceal his antipathy.

" Wine, Doctor ? " Zavalishine offered it with careless politeness. " Let me recommend this little white label. It's Orianda '93. Your glass, Demosthenes."

" I don't drink, Pavel Arkadievitch. You'll excuse me."

" This is as-ton-ishing. A young man who doesn't drink and doesn't smoke. It's a bad sign." Zaval-ishine suddenly raised his voice severely. " A bad sign. I'm always suspicious of a young fellow who neither drinks nor smokes. He's either a miser or a gambler or a loose-liver. Pardon, I'm not referring to you, Mr. Empedocles. Another glass, Doctor ? This is Orianda —really not half a bad sort of little wine. One asks oneself why one should get from the sausage-merchants different Moselle wines and other kinds of sourness, when they make such delicious wine right at home in our own Mother Russia. Eh, what do you think, Professor ? " He addressed the student in his provoking way.

Voskresenski gave a forced smile.

" Everyone to his own taste."

" ' De gustibus ? ' I know. I've had a little learning, too, in my time. Besides, somewhere or other—it doesn't matter where or how—the great Dostoievsky has expressed the same idea. Wine, of course, is nothing in itself, mere Kinderspiel, but the principle is important. The principle is important, I tell you," he suddenly shouted. " If I am a true Russian, then everything round me must be Russian. And I want to spit on the Germans and the French. And on the Jews too. Isn't it so, Doctor ? Am I not speaking the truth ? "

" Ye-es ; in fact—the principle—that is, of course,

yes," Illiashenko said vaguely in his bass voice and with a gesture of doubt.

"I'm proud of being a Russian," Zavalishine went on with heat. "Oh, I see perfectly that my convictions seem merely funny to you, Mr. Student, and, so to speak, barbarous. But what about it ? Take me as I am. I speak my thoughts and opinions straight out, because I'm a straight man, a real Russian, who is accustomed to speaking his mind. Yes, I say, straight out to everyone : we've had enough of standing on our hind legs before Europe. Let her be afraid of us, not we of her. Let them feel that the last decisive powerful word is for the great, glorious, healthy Russian people and not for those cockroaches' remains ! Glory be to God . . ." Zavalishine suddenly crossed himself expansively, looked up at the ceiling, and gave a sob. "Thank God that you can find now more and more of those people who are beginning to understand that the short-tailed German jacket is already cracking on the mighty Russian shoulders. These people are not ashamed of their language, of their faith, of their country, and confidently they stretch out their hands to the wise Government and say : 'Lead us.' "

"Paul, you're getting excited," Anna Georgievna remarked lazily.

"I'm not getting in the least excited," her husband snarled angrily. "I'm only expressing what every honest Russian subject ought to think and feel. Perhaps someone is not of my opinion ? Well then, let him answer me. I am ready to listen with pleasure to a different opinion. There, for instance, it seems funny to Mr. Vozdvijenski . . ." The student did not raise his downcast eyes, but became pale and his nostrils quivered and dilated.

"My name is Voskresenski," he said in a low voice.

"I beg your pardon, that's exactly what I meant to say : Voznesenski. I beg your pardon. Well, I just ask you this : instead of making wry faces, hadn't you better break down my arguments, show me my error,

207

prove that I'm not right ? I say this one thing : we're spitting into our own soup. They're selling our holy, mighty, adored country to any sort of foreign riff-raff. Who manages our naphtha ? The Sheenies, the Armenians, the Americans. In whose hands are the coal, the mines, the steamers, the electricity ? In the hands of Sheenies, Belgians, Germans. Who have got the sugar factories ? The Sheenies, the Germans, the Poles. And above all, everywhere, the Sheeny, the Sheeny, the Sheeny. . . . Who are our doctors ? Sheenies. Who are our chemists, bankers, barristers ? To Hell with the whole lot of you ! The whole of our Russian literature dances to the Sheenies' tune and never gets out of it. Why are you making such terrible eyes at me, Anitchka ? You don't know what that means ? I'll explain later. Yes, there's point in the joke that every Sheeny is a born Russian littérateur Oh, my goodness, the Sheenies, the Israelites, the Zionists, the Innocents oppressed, the Holy Tribe. I'll say just this." —Zavalishine struck the edge of the table loudly and fiercely with his outstretched finger—" I'll say just this : Here, wherever you turn, you're confronted with the mug of some noble affronted nation. Liberty, Language, National Rights. And we go into ecstasies under their noses. Oh, poor cultured Finland ! Oh, unhappy enslaved Poland ! Ah, the great tormented Jewish race. . . . Beat us, my pigeons, despise us, trample us under your feet, sit on our backs and drive ! B-ut no—— " Zavalishine roared in a threatening voice, growing suddenly scarlet and rolling his eyes. " No," he repeated, striking himself on the chest with all his force. " This scandal is going to end. Up till now, the Russian people has been only scratching himself, half asleep ; but to-morrow, with God's blessing, he will awake. And then he will shake off from himself the mischievous Radical in-tel-lec-tuals as a dog would a flea, and will squeeze so tightly in his mighty palm all these innocents oppressed, all these dirty little Sheenies, Ukrainians, and Poles, that the sap will spurt out from them on all sides. And to Europe he will merely say : ' Stand up, you dog.' "

" Bravo ! Bravo ! Bravo ! " the doctor broke in with a voice like a gramophone.

The schoolboys, who had been frightened at first by the shouting, burst into a loud laugh at this, but Anna Georgievna said with a look of suffering :

" Paul, why do you go on like this in front of the children ? "

Zavalishine drained a glass of wine at a gulp and poured out another hastily.

" Pardon, it slipped out. But I will say this, I was expressing my convictions just now, honestly and sincerely at least. Now let them—that is, I meant to say, let Mr. Student here, let him refute what I say, let him convince me. I'm ready for him. It would be very much more honest than to evade it by wry little smiles."

Voskresenski shrugged his shoulders slowly.

" I'm not smiling at all."

" Ah ! You don't even give yourself the trouble of answering ? Of course. That is the be-s-t of all. You stand so high above any discussion or proofs ? "

" No, not in the least above. But it's like this—we'll never understand each other. What's the use of getting angry and spoiling one's temper ? "

" Quite so. I understand. You're too high and mighty then ? " Zavalishine was getting drunk and beginning to roar. " Ah, it's a pity, a great pity, my precious youth. It would have been such a treat to enjoy the milk of your wisdom."

At this instant Voskresenski raised his eyes towards Zavalishine for the first time. Suddenly he felt a wave of keen hatred for his round, light, protruding eyes, for his red nose, that seemed to be torn at the nostrils, for his white, bald, retreating forehead and his preposterous beard. And instinctively, as if against his will, he began to speak in a faint, stifled voice that was almost a stranger's.

209

" You insist on dragging me into a discussion. But I assure you that it's useless. Everything that you were good enough to express just now with such fire, I have heard and read hundreds of times. Hostility to everything European, a rancorous spite against kindred races, ecstacy before the might of the Russian fist, and so on, and so on. . . All this has been said, written, and preached on every doorstep. But what has the people here to do with it all, Pavel Arkadievitch ?—that's what I don't understand. That's what I cannot understand. The people—that is to say, not your valet or your porter or your workmen, but the people who composes the whole of Russia—the obscure moujik, the troglodyte, the cave man, why have you buttoned him up in your national dreams ? He is silent because he is thriving. You had better not touch him. Leave him in peace. It is not for you or for me to guess at his silence—— "

" Allow me ! My knowledge of the people is no worse than yours—— "

" No," the student interrupted impertinently. " Allow me now, please. You were good enough, a few minutes ago, to reproach me for laughing at your verbiage. Well, I will tell you that there is nothing funny in it, just as there is nothing terrible. Your ideal, the a-all-Rus-sian f-ist squeezing the sap out of all the little peoples, is dangerous to no one, but is merely repulsive, like every symbol of violence. You're not a malady, not an ulcer, you are simply an inevitable, annoying rash, a kind of measles. But your comedy of the large Russian nature, all these symbols of yours—your Russian kaftan, your patriotic tears—yes, all this is really funny."

" Ah, ex-cellent. Go on, young man, in the same spirit," Zavalishine said caustically, with a grimace on his lips. " It's a delicious system of polemics, isn't it, Doctor ? "

For his part Voskresenski felt in his heart that he was speaking loosely, clumsily, and confusedly, but he could

not stop now. In his brain there was the sensation of a
strange, cold void. His feet had become slack and heavy
and his heart seemed to have fallen somewhere deep
down and to be quivering there and breaking from too
frequent strokes.

"What does the system matter? To the devil with
it!" he exclaimed, and this exclamation flew out unexpectedly in such a full, strong sound that he suddenly
experienced a fierce and joyous pleasure. "I have been
too silent during these two months to pick and choose
a system. Yes. One is ashamed and pitiful and amused
in turn at your comedy, Pavel Arkadievitch. You know
the strolling minstrels who sing in the recreation gardens
in summer? You know the sort of thing—the hackneyed
Russian song. It is something torturingly false, impudent,
disgraceful. The same with you: 'The Russian soup,
the Russian kacha—our mother Russia.' Have you
ever had a look at the people's soups? Have you ever
had a real taste of it? One day with something to eat,
and the next day with nothing at all. Have you tasted
the peasants' bread? Have you seen their children with
swollen stomachs and legs like wheels? And in your house
your cook gets sixty roubles a month, and the valet wears
dress clothes, and the sterliadka is steamed. That's how
you are in everything. Russian patience. Russian iron
endurance. But with what horrors of slavery, on what a
bloodstained road was this patience bought! It is even
ludicrous! Russian invincible health—give way to the
shoulder there!—the Russian giant strength—have we
got it in this huge, overworked, overstrained, famished,
drunken man? And then, to cap everything, the frantic
yell: 'Down with European coats and dress clothes!
Let us go back to our good, glorious, vast and picturesque
Russian national clothes.' And then, to the amusement
of your servants, you masquerade in a Russian kaftan at
seven roubles a yard with a moire lining. All your nation-
alism is silk-lined. My God! and when you start talking

211

about the Russian songs, what rubbish! In it you hear
the sea, and see the steppe, you catch the voice of the
forest and some kind of boundless daring. But there is
no truth in all this : you hear nothing, you feel nothing
beyond the sick groaning or the drunken hiccup. And
you do not see any kind of large steppe, because it has
no existence, and there is only a sweating face distorted
by torture, swollen veins, bloodshot eyes, an open, sanguinary mouth . . ."

"For you clergy it is easier to see from the belfry,"
Zavalishine sneered scornfully.

But the student only waved him aside and went on :

"Then Russian architecture came into fashion, if you
please. Carved cocks, some sort of wooden dressers,
mugs, ewers, sunflowers, armchairs and benches on which
it is impossible to sit, with idiotic covers. Good Lord!
but don't you feel how all this accentuates the frightful
poverty of our national life, the narrowness and the lack
of fantasy? A grey crepuscular creation, a Papuan
architecture. A game, that's what it is precisely. A
vile game, if all this is done purposely to lead the fools
and gapers by the nose ; a miserable one if it is merely a
fashionable fad, a sort of stupid disguise, as if the doctors
in charge of a hospital were suddenly to put on hospital
dressing-gowns and a dance a can-can in them. That's
what it is, your Russian fashion with the moire lining."

Something caught Voskresenski at the throat and he
became silent. Now for the first time he realised that,
in the course of his rambling speech, he had unconsciously
risen to his feet and was banging his fists on the table.

"Perhaps you'd like to add something more, young
man ? " Zavalishine asked with forced politeness and in
a voice of exaggerated softness. He was white, his lips
were grimacing and twitching and the ends of his full
beard shook visibly.

"That's all," the student answered in a dull tone.
"There's nothing else. . . ."

212

"Then kindly let me have the last word." Zavalishine rose from his place and threw down his napkin.

"Convictions are convictions, and fidelity to them is a respectable virtue. But all the same, I have to answer for my children, to my country, and my Church. Yes, I am obliged to defend them from evil, from deteriorating influences. And so—I ask you to forgive me—but one of us, either I or you, will have to retire from their education."

Voskresenski made a sign with his head without speaking. Pavel Arkadievitch wheeled round sharply and left the table with long strides. But he stopped at the door. He was stifling with rage. He felt that the student had shown a moral superiority in this absurd discussion, a superiority obtained, not by conviction of thought, not by arguments, but by a youthful, untrammelled and, though nonsensical, a beautiful passion. And he wanted, before leaving the room, to give the tutor the last insult, a heavier one, with more sting in it. . . .

"My man will bring you the money due to you upstairs," he said through his nose in a jerky, self-satisfied way. "And also, as arranged, your journey money."

And he went out, banging the door so noisily that the cut glass rang and vibrated on the table.

For a long time everyone was awkwardly silent on the balcony.

Voskresenski, with cold trembling fingers, was making bread pills as he bent low over the table. It seemed to him that even little six-year-old Vavotchka was looking at him with curiosity and contemptuous pity.

Shall I go after him and slap his face? Challenge him to a duel? How badly and miserably it has all turned out! Shall I give him back his money? Throw it in his face? Faugh! what a miserable business.

All these reflections flashed at random through his brain.

"Dear Sachenka," Anna Georgievna spoke in a caressing

213

voice as if to a child, " don't attach any importance to this. It really isn't worth it. In an hour he will admit that he was wrong, and he'll apologise. To tell you the truth, you, too, said a good deal to him."

He made no answer. He wanted, more than anything in the world, to get up at once and go somewhere far away, to hide in some dark, cool corner ; but a complex, torturing indecision chained him to his place. The doctor began to speak about something or other too loudly and in an unnatural, detached tone. " That's because he's ashamed on my account," Voskresenski thought to himself, and he listened, scarcely understanding the words :

" One of my acquaintances who knows Arabic very well used to compare Arabian sayings with our Russian ones. There are some most curious parallels. For instance, the Arabs say : ' Honesty is a diamond, which makes a pauper the Sultan's equal.' And in Russian it comes out : ' What about honesty if there's nothing to eat ? ' The same about hospitality. The Arabian proverb says . . ."

Voskresenski rose suddenly. Without looking at anyone, his eyes downcast, he went awkwardly round the table and rushed across the balcony to the flower garden, where there was a sweet and heavy scent of roses. Behind him, he could hear Anna Georgievna's troubled voice :

" Sachenka, Alexander Petrovitch, where are you going ? We're having dessert at once . . ."

III

In his room upstairs, Voskresenski changed his clothes, pulled out from under the bed his old reddish box plastered all over with labels, and began to pack. Into it he flung furiously books and lectures, squeezed in his linen, crumpled anyhow in his precipitation, and furiously tightened the ropes and straps. As his physical force, whipped up by the recent explosion of still unsatisfied anger, was spending itself, he became slightly cooler and calmer.

His packing finished, he drew himself up and looked round. All of a sudden he regretted leaving his room, as if in it he were leaving a part of himself. As soon as he woke up in the morning, he had only to raise his head from the pillow to see right in front of him the dark blue stripe of the sea just level with the windows. The light, pink, transparent blind would be gently trembling from the breeze and the whole room would be so full of morning light, so impregnated by a strong and invigorating sea air, that in the early days, on waking up, the student used often to laugh aloud from some inner unconscious joy of life.

Voskresenski went on to the balcony. Far out in front, a long narrow cape, rounded at the end, jutted out into the sea. This rounded part was called the Battery, and behind it, circling it sharply, a small steamer was heading out to sea. Its panting snorts, like the heavy breathing of a dog, could be heard distinctly. Under the white awning, dark human figures were distinguishable. The steam-launch rocked a little, but boldly clambered up each wave and rolled over it, tucking its nose gallantly into the next, while the severed water washed over its deck. And still further out, as if midway between the shore and the horizon, the black, powerful mass of a huge steamer, with funnels bent behind, was moving with perfect balance noiselessly and evenly. And there came to Voskresenski in that moment, as through a tiny little cloud of invading sorrow, that delightful, audacious longing which he always experienced when thinking of long journeys, new impressions, new faces, all the limitless stretch of the young untasted life that lay before him.

" To-morrow, I, too, shall find myself on board ship with others. I'll make fresh acquaintances, look at new shores, at the sea," he thought to himself. " It's good."

" Sachenka, where are you ? Come here." It was Anna Georgievna's voice.

He returned quickly to his room, buttoning on the way the collar of his Russian shirt, and arranging his hair. A formless, vague fright, a sort of dark, enervating presentiment stirred for an instant in his soul.

" I'm tired," Anna Georgievna was saying, slightly out of breath. " How nice it is in here, so cool."

She sat down on the ledge of the window. Against the background of the dazzling whitish-blue sky and the deep blue of the sea beneath, the short, full figure, in its white peignoir, outlined itself with a soft and elegant precision. Her rough, reddish curls lit up her head in that light with a deep golden gleam.

" Well, what is it, my angry sparrow ? " she asked, with tender familiarity. " Haven't you cooled down yet ? "

" Yes, I've cooled down. I'm going away at once," he answered in a surly tone.

" Sacha."

She pronounced his name in a low, strange, agitated tone that Voskresenski had never heard before in his life. He started and looked at her attentively. But she was sitting with her back to the bright light and it was impossible to distinguish her expression. For all that, it seemed to the student that her eyes were shining in an unusual way.

" Sacha, my own one," she said suddenly in a hurried, stifled voice. " No, no, dear, you won't go away. Do you hear ? Come here to me . . . to me, I tell you. Oh, what a big stupid you are ! Do you hear ? You mustn't think of going ! I don't wish it. My darling, you will stay . . ."

She seized his hands, pressed them tightly, and, without letting them out of her own, placed them on her knees so that, for an instant, he felt her firm and, as it were, sliding figure under the light rough material of her peignoir.

" You will stay ? Yes ? " she asked in a quick whisper, looking up into his face.

He raised his eyes and met her clouded, fixed, avid glance. A burning joy leaped from his heart, transfusing his breast, striking into his head and throbbing in his temples. All confusion and awkwardness had disappeared. On the contrary, it was a dreadful oppressive delight to gaze, so close and shamelessly, so endlessly, without pronouncing a single word, into those beautiful eyes, still shining with tears and senseless with passion. Half consciously he divined that her glance had fallen below his eyes, and he lowered his own to her full, bright, parted lips, behind which gleamed the moist whiteness of her teeth. Suddenly it seemed to him that the air in the room had become suffocating ; his mouth was dry and he could scarcely breathe.

" You will stay ? Yes ? True ? "

He put his arms round her and immediately felt the large beautiful body light and alive, obedient to every movement, every hint of his hands. A sort of burning, arid whirl caught him suddenly, crippling his will, his judgment, all his proud, chaste thoughts, everything in him that was clean and human. For some reason or other, he recalled the bathing before dinner and those warm, swinging insatiable waves.

" Darling, is it true, true ? " she was repeating ceaselessly.

Roughly, like a savage animal, he caught her up and lifted her in his arms. Then, as if in delirium, he heard her frightened whisper : " The door—for God's sake the—door—— "

Mechanically he turned round, saw the wide-open door and beyond it the darkness of the corridor, but he did not understand the sense of these words, the significance of this door, and he immediately forgot it all. The dark, half-closed eyes were suddenly so close to his face that their contour seemed indefinite, blurred, and they them-

217

selves became enormous, fixed, monstrously shiny, and quite strange to him. Hot rocking waves broke on him, drowning his reason, burning him as with fiery circling coils. . . .

Later on he woke up and heard with surprise her voice, which seemed to be imploring him about something :

" I adore you . . . my young, strong, beautiful . . ."

She was sitting on his bed beside him, leaning her head against his shoulder with a submissive, fawning air and trying to catch his eye. But he was looking away, frowning and pulling nervously with a shaking hand at the fringe of his rug which was hanging on the foot of the bed. An invincible disgust was growing in him every second towards this woman, who had just given herself to him. He himself understood the injustice and selfishness of this feeling, but he could not overcome it, even out of gratitude, even out of compassion. Her proximity was physically repulsive to him, her touch, the noise of her rapid, jerky breathing ; and though he blamed only himself for every-thing that had happened, a blind, senseless hatred and spite towards her was filling his soul.

" Oh, what a scoundrel I am ! What a scoundrel ! " he was thinking, and at the same time he was afraid of her reading his thoughts and feelings on his face.

" My darling adored one," she was saying tenderly, " why have you turned away from me ? Are you angry ? Is anything the matter with you ? Oh, my dear one, didn't you really notice that I loved you ? From the very beginning, from the very first day. . . . Ah, but no. When you came to us in Moscow I didn't like you. What an angry one, I thought. But then afterwards . . . But, dearie, won't you look at me ? "

The student mastered himself and managed to give her awkwardly from under his eyebrows a side glance. His very throat contracted, so disgusting seemed the reddened face, splashed with powder at the nostrils and chin, the small wrinkles round the eyes and the upper lip, never noticed until this moment, and, above all, her suppliant, anxious, culpable devotion—a sort of dog's look. A shudder of repulsion came over him as he turned his head away.

" But why am I not repulsive to her ? " he was thinking in despair. " Why ? Ah, what a scoundrel I am !

" Anna Georgievna—Nina," he stammered out in an unnatural, wooden voice, " you'll forgive me. . . . You'll excuse me. I'm agitated. I don't know what I'm saying. . . . Understand me. Don't be angry. . . . I must be by myself. My head is going round and round."

He made an involuntary movement, as if to turn away from her, and she understood it. Her arms, that had been clinging round his neck, fell helplessly along her knees and her head bent down. She sat like this for a few more minutes and then rose silently with a resigned expression.

She understood better than the student what was happening to him now. She knew that for men the first steps in sensual passion produced the same terrible sickly sensation on beginners as the first draughts of opium, the first cigarette, the first drunken bout. She knew, too, that until this he had been intimate with no other woman, that for him she was *the first ;* knew this from his own words before, felt it by his savage, severe shyness, his awkwardness and roughness with her.

She wanted to console, to calm him, to explain in tender motherly words the cause of his suffering, for she knew that he suffered. But she—ordinarily so bold, so self-assured—could find no words. She felt confused and shy like a young girl and she felt at fault for his fall, for his silent anxiety, for her thirty-five years, and because she did not know, and was unable to discover, how she could help him.

" Sacha, this will pass," she said at last, almost under her breath. " This will pass, believe me. Calm yourself. But don't go away. You hear me ? You'll tell me if you want to go away, won't you ? "

219

" Yes. . . . All right, yes—yes," he repeated impatiently, looking at the door all the time.

She sighed and left the room noiselessly. Then Voskresenski clutched his hair with both hands and fell with a groan face downwards on the pillow.

IV

The next day Voskresenski was on his way to Odessa on the large steamship *Xenia*. Disgracefully and weakly he had run away from the Zavalishines, unable to bear his cruel remorse, unable to force himself to meet Anna Georgievna again face to face. After lying on his bed until dusk, he had put his things together as soon as it was dark and then noiselessly, stealthily, like a thief, he had stolen through the back entrance into the vineyard, and from there had clambered out into the road. And all the time, on his way to the post station, when driving in the diligence that was packed with silent Turks and Tartars, all through the night at the Yalta Hotel, his shame, his merciless disgust for himself, for Anna Georgievna, for everything that had happened the day before, and for his own boyish flight, never left him for a single second.

" It has all turned out as if it were a quarrel, as if it were out of revenge. I have stolen something from the Zavalishines and have run away from them," he thought, angrily grinding his teeth.

It was a hot windless day. The sea lay quiet, caressing, of a pale emerald round the shore, light blue further out and touched only here and there by lazy little wrinkles of purple. Beneath the steamer, it was bright green, bottomless, light and transparent as air. Side by side with the steamer raced a flight of dolphins. From above, one could see perfectly how in the depths the powerful

220

winding movements of their bodies cut through the thin water, and how, at intervals, one after the other, in quick dark semi-circles, they leaped to the surface.

The shore receded slowly. Gradually the steep hills showed themselves and then became lost to view, palaces, vineyards, squat Tartar villages, white-walled villas, drowned in wavy green, and, in the background, the pale blue mountains, covered with black patches of forest, and over them the fine airy contours of the peaks.

The passengers were trooping to the taffrail that faced the shore, calling out the names of the places and the names of the owners. In the middle of the deck, near the hatchway, two musicians—a violinist and a harpist— were playing a waltz, and the stale, insipid melody sounded unusually beautiful and stimulating in the sea air.

Voskresenski searched impatiently for the villa that looked like a gynæceum. And when it appeared again behind the dense woods of the Prince's Park and became quite visible above its huge white fortress-like wall, he breathed faster and pressed his hands against his heart which had grown cold.

He thought that he could distinguish on the lower terrace a white spot, and he wished to think that she was sitting there now, this strange woman, who had suddenly become so mysterious, so incomprehensible, so attractive to him, and that she was looking out at the boat, sorrowful as he was, and with her own eyes full of tears. He imagined himself standing there on the balcony close beside her, not his self of to-day, but that of yesterday, of a week ago—that former self which would never return to him. And he was sorry, unbearably, achingly sorry for that phase of life which had gone from him for ever and would never return, would never repeat itself. With an unusual distinctness, his eyes veiled in a rainbow-like mist of tears, Anna Georgievna's face rose in front of him, no longer victorious, or self-assured, but with a gentle, suppliant expression, self-accusing ; and she seemed to him now small, hurt, weak, and close to him, as though grafted on to his heart for ever.

And with these delicate, sad, compassionate sensations there was blended imperceptibly, like the aroma of a fine wine, the memory of her warm, naked, arms, her voice trembling with sensual passion, her beautiful eyes glancing down to his lips.

Hiding itself behind the trees and villas, then showing itself again for a moment, the gynæceum receded further and further and then suddenly disappeared. Pressing his cheek against the taffrail, Voskresenski looked for a long time in that direction. All this, indeed, had passed like a shadow. He recalled the bitter verse of Solomon, and he cried. But these tears, the tears of youth, clear and light, and this sorrow, were blessed.

Below deck, in the saloon, the lunch bell sounded. A chattering, noisy student, whose acquaintance Voskresenski had made in the port, came up behind him, tapped him on the shoulder and shouted out gaily :

" I've been looking for you, my friend ; you have provisions, haven't you ? Let's have a glass of vodka."

THE JEWESS

" **W**E'VE passed it, pa-assed it," a child's feeble
voice rang pitifully. " Right ! " shouted an
angry bass behind. " To the right, right,
r-r-right," gaily and swiftly sounded a chorus in front.
Someone ground his teeth, someone whistled piercingly.
. . . A band of dogs broke into a thin bark, at once angry
and joyful. " O-o-o ! Ha-ha-ha ! " the whole crowd
laughed and groaned alternately.

The sledge was tossed up and plunged into a hollow of
the road. Kashintzev opened his eyes.

" What's this ? " he asked, with a start.

But the road remained deserted and voiceless. The
frosty night was silent above the endless dead white
fields. The full moon was in the middle of the sky and
a fully outlined dark blue shadow sliding along the sledge,
broken by the open snowdrifts, seemed squat and monstrous. The dry, elastic snow squeaked, like india-rubber,
beneath the runners.

" Ah, but that's the snow squeaking," Kashintzev
thought. " How odd ! " he said aloud.

At the sound of his voice the driver turned round.
His dark face, the beard and moustache whitened under
the frost, looked like the mask of some rough wild animal
plastered over with cotton wool.

" What ? Two more versts, nothing much," said the
driver.

" This is snow," Kashintzev was thinking, once more
yielding to drowsiness. " It's only snow. How strange ! "

223

"Strange, strange," lisped one of the little sledge-bells restlessly and distinctly. "Strange, stra-ange, stra-ange. . . ."

"Oh, oh, oh, just look!" a woman shouted in front of the sledge. The crowd that was coming in a mass to meet him all started talking at once, crying and singing.

Once more, as though roused to fury, the dogs barked.

Somewhere in the distance a locomotive droned. . . . And immediately, in spite of his drowsiness, Kashintzev recalled with extraordinary vividness the station buffet, with its pitiful, dusty display—clusters of electric burners under a dirty ceiling, the soiled walls broken by enormous windows, artificial palms on the tables, stiffly-folded napkins, electroplate vases, bouquets of dry, feathery grass, pyramids of bottles, pink and green liqueur glasses.

All that was last night. His medical colleagues were seeing him off. Kashintzev had just been appointed to a new post—that of junior doctor in a far-off infantry regiment. They were a party of five, and they dragged the heavy station chairs round to the doctors' usual little table in the corner. They drank beer and talked with a forced heartiness and assumed animation, as if they were acting a seeing-off scene on the stage. The handsome and self-assured Ruhl, his eyes flashing in an exaggerated way, glancing round for applause and talking so that strangers could hear him, said in his familiar, affected voice:

"That's it, old man. Our whole life from birth to death consists only of meeting and seeing one another off. You can write this down as a souvenir in your note-book : 'Evening aphorisms and maxims of Dr. von Ruhl.' "

He had scarcely finished speaking when the fat railway official, with the face of an angry bulldog, showed himself at the door, shaking his bell and shouting in a sing-song voice, with abrupt stops and chokes :

"Fi-irst bell. Kiev, Jmerinka, Odess. . . . The tra-ain is on the second platform."

And now, squatting uncomfortably on the low seat of the tugging sledge, Kashintzev laughed aloud from pleasure—so very bright and clear were these recollections. But immediately the tiring, relentless impression of the endlessness of this dreary road returned to him. From the moment when, in the morning, he had alighted at the small railway station to get into this post sledge only six or seven hours had elapsed, but he seemed to have been driving like this for whole weeks, or months ; he seemed to have had time to change, to grow older, duller and more indifferent to everything since the day before. Somewhere on the way he had met a beggar, drunk and in rags, with a broken nose and a shoulder naked to the frost ; somewhere he had seen a long thin horse with an arched neck and a chocolate-coloured, thick velvety coat plunging and refusing to be harnessed ; someone, it seemed, had said pleasantly a long, long time ago : " The road is good to-day, your honour ; you'll be there before you have time to look round." Kashintzev at that moment had been contemplating the snow-plain which was reddened by the evening sunset. But now all this was muddled and had receded into a kind of troubled, unreal distance, so that it was impossible to remember where, when, and in what order it had all happened. From time to time a light sleep would close his eyes, and then to his befogged senses there would become audible strange shrieks, grindings, barks, shouts, laughs, and mumblings. But he would open his eyes and the fantastic sounds would transform themselves into the simple squeaks of the sledge-runners and the tinkling of the sledge-bells, while to right and left the sleeping white fields extended, now as always, and in front of him protruded the black bent back of the driver, and still the horses' haunches moved regularly as they swished to right and left their knotted tails.

" Where shall I take you, your honour ; to the post office or to the shelter ? " the driver asked.

Kashintzev raised his head. He was driving now

along a straight street in a village. The beaten-down road in front gleamed in the moonlight like burnished blue steel. On both sides of the road dark, piteous little houses, overladen by their heavy snow hats, peeped out of the deep white drifts. The village seemed to have died out of existence ; not a dog barked, there were no lights in the windows, no one could be seen on the road. There was something terrible and sad in this numbness of human habitations that, lost in the deep snow, appear to nestle fearfully against each other.

" Where's that—the shelter ? " Kashintzev asked.

" Your honour doesn't know ? Movsha Khatzkel's shelter. Gentlemen always stop there. You can get tea, eggs, a snack of some kind. One can spend the night there, too ; there are five rooms. "

" Well, all right, let's go to the shelter."

Now for the first time at the thought of food and warm lodgings Kashintzev realised how very cold and hungry he had become. And the low, blind little houses, buried in the snow, were still coming to meet him and still receding, and it seemed that there would be no end to them.

" When shall we get there ? " Kashintzev asked impatiently.

" Very soon. It's a long village, a verst and a half. Now, young ones," the driver shouted ferociously at the horses in his raucous voice, and, raising himself slightly, he whirled his knout over his head and tugged at the reins.

In the distance a red spot of light was discernible and began to grow, now hidden by some unseen obstacle, now flashing out again. At last the horses, like toys whose windings had run down, stopped of their own accord at the travellers' house and at once weakly lowered their heads to the ground. The vaulted, semi-circular entrance formed an enormous gaping corridor through the whole house, but further on, in the yard, brightly lit up by the moon, one could see carts with their shafts raised, straw strewn on the snow, and the silhouettes of horses under the flat sheds. On each side of the yard entrance two windows, covered with snow, shone with a warm, inviting light.

Someone opened the door, which squeaked piercingly on its hinges, and Kashintzev entered a room. White clouds of frosty air, which apparently had been waiting just for this, rushed behind him in a mad whirl. At first Kashintzev could distinguish nothing ; his spectacles were immediately covered with vapour and he could see in front of him only two shiny, blurred rainbow circles.

The driver who had followed him shouted :

" Listen, Movsha, here's a gentleman for you. Where are you ? "

From somewhere or other there emerged a short, thick-set, light-bearded Jew in a high cap and a knitted tobacco-coloured waistcoat. As he came he munched something and wiped his mouth hurriedly with his hand.

" Good-evening, your honour, good-evening," he said amicably, and at once, with an air of compassion, he shook his head and smacked his lips : " Tze, tze, tze ! How frozen your honour is, good gracious ! Just let me take your coat, I'll hang it on a nail. Will your honour order tea ? Perhaps something to eat ? Oh, how frozen your honour is ! "

" Thank you, yes," Kashintzev ejaculated. His lips were so shrivelled from cold that he moved them with difficulty ; his chin had become motionless as though it didn't belong to him, and his feet seemed to him soft, weak, and sensitive as if in cotton wool.

When his spectacles had quite thawed, he looked round. It was a large room with crooked windows and an earthen floor, plastered with pale blue lime which, here and there, had fallen out in large chunks, leaving the wooden shingles bare. Along the walls narrow benches were stretched and wet slanting tables, greasy from age. Almost under the very ceiling a lamp was burning. The smaller back

227

part of the room was partitioned off by a many-coloured chintz curtain, from which there emanated the odour of dirty beds, children's clothes, and some sort of acrid food. In front of the curtain a wooden counter extended.

At one of the tables opposite Kashintzev sat a peasant in a brown Ukrainian overcoat and a sheepskin cap, his untidy head leaning on his sprawling elbows. He was drunk with a heavy, helpless drunkenness, and he rolled his head on the table, hiccupping and blubbering out something incomprehensible in a hoarse, soaked, bubbling voice.

" What are you going to give me to eat ? " Kashintzev asked. " I feel very hungry."

Khatzkel hunched his shoulders up, spread his hands apart, winked with his left eye, and remained in this position for several seconds.

" What am I going to give his honour to eat ? " he repeated; with a sly penetrating air. " And what does his honour want ? One can get everything. One can put the samovar on, one can cook eggs, one can get milk. Well, you understand yourself, your honour, what is to be got in such a scabby village. One can cook a chicken, but that will take a very long time."

" Give me eggs and milk. And what else ? "

" What e-else ? " Khatzkel seemed surprised. " I could offer your honour a stuffed Jewish fish. But perhaps your honour doesn't like Jewish cooking ? You know, an ordinary Jewish fish which my wife prepares on the Sabbath."

" Give me fish, too. And a liqueur-glass of vodka, please."

The Jew closed both his eyes, shook his head, and smacked his lips with an air of consternation.

" No vodka," he whispered. " You know yourself how strict they are nowadays. Are you going far, your honour ? "

" To Goussiatine."

228

" May I ask if your honour is in the police service ? "

" No, I'm a doctor, an army doctor."

" Ah, his honour is a doctor. That's very nice. On my conscience, I'm very sorry that I can't get you any vodka. Still . . . Etlia," he shouted, moving away from the table, " Etlia ! "

He disappeared behind the curtain and spoke rapidly in Yiddish as though he were angry. After this he kept on appearing and disappearing, and apparently bustled about a great deal. By this time the peasans who was sprawling at the table, raised his head and, with his wet mouth wide open and his eyes glassy, began to sing hoarsely, with a snapping gurgling in his throat.

Khatzkel rushed up to him and shook him by the shoulder.

" Trokhim, listen, Trokhim. . . . I have asked you again and again not to yell like this. His honour there is getting angry. . . . Well, you've had a drink and all is well. God give you happiness, and just you go quietly home, Trokhim."

" Sheenies," the peasant suddenly howled in a terrible voice, and he banged his fist on the table with all his might. " Sheenies, you devil's spawn ! I'll k-kill . . ."

He fell heavily face forward on the table, still jabbering.

Khatzkel, with a pale face, sprang away from the table. His lips grimaced in a scornful but at the same time troubled and helpless smile.

" You see, your honour, what my bread's like," he said bitterly, addressing Kashintzev. " Tell me what I can do with a fellow like that ? What can I do ? Etlia ! " he shouted in the direction of the curtain. " When are you going to serve his honour ? "

Once more he dived into the curtained part of the room and immediately returned with a dish on which lay a fish, cut in thin slices and covered with a dark sauce. He also brought back a large white loaf with a thick solid crust speckled with black grains of some aromatic seasoning.

" Your honour," Khatzkel said mysteriously, " my wife in there has found some vodka. Taste it ; it's a good fruit vodka. We drink it at our Easter and it's called Easter vodka. There ! "

He drew from his waistcoat a tiny narrow-necked decanter and a liqueur glass which he placed in front of Kashintzev. The vodka was of a yellowish colour and had a slight smell of cognac, but when the doctor had swallowed a glass it seemed to him that all his mouth and throat had been filled with some burning, scented gas. He felt at once in his stomach a sensation of cold, and then of a gentle warmth, and he was seized with a terrific appetite. The fish proved to be extremely good and so spiced that it made his tongue smart. How do they prepare it ? The cautious thought flashed through his brain, and then and there he laughed as he recalled one of Dr. von Ruhl's familiar evening aphorisms : " One must never think about what one eats or whom one loves."

Khatzkel was standing at a little distance, his hands folded behind his back. Apparently guessing the train of Kashintzev's thoughts, he said with an obliging and kind expression :

" Perhaps your honour imagines that this is prepared in some dirty way ? No such thing. . . . Our Jewish women do everything according to the holy books, and everything is written there : how to clean, how to cut it, and when to wash one's hands. And if it isn't done just like that, it is considered a sin. Your honour must eat his fill. Etlia, bring in more fish."

From behind the curtain a woman appeared and stood at the counter covering her head with a large grey shawl. When Kashintzev turned towards her he had the impression of receiving an invisible blow in the chest and of a cold hand squeezing his palpitating heart. Not only had he never seen such a dazzling, superb, perfect beauty, but he had not even dared to dream that there existed such in the world. Before, when he happened to see the little

230

heads of beautiful women in the pictures of well-known artists, he was inwardly convinced that these regular, faultless features had no existence in nature, but were the mere fictions of a creative imagination. All the more surprising and unreal, then, was this dazzling, beautiful face which he now beheld in a dirty lodging-house, reeking with the odours of unclean habitation, in this bare, empty, cold room, behind the counter, close to a drunken, snoring peasant who hiccupped in his sleep.

" Who is this ? " Kashintzev asked in a whisper. " There, this . . ." he was on the point of saying " Sheeny " from habit, but he checked himself and substituted " this woman ? "

"Who ? That ? " Khatzkel asked negligently, with a nod in her direction. " That, your honour, is my wife."

" How beautiful she is ! "

Khatzkel gave a short laugh and shrugged his shoulders scornfully.

" Your honour is mocking me ? " he asked reproachfully. " What is she ? A poor, ordinary Jewess and nothing else. Hasn't your honour seen really beautiful women in great cities ? Etlia ! " he turned to his wife and said something rapidly in Yiddish, at which she suddenly burst out laughing, her white regular teeth gleaming, and she moved one shoulder so high that she seemed to want to rub her cheek against it.

" Is your honour a bachelor or married ? " Khatzkel asked with wheedling prudence.

" No, I'm a bachelor. Why do you ask ? "

" No, it's just like this. . . . So your honour is a bachelor ? And how is it, your honour, that a solid, learned man like you wouldn't marry ? "

" Oh, that's a long story. . . . For many reasons. Still, I don't think it's too late even now. I'm not so old, am I ? "

Khatzkel suddenly moved up close to the doctor, glanced

round the room with a frightened air, and said, lowering his voice mysteriously :

" And perhaps your honour will spend the night here ? Don't be afraid, please ; the best gentlemen always stop here ; yes, the best gentlemen and the officers."

" No, I must hurry on. There's no time."

But Khatzkel, with a cunning, penetrating, and tempting air, half closed one eye after the other and continued to insist :

" It would be better, on my word, to stay, your honour. How can your honour go in such cold as this ? May God strike me dead if I'm not speaking the truth. . . . Just listen to what I'm going to tell you, your honour. . . . There's a retired governess here. . . ."

A swift, mad thought flashed through Kashintzev's head. He took a stealthy glance at Etlia, who, indifferently, as though not understanding what the talk was about between her husband and his guest, was gazing out through the powdered white window ; the next instant he felt ashamed.

" Leave me alone ; get out," curtly ordered Kashintzev.

It was not so much through Khatzkel's words as through his expression that he understood his drift. But he could not get angry as probably he would have considered it his duty to get angry under other circumstances. The warmth of the room, after a long cold journey, had made his body soft and tender. His head was swimming quietly and gently from the vodka ; his face was burning pleasantly. He was inclined to sit still without moving ; he experienced a languid sensation of satiety, warmth, and a slight drunkenness. He refused to think of the fact that in a few minutes he must again enter the sledge and continue his dull, endless, frosty route.

And in this curious, happy, light-headed condition it gave him an inexpressible pleasure, from time to time, as if by chance, as if deceiving himself, to rest his eyes on the beautiful face of the Jewess and think about her,

not merely vaguely but in formulated words, as though
ae were talking with some invisible person.

" Can one describe this face to anyone ? " he asked
himself. " Can one transmit in ordinary, pale, everyday
language those amazing features, those tender, bright
colours ? Now she is almost facing me. How pure
how astoundingly delicate is the line that goes from the,
temple to the ear and then downward to the chin, marking
the contour of the cheek ! The forehead is low, with
fine, downy hair on each side. How charming, and
feminine, and effective this is ! The dark eyes are enormous, so black and enormous that they appear made up,
and in them, close to the pupils, living, transparent, golden
dots shine like spots of light in a yellow topaz. The eyes
are surrounded by a dark, scarcely-defined shadow, and
it is impossible to trace this dark shadow, which gives
the glance such a lazy and passionate expression, into the
tawny, deep colour of the cheeks. The lips are red and
full, and, though they are closed just now, they have the
appearance of being open, of offering themselves. On
the slightly shaded upper lip there is a pretty mole just
at the corner of the mouth. What a straight, noble nose
and what fine, proud nostrils ! My dear, beautiful one ! "
Kashintzev kept repeating to himself, and so overcome was
he that he wanted to cry from the ecstasy and tenderness
which had seized hold of him, compressing his chest and
tickling his eyes.

Above the bright, tawny colour of the cheeks brown
stripes of dried dirt were visible, but to Kashintzev it
seemed that no kind of negligence could disfigure this
triumphant, blossoming beauty. He also noticed, when
she came out from behind the counter, that the hem of
her short, pink chintz skirt was wet and dirty, flapping
heavily at every step. On her feet were enormous worn-
out boots, with flaps sticking out at each side. He noticed
that sometimes, when talking to her husband, she quickly
pulled the tip of her nose with two fingers, making, as she

did so, a snorting noise, and then, just as quickly, passed
her index finger under her nose. For all that, nothing
vulgar, or funny, or pitiful could spoil her beauty.

" What does happiness consist of ? " Kashintzev asked
himself, and answered immediately : " The unique happiness is to possess a woman like this, to know that this
divine beauty is yours. Hum . . . it's a trivial, army
word—' to possess '—but what compared to this is all the
rest of life—a career, ambition, philosophy, celebrity,
convictions, social questions ? In a year or two, or three,
perhaps, I shall marry. My wife will be from a noble
family, a lean girl with light eyebrows and curls on her
forehead, educated and hysterical, with narrow hips and a
cold, bluish figure, pimpled all over like a plucked hen.
She will play the piano, talk on current questions, and
suffer from feminine maladies, and both of us, mere male
and female, will feel towards each other indifference if not
disgust. And perhaps the whole goal, the whole purpose,
the whole joy of my life, consists, by any means, true or
untrue, in taking possession of a woman like this, stealing
her, taking her away, seducing her—what does it matter ?
Even if she is dirty, ignorant, undeveloped, greedy, God
in heaven ! what trifles these are compared with her
miraculous beauty."

Khatzkel approached Kashintzev once more, thrust
his hands into his trouser-pockets and sighed :

" Do you happen to have read the papers ? " he asked
with hesitating politeness. " Is there anything new
about the war ? "

" Everything is just the same. We retreat, we are being
beaten. However, I haven't read the papers to-day,"
Kashintzev answered.

" Your honour hasn't read them ! What a pity ! We
here, you know, live in the steppes and learn nothing of
what is going on in the world. They've been writing,
too, about the Zionists. Has your honour heard that
there has been a congress of them in Paris ? "

" Certainly, of course."

Kashintzev looked at him more closely. Under his external cunning one detected something starved and puny which spoke of poverty, humiliation, and bad food. His long neck, above his worsted scarf, was thin and of a dirty yellow colour. On it two long strained veins, with an indentation between them, stuck out on each side of his throat.

" What is your ordinary occupation here ? " Kashintzev asked, seized with a sense of guilty pity.

" We-ell ! " Khatzkel shrugged his shoulders hopelessly and scornfully. " What can a poor Jew do within the pale ? We scratch a living somehow or other. We buy and sell when there's a market. We fight each other for the last little morsel of bread. Eh ! what can one say ? Is anyone interested in knowing how we suffer here ? "

He waved his hand wearily and withdrew behind the curtain, while Kashintzev resumed once more his interrupted thoughts. These thoughts were like the moving, multi-coloured images which come to one in the morning when one is on the border between sleep and awakening—thoughts which, before one wakes up completely, seem so fantastically malleable and at the same time full of such deep importance.

Kashintzev had never experienced such pleasure in dreaming as he did now, mollified by the warmth and the sense of satiety, leaning with his back against the wall and stretching his legs straight in front of him. In this pleasure, a sort of not very well-defined spot in the design of the many-coloured curtain had a great significance. He had unfailingly to find it with his eyes, stop at it, after which his thoughts of their own accord began to flow evenly, freely, and harmoniously, without any obstruction of the brain-cells—thoughts that leave no trace behind them and bring with them a kind of quiet, caressing joy. And then everything would disappear in a pale, bluish, hesitating fog—the papered walls of the lodging-house, its crooked tables, its dirty counter. There would remain only the beautiful face which Kashintzev saw and even felt, in spite of the fact that he was looking not at it, but at the vague, indistinguishable spot in the curtain.

What an extraordinary, unattainable race these Jews are, he was thinking. What is the Jew fated to experience in the future? He has gone through decades of centuries, without mixing with anyone else, disdainfully isolating himself from all other nations, hiding in his heart the old sorrow and the old flame of the centuries. The vast, varied life of Rome, of Greece, of Egypt, had long ago become the possession of museums, had become a delirium of history, a far-off fairy-tale. But this mysterious type, which was already a patriarch when these others were infants, not only continues to exist, but has kept his strong, ardent, southern individuality, has kept his faith with its great hopes and its trivial rites, has kept the holy language of his inspired divine books, has kept his mystical alphabet from the very form of which there vibrates the spell of thousands of years ago. What has the Jew experienced in the days of his youth? With whom has he traded and signed treaties? Against whom has he fought? Nowhere has a trace been left of his enigmatic enemies from all those Philistines, Amalakites, Moabites, and other half mythical people, while he, supple and undying, still lives on, as though, indeed, fulfilling someone's super-natural prediction. His history is permeated by tragic awe and is stained throughout by his own blood : centuries of prison, violence, hatred, slavery, torture, the funeral pyre, deportation, the denial of all human rights—how could he remain alive? Or have the fates of a people indeed their own incomprehensible goals that are for ever hidden from us? How can we know? Perhaps it pleased some Higher Force that the Jews, having lost their own country, should play the rôle of a perpetual leaven in the gigantic fermentation of the world.

There stands this woman whose face reflects a divine beauty, that inculcates a holy enthusiasm. For how many thousands of years must her people have refrained from mixing with any other race to preserve these amazing biblical features ? With the same plain fichu on the head, with the same deep eyes and sorrowful line near the lips, they paint the Mother of Jesus Christ. With the same pure charm shone the gloomy Judith, the sweet Ruth, the tender Leah, the beautiful Rachel and Hagar and Sarah. Looking at her, you believe, feel, and almost see how this people reverts in its stupendous genealogy back to Moses, to Abraham, and higher, still higher— straight back to the great, terrible, avenging biblical God.

" With whom was I discussing not long ago ? " Kashintzev suddenly remembered. " I was discussing the Jews, I think with a staff colonel in the train. No, it was with the town doctor from Stepany. He was saying : ' The Jews have grown decrepit, the Jews have lost their nationality and their country. The Jewish people must degenererate because it is penetrated by no drop of fresh blood. There are only two courses left to it—either to become fused with other nationalities, renewing its sap in them, or perish.' Yes, then I could find no reply, but now I should bring him up to this woman behind the counter and say : ' There it is, just look at the security for the immortality of the Jewish people ! Khatzkel may be puny, pitiful, and sickly. I admit that the eternal struggle for life has stamped upon his face the cruel traces of cheating, cowardice, and distrust. For thousands of years he has been " scratching a living " somehow or other, has been stifling in different ghettos. But the Jewish woman guards ever the type and spirit of the race, carries carefully through streams of blood under the yoke of violence, the holy fire of the national genius, and will never allow it to be extinguished.' As I look at her there I feel the black abyss of centuries opening itself behind her. There is a

miracle, a divine mystery here. Oh, what am I in her eyes
—I, the barbarian of yesterday, the intellectual of to-day—
what am I in her eyes ? What am I in comparison with this
living enigma, perhaps the most inexplicable and the
greatest in the history of humanity ? "

Suddenly Kashintzev came to himself. There was
a certain agitation in the lodging-house. Khatzkel was
running from one window to another and, with his palms
pressed against his temples, was trying to distinguish
something in the darkness outside. Etlia, disgusted and
angry, was pulling the collar of the drunken peasant,
who still kept lifting and lowering his red, senseless face,
swollen with sleep, and pouches under the lids, while he
snorted savagely.

" Trokhim, listen—well, Trokhi-im. I say to you,
get up ! " the Jewess was urging impatiently, murdering
the Ukrainian language.

" Hush ! The police inspector," Khatzkel muttered
in a frightened whisper. He smacked his lips repeatedly,
shook his head in despair, rushed impetuously to the
door, and threw it open exactly at the moment when a
tall police official, freeing himself from the collar of his
thick sheepskin coat, was in the act of entering the room.

" But listen, Trokhim, get up," Etlia said in a tragic
whisper.

The peasant raised his bloodshot face and, twisting
his mouth, began to yell.

" What's this ? " the inspector roared fiercely, with
rolling eyes. Indignantly he threw his sheepskin coat
into the hands of Khatzkel, who had run up to him. Then,
puffing his chest out like a wheel, he strutted a few steps
forward with the magnificent air of an opera colonel.

The peasant got up, staggering, and flopping against
the table with his hands, his body, and his feet. Something like conscious fear flashed into his bluish, swollen face.

" Your high . . . honour," he muttered, shambling
helplessly where he stood.

" Out," suddenly thundered the inspector, in such a terrible voice that the nervous Kashintzev started and huddled himself up behind his table. " Out with you at once."

The peasant swung forward and feebly stretched his hands out so as to clutch and kiss authority's right hand, but Khatzkel was already dragging him away to the door, by the back of his collar.

" You," shouted the inspector, fiercely flashing his eyes on Etlia, " deal in vodka ? Without a licence ? You receive horse-stealers ? Be ca-areful. I'll have you run in."

The woman raised her shoulders in an ugly way, bent her head sideways and, with a pitiful and submissive expression, closed her eyes as if she were expecting a blow from above. Kashintzev felt that the chain of his light, agreeable, and important thoughts had suddenly broken and could not be mended ; he felt awkward, ashamed of these thoughts, ashamed in his own eyes.

" May God punish me, Colonel, your honour," Etlia was swearing with passionate conviction. " May God strike me blind and not let me see to-morrow's daylight and my own children ! His honour, the colonel, knows himself what can I do if a drunken peasant will turn in here ? My husband is a sick man and I am a poor weak woman."

" All right." The inspector stopped her severely. " That's enough."

At that moment he noticed Kashintzev, and then and there tossing his head back with the air of a conqueror, he puffed his chest out and flourished his immaculate light whiskers to right and left. But suddenly a smile showed itself on his face.

" Basil Basilitch ! Old crocodile ! This is a bit of luck," he exclaimed, with theatrical joviality. " The deuce knows how long it is since we've seen each other. I beg your pardon." The inspector stopped abruptly at the table. " I believe I have made a mistake."

He brought his hand up smartly to the peak of his cap. Kashintzev, half rising, did the same rather awkwardly.

" Be magnanimous and forgive. I took you for my colleague the Poitchanov inspector. What an absurd mistake ! Once more—I beg your pardon. However, you know the uniforms are so alike that. . . . In any case, allow me to introduce myself : the local inspector and, so to speak, the God of Thunder—Irissov, Pavel Afinogenytch."

Kashintzev rose once more and gave his name.

" As everything is so unusual, permit me to sit near you," Irissov said and again he smartly touched his cap and clicked his heels. " Very pleased to meet you. You there, Khatzkel, bring me the leather case in my sledge ; it's underneath the seat. Forgive me, are you going far, doctor ? "

" To Goussiatine. I've just been posted there."

" Ah, in an infantry regiment ? There are some devilish good fellows among the officers, though they drink like horses. It's a scabby little town, but, as localities go, it's residential in a way. So, we'll meet each other ? Delighted. . . . And you've just been . . . ha, ha . . . a witness of the paternal reprimand that I was giving."

" Yes—partly." Kashintzev forced himself to smile.

" What's to be done ? . . . What's to be done ? That's my character. I like to be a little severe. . . . You know I'm no lover of all sorts of fault-finding and complaints and other absurdities of the kind. I do my own punishing myself."

The inspector was representative, as provincial ladies say—a tall, handsome man, with smart whiskers, growing sideways *à la* Skobeleff, and a high, white, tranquil forehead. His eyes were of a beautiful blue, with a constant expression of languor, a sort of immodest, unmanly, capricious fatigue ; his whole face had a delicate, even porcelain pink hue, and his raspberry-coloured, supple lips kept moving coquettishly and stretching themselves like two red, mobile worms. One could see by every indication that Inspector Irissov was the local *beau*, dandy, and lady-killer, an ex-cavalry man, probably a gambler and a hard liver, who could go three days running without sleep and who never got drunk. He spoke quickly and distinctly, had the air of paying an exaggerated attention to the words of his interlocutor, but apparently listened only to himself.

" I'm a father to them all, but a strict father," the inspector went on, raising his finger impressively. " Put the case here on the table, Khatzkel. I'm strict, that's true. I won't allow myself to be sat on, as the others do, but then I know everyone of my . . . he-he-he ! . . . subjects, so to speak, by heart. You saw that little peasant just now ? He's Trokhim, a peasant from Oriekh, and his nickname is Khvost. Do you think that I don't know that he's a horse-stealer ? I know perfectly well. But until the right time I keep silent and one fine May morning—Trokhim Khvost will have disappeared from circulation. Then just look at this very Khatzkel. Isn't he a scabby little Jew ? And, believe me, I know how the rascal lives. What ? Am I not telling the truth, Khatzkel ? "

. " Oh, my God, can his honour the inspector say what is untrue ? " Khatzkel exclaimed in servile reproach. " Every one of us, poor, unhappy little Jews, prays constantly to God for his honour the inspector. We always say among ourselves : ' What do we want with a real father when our good, beloved inspector is better to us than our own father ? ' "

" You see ? " the inspector said carelessly, with a significant twinkle in his eyes, as he pointed at Khatzkel over his shoulder. " That's the voice of the people. Don't worry, that's how I hold them. What ? Wasn't I telling the truth ? "

" What can I say to that ? " Khatzkel had shrivelled he was squatting almost on his heels, stretching not his, hands as though pushing away from him a sort of monstrous, unjust accusation. "We haven't time to think of anything that his honour the inspector doesn't know already beforehand."

"You hear him?" the inspector said curtly. "'Help yourself,' said Sobakievitch, to quote Gogol." He pointed to the open case. "Won't you have some roast duck? Ripping duck. Here is vodka. These are patties with fish and onions. Here's some rum. No, don't be suspicious; it's real Jamaica rum and even has the real smell of bugs about it. And this—please don't laugh at me— this is chocolate, a dainty for the ladies, so to speak. I recommend it to you; it's the most nourishing thing when one's travelling. I've learned that from sad experience on my ungrateful service. Please help yourself. . . ."

Kashintzev politely declined the invitation, but the inspector would take no refusal. There was nothing for it but to drink a glass of rum, which smelled of anything but rum. Kashintzev felt ill at ease, awkward and melancholy. He glanced stealthily from time to time at Etlia, who was talking in an animated whisper with her husband behind the counter. Her fantastic charm seemed to have left her. Something pitiful, humiliated, terrible in its very ordinariness, was now stamped on her face, but, all the same, it was poignantly beautiful as before.

"Ha, ha, that's your game, is it?" the inspector exclaimed suddenly, munching some chicken and noisily moving his moist, supple lips. "A pretty little Jewess, what?"

"Extraordinarily beautiful. Charming," came involuntarily from Kashintzev.

"Ye-es. . . . Fine game. But . . ." The inspector waved his hands, sighed artificially, and closed his eyes for a second. "But there's nothing doing there. It's been tried. It simply isn't possible. It's impossible, I tell you. Though the eyes see . . . But there, if you don't believe me, I'll ask him at once. Eh, Khatzkel?"

242

"For God's sake, I entreat you," Kashintzev stretched his hand out imploringly and rose from the bench, "I implore you not to do this."

"Oh, rubbish ! . . . Khatzkel."

At this minute the door opened and the new driver, with his whip in his hand, and his cap, like the national Polish headgear, on his head, came into the room.

"For which of you two gentlemen are the horses for Goussiatine ? " he asked. But recognising the inspector he hastily pulled off his cap and shouted in a military way : "We wish you health, your very high honour."

"Good-day, Iourko," the inspector answered condescendingly. "But you ought to stay a little longer," he said regretfully to the doctor. "When shall I get another chance of a chat with an intellectual man like you ? "

"I'm sorry, but there isn't time," Kashintzev said as he hurriedly buttoned his coat. "You know what it is yourself, the service ! How much do I owe ? "

He paid, and shivering in advance at the thought of the cold, the night and the fatiguing journey, he went to the door. From a naïve habit, that he had kept since childhood, of guessing the future by trifles, he thought as he grasped the handle of the door : "If she looks at me it will come to pass." What was to come to pass he did not know himself, any more than he knew the name of this dulness, this fatigue, this sense of undefined disillusion which oppressed him. But the Jewess did not look round. She was standing with her miraculous, ancient profile, illumined by the lamplight, turned towards him, and was busy with lowered eyes over something on the counter.

"Good-bye," said Kashintzev, as he opened the door.

Elastic clouds of vapour rushed in from the street veiling the beautiful face and inundating the doctor with a dry cold. In front of the steps stood the post horses, their heads hanging dejectedly.

They passed another village, crossed a little river over

the ice and once more the long, melancholy road stretched
itself out with its dead white fields to right and left.
Kashintzev dozed. Immediately the strange, misleading
sounds in front and behind and on both sides of the sledge
began to speak and sing. The band of dogs broke out
into barks and yelps, the human crowd murmured, the
children's silvery laughter rang out, the little bells chattered
madly, pronouncing distinct words : " One's first duty—
severity, severity," shouted the inspector's voice.

Kashintzev knocked his elbow against the side of the
sledge and returned to consciousness.

On both sides of the road were running to meet him
the tall, dark trunks of the pines, stretching out over
the road their snow-laden branches, like enormous white
paws. Among them, a long way off, in front, there seemed
to gleam stately, slender columns, official walls and balconies,
high white walls with black gothic windows, fantastic
outlines of some sleeping, enchanted castle. But the
sledge turned with the winding of the road and the phantom
castle transformed itself into black files of trees and arches
shaped by their snowy branches.

" Where am I ? Where am I driving to ? " Kashintzev
asked himself in perplexity and fear. " What has just
happened to me ? Something so big, so joyful, so important ? "

In his memory there swam out, with amazing clearness,
a charming feminine face, a delicate outline of cheeks
and chin, liquid, tranquilly passionate eyes, a beautiful
curve in the blossoming lips. And suddenly the whole
of his life—all that had passed and all that lay in front—
outlined itself to him in a sad loneliness, like this night
journey with its boredom, cold, emptiness, and isolation,
with its enervating, dreamy delusions.

In passing, the superb beauty of this unknown woman
had lit up and warmed his soul, had filled it with happiness,
with beautiful thoughts, with a sweet unrest. But this
strip of life had already run away from him, disappearing

behind him, and from it there was left only a memory, like the light in a chance station that disappears in the distance. And in front one sees no other light ; the horses continue their regular trot, and the indifferent driver—Time—dozes indifferently on his seat.

This book, designed by
William B. Taylor
is a production of
Edito-Service S.A., Geneva

Printed in Switzerland

R 1